LIZZY

*The Elizabeth Keckley Story, from Slavery
to Being America's 1st Couturier*

C. GEORGINA C.

This book is dedicated to Eloise and Faye; my daughters who are the center of my Universe.

May you always keep the light illuminated in your soul. You have a right to be here, no less than the Moon and the Stars. Above all, you have a right to be happy. Seek refuge in knowing your ancestors stand before you and beside you. They watch over you and reside within you. In times of uncertainty, call upon them for they are ever near and ever ready to be your guides, your advocates and way pavers.

May you always listen to your instincts, for there is the Angel stewarding your souls. Be courageous enough to run towards your fears. May you embrace failing for it is in your failure that you will learn to succeed.

May you let God run through you in your thoughts, words and actions so that you can live a life harming none.

Be mighty enough to lasso your dreams and draw down the moon and bring peace as close to your heart - for in your heart lies my love eternal.

And when the road ahead seems unclear, may you look inside your heart for the North Star to guide you. It never fails. May Elizabeth Keckley's story and all the stories of your ancestors ignite your souls and move you to reach your fullest potential. May you carve your own paths and live a life you are proud of. There is no time limit to this thing. Do what makes you happy.

I am with you forever and a day. May you love without limits.

I love you always, Mommy

PROLOGUE

(On April 9, 1865, after too many agonizing and tumultuous years, the Confederate Army under the leadership of Jefferson Davis had surrendered. The war was finally over.)

Washington, D.C. April 15, 1865; 12:30 a.m.

A loud bang shook me, yet I couldn't wake myself up from a terrible nightmare. I heard cries outside but I was paralyzed, transfixed upon the bed and laid there in a cold sweat. It was as if I was once again possessed with the incubus that tormented me for 47 years. I attempted to scream. Nothing but the force of the demon kept at me. Suddenly, I awoke disoriented but relieved by the pounding coming from my door.

"Who is it?" I trembled as I called out. It was my neighbor, Mrs. Brown whose face jumped at me when I opened the door.

"Lizzy...The President has been shot," her dilated eyes frightful and spooked. She was panicked and stricken by the shock of the news.

"Mrs. Brown, who told you this?" I asked as I gathered my coat while scrambling to tie my shoes. I stood, looked out the window and saw the raging pandemonium on Twelfth Street right outside, people running in all directions- sobbing and yelling at the same time. Men, women and children aimlessly wandered the streets in their nightclothes.

"The President has been shot! God help us!" said an elderly man raising his arms in the air as he knelt on the ground in deep prayer.

I stepped outside my door and already the streets were filled with heavily armed soldiers. Alert were their prying eyes and prodding bayonets. An armed officer declared that there was a wrongdoer amongst us. A joyous moment in the nation, a celebration and the end of the war has now turned into mayhem and madness.

Earlier that evening, I attended to Mrs. Lincoln and dressed her for the Ford Theater in a gown I made that fitted her beautifully. She expressed her excitement at the chance to enjoy some time with her husband.

The copper colored taffeta gown featured a fitted bodice with black and white lace that trimmed the edges of the pagoda sleeves. A delicate lace collar finished with silk cording accentuated Mrs. Lincoln's soft neck. She thanked me profusely and I was pleased to see her satisfaction.

It was now close to midnight. I hastened to leave and saw Mrs. Brown in one corner of my room, curled up like a child. She was shaking and mumbling at the same time.

"Who shot him?" I asked with no response from her. By now, Mrs. Brown was suffering some kind of stupefaction. I asked again but this time articulating the words slowly as I stared into her tearful eyes, *"Mrs. Brown, listen to me. Who shot the President?"*

Snapping out of it, she replied: *"It was the actor they said, John Wilkes Booth and the President's army is on a search for him now."*

"I must go to the White House now. Mrs. Lincoln needs me," I said hastily without realizing that I grabbed Mrs. Brown so tightly causing her to let out a deafening whelp. Within seconds I was outside just a couple blocks from Twelfth Street making my way through the chaos and confusion of the crowd.

A carriage drove past me almost knocking me over when I heard someone announce out loud: *"A twenty-thousand-dollar reward has been issued for the murderers!"*

Murderers? What does this mean? Does this mean the President is dead? Who else was killed? What about my dearest friend, Mrs. Lincoln? Is she alive? Did the murderers kill her too? How could anyone do this?

My heart was racing and I was in a daze. Lost in the panic-stricken crowd, I found myself standing in the middle of the street momentarily having lost my sense of purpose. I felt paralyzed until someone grabbed me by my shoulders and screamed into my face, *"Lady, all the colored people are headed to the front of the White House. You must go now! You are not safe out here!"*

I sprinted forward weaving in and out through all the routes I had grown accustomed to in order to get to the White House. Through the alleys and shacks, the downtrodden neighborhoods where the colored people lived, I ran as fast as I could until my chest swelled in pain. I was met with scrutinizing eyes and the menacing shouts of the folks who knew I was from a different grain.

I decided to head back home to beseech the assistance of my landlords, Mr. and Mrs. Walker Lewis; free Negro citizens who owned the boarding house where I stayed and operated my dress shop. My hope was to convince them to take me by horse carriage to the White House to avoid discriminating and suspecting eyes. As I made my way back home, the rain fell from the dark expanse above us that loomed over the nation's capital like Satan's wrath, and I felt a heavy weight pressing down upon my shoulders.

My head was pounding causing my vision to become one big blur. The nightmare I thought had recently ended was on the precipice of just beginning.

An hour later, drenched and exhausted, I arrived at the Lewis's home. I explained that I could get to the White House using a different route but would need their help in doing so. I was relieved when they willingly obliged to help me as they hastened themselves to get dressed for the trip. Mr. Lewis pulled out a gun from the closet and put it inside his raincoat.

"Take this," he said handing me a brightly lit lantern. Mrs. Lewis carried a satchel with another gun inside it as she motioned for me to

follow her where the horses were waiting.

It was one o'clock in the morning as the audible sound of the chimes rung from Mrs. Lewis' living room clock while we boarded inside the carriage. It took Mr. Lewis a few minutes to calm his horses down for they too, felt the urgency in the air and showed no signs of alleviation from the anxiety in the atmosphere.

"Heeyah! Onward!" Mr. Lewis yelled at his horses with a crack of his whip immediately sending shivers down my spine; its explosive clap reminiscent of the lashings I once endured seemed all too familiar again. I shuddered in recollection.

Regaining my focus, I directed Mr. Lewis to drive his carriage towards the back way and through the side streets far away from the growing crowds. Every one of them wet, tired, inconsolable, angry and in shock; men, women, and children all strewn about the streets of the capital aimlessly wandering about like helpless ants separated from their colony. Soldiers were executing their orders to secure the streets. White House staff members emerged from their stations as they removed the flower garlands decorating the light posts and began replacing them with black banderoles.

"Why are they so quick to remove them? What does all this mean, Mrs. Lewis?" I asked but received no response for she too, had the same question ruminating in her head.

Finally, upon arriving at the White House property by the livery, we were stopped by four soldiers with their bayonets directly pointed at each one of us. *"Stop right there! Put your hands up or I will shoot! Identify yourselves immediately!"* a soldier demanded.

"We come in peace. My name is Elizabeth Keckley. I am Mrs. Lincoln's dressmaker. These are the Lewis's, and they are my landlords who helped me get to Mrs. Lincoln upon hearing the news of the President. I must attend to Mrs. Lincoln now. My papers are inside my coat pocket if you would like to inspect them," I said as I directed him to take my official White House employment papers inside my pocket. The soldier took

the paper and read it line by line carefully.

With our hands still up, his eyes never blinking and transfixed onto mine, he put the papers back inside my pocket and said, *"The President has been shot and we are taking every measure to secure the space for the safety of the President, his family and his Cabinet. You have no official business coming to the White House and I don't care if you are Mrs. Lincoln's dressmaker. No one is sewing a dress for anyone right now, so I suggest you all turn back around immediately before I arrest all of you for trespassing. Now go! Get!"* he ordered with force and blood-curdling intensity.

Fearing for our lives, we hurried home with heavy hearts and great trepidation. Desperate and feeling defeated, I couldn't help but worry for Mrs. Lincoln. The thought of her undergoing this without me was unbearable and disconcerting. I was determined to get to her and stayed up all night in earnest prayer trying to devise an alternate route plan. The hours dragged longer than I could ever imagine until sunrise came and I heard a knock on the door.

It was 6:00 a.m. when soldiers from the White House stood outside my apartment and handed me a note that read, *"Lizzy, please come. Do not delay."* Mrs. Lincoln's shaky handwriting showed all evidence of her distress.

The streets were bumpy and slippery from the downpour of the previous evening. The smell emanating from the Potomac River consumed what little breath was left inside my lungs in a most offensive and virulent kind of way. Never have I seen the city so dull, morose and dreary. It was hell on earth.

Amidst all the confusion, my mind escaped my personhood as I embarked into Mrs. Lincoln's carriage. I was still living in my nightmare and the sound of the horses' hooves hit the ground in a crescendo of thundering blows that sent me back to the time I prayed and wished to forget.

Mrs. Lincoln's cries were drawing me closer, yet everything moved ever so slowly, where the clock was turning backwards, and there was nothing I could do to stop it.

I felt myself sucked back into my dark past rather than towards the present when my dearest friend, Mrs. Mary Todd Lincoln needed me most.

I was consumed with worry, but at least I knew she was alive; yet I could not escape from the reality that the President had been shot - and I was numb at the thought that maybe he was gone.

CHAPTER 1

A Black Dress and White Apron

Master Colonel Armistead Burwell was born in the year of 1777 in Dinwiddie County, Virginia. He was the son of Mr. John Burwell and Mrs. Anne Powell, and was the third of six children. The Burwells were among the First Families of Virginia and were known to own several plantations in Virginia and North Carolina.

Mr. John Quincy Adams, a lawyer, served as the 6th President of the United States once described the Burwells as *"typical Virginia aristocrats of the time and were rather bland, somewhat imperious and politically simplistic."*

Master's father was John Burwell; the sibling of William Armistead Burwell, who served as President Thomas Jefferson's Secretary and was a member of the United States House of Representatives. The Burwells considered themselves as patriots with many of its male members enlisted in the American Revolutionary War and the War of 1812, the latter of which Master Colonel Burwell led, along with his troops in the United States Army towards a victorious end at the age of 35.

Master Burwell was a stern burly white-haired man with a protruding stomach. He maintained a permanent scowl on his face that was further emphasized by his raspy cigar-smoking voice.

He was a brisk, abrupt, coarse and an unforgiving man whose business matters were constantly debatable and often uncertain. What was not debatable nor questionable was the origin of my parentage. He was my biological father; a staggering revelation that later came from my mother while I sat by her bedside during the final hours of her life.

My mother was an enslaved woman by the name of Agnes Hobbs (known as Aggy) who became pregnant by Master Colonel Burwell. Four years after my birth, the Colonel's wife, Mrs. Mary Cole Turnbull Burwell became pregnant with their tenth child. Throughout my life, stories have been told about the nature of how my mother's pregnancy came to be and suffice it to say that my arrival into this earth was not spawned out of mutual respect or love. My mother became the object of Colonel Burwell's impulsions wherein he repeatedly and forcibly assaulted and raped her. These are the truths I wished I never had to tell but are necessary to explain my existence.

I was born on the last month of the coldest season in Dinwiddie County, Virginia just South of Petersburg on February 1818 where it rained for eleven torrential consecutive days.

My mother said that I was born on the month when daytime seemed like an eternity that kept us working more. It was wet, cold and unbearably difficult.

Despite having Colonel Burwell as my biological father, I was nonetheless born a slave. In the South, a child birthed by a female slave was immediately be deemed a slave. My mother's future husband, George Hobbs worked in a different plantation not far away from the Burwells and although I was not his child, George Hobbs loved me like his own and dedicated himself to my mother. He was the only father I knew and loved.

"Oh Aggy, she sho' is beautiful like you. Look at them hands she's got. Them hands are special hands indeed. From this day forth, you is my Little Lizzy," Mr. Hobbs said as he welcomed me into the world as his very own.

"She must know how much you love her George, just look at how she is looking into your eyes," mother said.

"She shall be Elizabeth Hobbs, her father's daughter," she continued to say as she nursed me to a deep and peaceful slumber.

I am thankful to her for having made the decision to name me the daughter of Hobbs. Later, I deduced that it was my mother's way of resisting the oppression that bound her.

Until the time of my marriage, my name was Elizabeth Hobbs and recorded in the plantation books as:

"Lizzy, A child of Aggy/Feb. 1818," as Master Burwell's mother dictated to the record keeper out loud for the entire plantation to hear.

"And let us not bother ourselves with the matter of who this child's father is for it is not anyone's concern as she is the child of a slave and my son's rightful property and that's all that we need to be concerned with, do y'all understand?" she scoffed as the sweat collecting on her brows landed upon the parchment paper from which my record as 'property' owned by Colonel Burwell became indelibly clear.

"Just as well," my mother mumbled under her breath for she would rather die a thousand deaths than have me named the slave child of her oppressor, Master Colonel Burwell.

My entry into the world was of no unusual circumstance in every plantation in the South where children fathered by their masters were regarded as additional property.

Master's wife, Mistress Mary Cole Turnbull Burwell was a thin, pale-skinned woman with crooked teeth. Add to this was the fact that I resembled my master in many ways, which caused much discord to my mistress who loathed mother for this very reason alone. My mother was undoubtedly beautiful, and my mistress disdained her for being the subject of Master Burwell's attention, adulation and obsession.

"As soon as this child can stand on two feet, she shall immediately

have much work to do. I have no plans of feeding another free loading niggress in this house now you hear? I have too many hogs to tend to before the next season of auction begins," my mistress exclaimed with her blue eyes piercing right through my mother's weary heart.

"Ugly She-Devil. Evil grouch. Despicable bellyache! Disgusting infected festering sore! Smelly swine! I hate her! With all my heart I hate her!" I used to say to myself when I grew a little bit older whenever Mistress would walk by and of course, minutes later I would find myself asking for God's pardon in prayer.

I must have been only 3 days old when Mistress barked orders to Mother: *"Do you hear me Aggy? And in two days you shall resume your duties because there is no need for you to rest anymore. We have much work where the crops are concerned, so best to start weaning that child off hastily today! Now would you sit up and stop carrying on like you've been through hell and back? I can't have you niggers getting too comfortable around here!"* stomping her feet to the ground to emphasize the seriousness of her demands; her face reddened from the blood curdling hatred that seemed to have consumed every living white person in the South.

I found this behavior odd to put it mildly, and rather un-evolved. It was a character that was savage and inhumane. I was convinced it is a characteristic spawned from the devil himself. To possess such ease (and pleasure) in dehumanizing someone led me to believe that the Burwells were the devil incarnates wreaking havoc on earth.

I grew up with many other children enslaved; some still attached to their mother's breasts but already given a fate of servitude before they could even walk.

My mother was favored by Master Burwell and was given permission to learn how to read and write- an unusual, rare and unlawful granting in those times. She had many God-given talents that made her highly valuable to the Burwell family. She was a swift mover in the fields with a high tolerance for the heat of the sun and the firmness to withstand the deathly chill of the winter months.

She was built with strong arms and shoulders that could carry heavy bales of hay and wide hips that hoisted baskets of grain on each side. Mother was a beautiful sturdy woman with skin that glistened at the touch of the sun. She had eyes that could hypnotize even the most scornful soul. She was splendidly built and had well-balanced hands, arms, legs and feet. Her bosom was set and held high, and she possessed a neck that could outshine any graceful creature in God's kingdom. Most people would describe her as an unusually breathtaking woman with hair that reached past her shoulders as the soft light brown curls framing her oval-shaped face mimicked the face of an angel.

Later, as I reached the age of fourteen, everyone considered me to look like my mother in an exacting way. This of course, made me so very happy for in my eyes, my mother was the most beautiful woman I have ever known.

Master Burwell never left his gaze upon her. Secretly, I wished for the sun's rays to eventually blind his undressing eyes or prayed for lightning to strike and render him dead immediately and gone forever and a day.

The Burwell home was large enough to fit several families in it. The voluminous drapes that hung from the ceiling to the floor caused me to often wonder what purpose they served other than to collect dust which in turn, we slaves had to clean.

The home was provisioned with two kitchens, a formal dining room, a sitting room to receive guests, and several bedrooms upstairs. It was grand in size with furnishings that Master Burwell had his slaves craft from wood taken from the mature trees in the plantation.

In the study, the wooden floor was covered with a woolen rug in deep saturated colors of red, blue and gold. Every month, our Mistress would summon Mother to clean the jacquard rug that had to be rolled out of the home and left outside to be cleaned. This was quite heavy for one person to lift by herself, yet Mistress forbade anyone to help my Mother and demanded that she carry the rug outside without any assistance from anyone in the Burwell plantation. There were a few rugs in the home that required cleaning every so often as well as the wooden floors of the house comprising two levels that were quite expansive.

Mother created for herself a routine by which to provide her some ease and organization to the workload she was charged to accomplish daily. This applied to the order of business pertaining to Mistress Burwell's rugs. First, Mother would scrub the rugs that she laid outside the home next to the barn where the horse carriages were stationed.

"Jacquard rugs were named after a Frenchman named Joseph Marie Jacquard," Mother said one morning with a blank look on her face, the sweat rolling down and into her eyes that eventually caused them to sting, the heat from her body escaping her skin causing a silhouette of her magnificent beauty from my view across the hallway of the main room.

Even in the moments of her strife, she remained beautiful. Her soft curls soaking with sweat that fell ever so gently above her brow was a sight for sore eyes. Her tired hands scrubbed vigorously with fingers that looked like the tapered candles from the candelabra at the center of Mistress Burwell's dining table in the main room.

Her voice was soft like a feather and possessed a quality that could sooth any weary soul. When she sang a hymn, it sounded like a hallowed choir where the cherubims and seraphs joined along in praise of God's angel. On the rare occasion when she smiled, she radiated such brilliance that could light the path of acres upon acres of land and beyond. Mother was divine in every possible way, and it delighted me to think that everyone thought I looked, moved and sounded just like her.

While the rugs dried, Mother began the task of scrubbing the wooden floors down. She did this with soap and water using a hard brush made from bore bristles to remove the dirt that had collected in between the planks. Once the entire floor was cleaned, Mother would polish it with oil and wipe it down thoroughly to ensure that no one in the Burwell home fell or slipped.

"Oh child, would you please wipe your mother's eyes...they are burning me Lizzy," she asked for she could not wipe her eyes with her own hands as they were soaked in soap. In my young mind, I cursed the rug-making Frenchman named Jacquard who invented such a cumbersome and useless thing for it was a source of pain and suffering for my poor mother.

My mother's hands would be raw by the time all the rugs were finally washed clean and the floors were polished and dried. She had to move quickly to finish washing them in order to catch the sun's drying power, then hurry herself to roll them back up and carry them one by one into the first floor and then the more difficult task of carrying them up the long staircase of to the second floor of the home before sundown. Relishing my mother's hardship, Mistress Burwell would make a point of standing in front of the window while watching my mother toil away. If Mistress were in a foul mood, she would make my mother repeat the process giving the reason, *"You did not clean it properly Aggy! Do it again!"*

Sometimes my mother quietly cried as she cleaned those rugs. I couldn't bear to watch her and instead would run to the fields and force myself to fall asleep under the sway of the branches from an old oak tree while I solemnly prayed for a miracle. There, with permission from the good old oak tree, I etched a symbol of that only I could discern.

I make mention of this old oak tree and all the trees that surrounded the Burwell plantation not only for the practical use it served in offering shade during the hot summer months, but also for the refuge it gave many runaway slaves during those pitch-black nights where they climbed up its branches to get a momentary night's rest. Even for but a few hours until it was time to journey into the unknown, these branches became life-saving stand-ins during some of our most desperate times of our survival.]

An elderly slave once told me the story of a time when several slaves owned by a man named Dandridge some miles from Master Burwell's property ventured out in the middle of the night in pursuit of freedom. It was a well-known implementation of the slave catchers to let loose the bloodhounds when word of a runaway was made known. To avoid detection, the runaways would rub their bare feet or the soles of their shoes with a tincture of oils and botanicals to deter the hounds from tracing their steps. It was also necessary for them not to brush up against any shrubbery or branches to avoid their scent to be discovered and tracked.

Their only guide were the stars, specifically the North Star where many believed it to be the guiding soul of the ancestors who led them to safer grounds. They believed the trees' branches pointed them in the right direction and so it explains why often their faces were looking up to the dark expanse of the night sky. They were looking into the road map towards freedom.

Among the enslaved children in the Burwell property, I was always the one who used to conjure dresses in my head that eventually led me to create skirts made from the leaves of the same old black oak tree. I would weave and sew the leaves, flowers, twigs and branches all together to create a full hoop skirt that I, and many of my friends enjoyed playing dress-up with.

Mother was also adept in the kitchen and prepared delicious fares of sophisticated quality. Able to read and write, she learned about certain dishes and served meals of curious nature that were often given accolades and compliments by many of Master Burwell's guests. On occasions of utmost importance, her cooking would be called upon by special request. Ever thoughtful was she to set aside and sneak small pieces and bits for me to eat and enjoy at evening's end. She introduced me to these fine foods for she believed that one day I would eventually make good use of my life.

Her ability was vast in that she was also a proficient and fine dressmaker highly skilled in the art of embroidery and needlepoint. She sewed all the clothing for the slaves as well as every garment the

Burwell family wore. She knitted everything in the household with exacting dexterity, skill, proficiency and speed. Mother possessed the most discerning level of good judgment both in the form of her handiwork as well as its functionality. Early on even as a child, I learned the importance of balancing beauty and purpose, applying this approach of balance in form and function in my future life as an expert dressmaker.

During this time, Virginia, Alabama, Louisiana, Georgia, Mississippi and both North and South Carolina all passed Anti-Literacy laws. These laws were designed to make teaching Negro slaves to read and write a crime punishable by fines and imprisonment for white persons engaged in such behavior, and severe beatings, flogging, and death for the slaves caught reading or writing.

One morning, Master Burwell summoned my mother to his study and said: *"Aggy, this child seems to have some wit about her. I reckon she would take to the books quite easily. Teach her the books right away and hush your mouth to the others about this, including your Mistress. She will have the foreman shoot the gizzards out of you!"*

"Yes Master," mother acknowledged and as if his warnings were not sufficient, he adds: *"Leave no trace of it behind and make no mistake about it when I warn you, you and that child will be severely punished if you are caught!"*

One would think this was an act of kindness, when in truth, Master Burwell was a self-seeking man where his character was concerned and I am certain this was a decision that in his eyes would benefit him, rather than me in the long run. Needless to say, mother and I treaded very carefully and kept eyes behind our backs.

Mother would have secretly taught me how to read and write regardless but she obliged to her master's instructions simply to appease him and avoid the sting of a lashing. Aside from helping me focus on my books, she also shared her trade secrets to me especially in the fine art of dressmaking, a self-taught skill she learned through her own God-given gifts and through her readings of catalogues and pattern books she managed to sneak to read while cleaning Mistress' bedroom.

At age three, I already learned how to recite the alphabet and was quite proficient in writing my letters using a makeshift tablet my mother made for me out of wood and coal. These writing tools had to be cleared of its markings by soaking it in the laundry water mixed with soap after every use. Once it was cleaned from any evidence, mother would dry it and place the tablet atop the fireplace strategically placing an oil lamp directly on top of it to simulate its purpose as a catchall from the drippings of the lamp's oil. Eventually, mother got rid of the tablet and coal after feeling suspicious that someone might have been tipped off. Instead, she had me write my letters using my saliva. Being of brown complexion, the saliva would make an evident mark on my skin particularly my upper leg that served as my writing tablet. Mother would do the same by forming sentences on her skin with her saliva and I would read them to her before the markings would fade. This kind of improvisation was common amongst us slaves, where we found clever ways to make life a little less tedious and wearisome. Odd as it may seem, what fun those times were despite the anguish and the ever constant fear we felt.

Master Burwell outwardly regarded me as his 'earliest and fondest pet,' however let not these words fool one for he was a taskmaster of the tallest order. Dare I also say that he was ultimately jealous of my mother's affection towards her husband George, often punishing her with a beating for no offense whatsoever. The lashings my mother endured were so barbaric in nature that it is difficult to articulate into words without being accused of falsification.

One morning, as mother was tending to the hennery behind the Burwell home, Mistress Burwell, in a fit of jealousy and rage, arrived prepared to give my mother a lashing.

"Remove your dress Aggy," she said as she ordered Uncle Willie and Garrett, the teenage son of one of mother's cousin to tie her hands and feet against one of the tree trunks outside the hennery.

"Mistress, but what offense have I committed?"

"I owe you no explanation Aggy!" and with that she proceeded to deliver thirty-nine blows to my mother's back rendering her unconscious. When Mistress was done, she ordered one of the foremen to douse her with a bucket of salt water. This painful and excruciating process was believed by white folk to allow the brined water to heal the wounds quickly (for certainly they wanted their slaves to be able to return to work immediately) and in a twisted kind of deranged incongruity of the mind, designed to inflict more pain and suffering.

It was a common practice for many slave owners to hire out individuals specifically trained to execute the lashings for fear of the social stigma they would have to sustain once their peers found out of their wrongdoings. These specialists were called 'slave-breakers' who were hired to subdue, subjugate, and break slaves who were too bold, too brave, too smart, too powerful or as mother would say. too 'threatening.' Cowardice was a common theme amongst these slave owners who had no problem employing someone else to do their bidding for them, and for some reason made them feel absolved of any feeling of guilt, transgression or shame.

The Southern Whites and their avarice for wealth building continued to propagate the institution of slavery for hundreds of years prior to my existence driving America's economy at the forefront.

From cotton gins and to sugar refineries, tobacco mills, coal and gold mining enterprises to railroads and fishing industries to steamboat manufacturing and more, my people toiled and labored every waking moment of their lives to advance wealth for white slave owners who found every possible angle to legalize this gluttonous and predatory money-making scheme at the expense of human lives. I witnessed this assault and molestation against my people from the day I was born.

One day in Edward County, Virginia in the year of 1823, my master's wife, gave birth to a bouncy black-eyed baby daughter whom they named *'Elizabeth Margaret.'* It was strangely pleasing to me that she and I shared the same name, although mother always felt the mistress was unforthcoming and deeply jealous to the extent of naming her own child with an identical name. It was equally confounding to me that she and I shared the same father and that we were for all matters of common sense and science, sisters by blood – yet living two drastically contrasting lives.

On that day, Master Burwell's debatable and often uncertain business matters became more aimless when I was given the responsibility of taking care of this newborn child, my half-sister.

I was very young myself, barely weaned from my own mother, at the age of four years old. Nonetheless, I remember clear as day, the happiness I felt because I was finally no longer delegated to work by washing laundry and walking miles to fetch water from the well under the hot vulgar sun nor walk to the well back and forth in the dreadful cold during the winter months, nor collect eggs from the cranky hens who just like me, hated life at the Burwell plantation. Never mind the fact that my hands were barely big enough to collect these eggs without ever breaking them.

I was ecstatic about being appointed to work inside the household of my master from now on. Amongst us slaves, to be a 'house slave' was a preferable station and I was ecstatic about this new role.

At least I thought, I would be surrounded in all the beauty and splendor of the Burwell home and perhaps would have the occasional opportunity to play with the toys already set aside for the newborn baby girl. I especially yearned to sit on the wooden rocking horse that was beautifully hand carved by mother's friend's son, little Albert, who was only eleven years old yet so handy at woodwork. Albert was a stout boy who was often the subject of Mistress Burwell's scrutiny for she questioned how it was possible for Albert, a slave to appear well fed. His weight caused Mistress much suspicion and I feared for

Albert's safety.

"He looks like one of our hogs, doesn't he Armistead?" she would say to intimidate and mock him.

"Maybe we should sell him along with the other hogs at the next auction?" letting out an evil laugh that echoed throughout the Burwell house like the devil himself. How I hated this half-woman half-devil.

Although terrified by what he heard, Albert did not let anything take him away from his woodwork. What sewing was to me was carpentry and woodwork to Albert.

The wooden rocking horse Albert was making was a dark brown pony with a flaxen mane and tail. Its saddle made from the same wood was hand carved ornately. Gleaming from a fresh coat of varnish, the smell it emitted was like a soothing balm to my soul. With meticulous attention, Albert hand painted the rocking horse in red, gold and green colors. It was one of the most beautiful things I had ever seen. Albert possessed a skill so great that one would never believe the rocking horse was made by an eleven year old boy.

Later in my life as a dressmaker, I created a gown that was reminiscent of my cousin's artistry. It was a rich brown silk taffeta gown that I trimmed in gold satin piping at the neckline and surrounded the hem with gold lace trims.

Although my time with him was brief, my recollections of him sustained me throughout my life and I would often reminisce of our days gone by.

He said, *"Lizzy, I'se gon' make one for ya jes like dis wun here, would you like dat?"* to which I replied, *"Oh my Albert, that would be most wonderful, and for that I can share with you this delicious corn pone I snuck out of mistress' basket. Hahahaha, see?"*

Laughing out loud, I handed him the freshly made treat drenched in the stickiest sweetest syrup. He smiled and seemed mighty proud of his work as he relished each delicious bite of his sugary bit. Sticky-faced and satiated, we both stood there admiring the shiny steed one last time before one-eyed Scipio, (an old blacksmith whose left eye was gouged out of its socket on account of being accused of inappropriate behavior towards one of master Burwell's distant female relatives) proceeded to take the rocking horse into the main house on the second floor where the baby's nursery was located.

I wish to mention here that throughout Scipio's life, he denied any of the accusations made against him. This is evidenced by the fact that Scipio, as large and masculine as he appeared, was a man who preferred the company and friendship of other men. Amongst us, this was an understanding we kept in the strictest of confidence to protect and preserve his life.

While the facts are rumored and somewhat unconfirmed, talk of a male friend of the Burwell family was visiting from another part of town. One night, he entered Scipio's cabin and made advances to Scipio of which he refused to oblige.

Shamed by this, the man accused Scipio of inappropriate behavior against his wife that led to Scipio being flogged and beaten the next day. As if this was not enough, the overseer wanted to make a statement to all slaves by gouging out Scipio's eye with his bare hands. I was too young to remember but according to my mother, witnessing this was one of the most violent and horrific experiences of her life.

Albert and I walked back to our respective cabins at sundown and before I could say goodbye, noticed that Albert eyes were red and swollen for he had been crying all the way as we walked home.

"Why are you crying Albert?" I asked.

"Oh Lizzy, I'se been wurkun' on dat rockin' horse for nearly seben monts now 'n I'se growed to wish wun fo' me too. It sho' bring sum joy to my spirits to rock it back and forth. It mayk me feel so free," he replied trying very hard to hold back his tears.

"I am going to be the little baby's maid now and maybe you can come help me sometimes?" I said slowly.

With my hand still gently resting on his shoulder, he slowly walked towards the door of his cabin, turned around to face me and took my hand from his shoulder, opened my palm to give me a bundle of the flaxen horsehair that he braided and tied together with a string at the ends.

"You can hab dis Lizzy. I was gon' use it for the next rockin' horse I was gon' mayk but I don't know 'bout dat no mo. Here, maybe you can mayk sum good use for it."

Albert entered his cabin and never said goodbye. Two years after that day, Albert was sold at an auction and was purchased by a wealthy white family and we never heard what came of him again.

The following morning, I was summoned to meet my mistress on the second floor of the main house. Mother had given me a litany of what not to say, what not to do, who not to look at and more of these what not regulations.

Scipio stood at the steps of the main house holding the mistress' dog down to control it. It was a dog with no name, although I thought the name Satan would be most appropriate. He was a vicious dog who would be let loose to attack anyone in the plantation who Master Burwell deemed punishable by dog bites. Not many would live more than a few days after being attacked by this rabid beast and of course I had no intention of being his next victim.

"I'm scared Scipio," I cried looking up at him with my arms outstretched as if to carry me to safety.

"Oh no little Lizzy, you go on, skedaddle and skoot on upstairs. Mistress Burwell is waiting for you. He ain't gon' hurt you. I'll make sure of it," he said trying to cheer me up as he looked down at the nameless dog followed up with one hard kick to the mongrel's ribs that eventually silenced its frothing rabid mouth. In my mind, I envisioned the dog to be my mistress and what pleasure the thought

it gave me.

Mistress Burwell stood inside the baby's room dressed in a silken robe over a nightgown that appeared too small for her still alarmingly swollen belly. (This confused me at the time considering she had already given birth and wondered if there was another half-devil in there.)

"That is curious." I said under my breath as I stared at her stomach hoping to find an answer to the mystery of her condition.

Noticing my stare, my mistress said, *"I beg your pardon Lizzy, did you say something just now?"* I pretended not to hear her whatsoever remembering my mother's distinct instructions on what not to do, what not say, and who not to look at.

She then handed me a rather strangely ill-fitting black dress that seemed to be meant for a girl twice my age. It accompanied a white apron that had ruffles at the hemline. The apron's straps had to be wrapped around me three times for it not to drag to the ground. She also gave me a used pair of black leather shoes that were also far too big.

I deduced that this was a matter of utility in the event of my inevitable growth. I tumbled over and fell flat on my face after putting the shoes on to take the first steps. My feet kept slipping and sliding inside them despite numerous attempts to properly walk with them. In frustration, my mistress grabbed a handful of cotton and several sheets of writing paper from her study, crumpled them into small pieces and stuffed my shoes with it.

"Now stop this non-sense!" she screamed as if I had offended her causing the baby to wake up and cry. My master's mother came running to the room to see about the commotion and when she noticed the baby was fine, gave me a stinging glare and went back to her room.

In my head I thought to myself, *what non-sense was she speaking of? Was she talking about the non-sense of her inadequate ability to know that the shoes were made for a person twice my age? Was this the non-sense she meant? Or was it the non-sense of having a four year old child take charge of her newborn infant?* I remembered my mother's what not to do, say or look at instructions and dismissed the idea of challenging the she-devil. Instead, I reverted my focus on organizing the crumpled up paper and balls of cotton pressing on my toes.

"There! Are you happy now you miserable little darkie. Those shoes fit you just fine Lizzy. You ought to feel grateful for having something on your feet! Let me see you walk with them while holding the baby. Go on and don't be foolish! You are lucky to have shoes don't you see?" she barked, just like the dog with no name at the threshold whose loud growls and threats still managed to echo down the halls of my master's house.

Nervously and carefully, I proceeded to lift the baby and cradled her in my arms. The smell of her sweet breath distracted me for a minute as I stared into her beautiful eyes.

"Leeeeeeeeezzzzzzzy! What in the hell are you waiting for? Waaaaaaalk I said!" my mistress yelled causing the room to shake sending waves of shock down my spine that I nearly dropped the baby.

"Yes M'am, I'm sorry." I almost cried as I carefully took each foot in front of the other while learning to balance the newborn baby in my arms; all the while remembering my mother's words.

"Now Lizzy," said my mistress with a stern look on her face *"You are to always wear this..."* pointing to my new dress, and the voice in my head was my now my mother's, *"Lizzy, do not say a word unless asked to speak."*

Once again my mistress spoke, *"And you must not dirty your dress because you are now in charge of the baby..."* and the voice in my head was back to my mother's, *"Lizzy, do not touch anything."*

"Lizzy, the baby must always remain clean, and that means you need to change her often," she scoffed as the voice in my head was again my

mother's, *"Lizzy, do not look at anyone. Keep your eyes on the ground."*

"Yes M'am." I managed to utter still pondering the size of her curiously large belly. *How is it possible that the beautiful doe-eyed infant baby came out of her at all?* This curiosity became one of the greatest mysteries surrounding my childhood.

Despite my anxiety, I was quite thrilled at the idea of a new frock as the one I had already began to fray and was rather drab. Slaves were not supplied with much to begin with, and clothing was allotted only twice a year if the master was so inclined. The textile was purchased from the Petersburg factory by several bolts once a year. Small children in the plantation were usually naked and later by around age ten, boys were given breeches or short trousers and later, long trousers as they became older.

Girls would be given adult sized sheaths once they began to menstruate. Shoes were not often allotted, nor were hats. On most days, men and women wrapped their heads with a piece of fabric as a measure of protection from the heat. All the clothing in the plantation from the children to its oldest member, were assigned to be sewn by my mother, who never complained despite the arduous work it involved.

I learned that our ancestors wrapped their heads in the finest woven material to signify our long line of royalty. I questioned the accuracy of this account because in my young mind, how do Kings and Queens end up in a life of anguish; where they've become enslaved and subjugated their whole life with no hope for freedom whatsoever? I regarded this kind of storytelling as an escape from the darkness of our reality and to offer the younger generations a ray of hope and the will to live. As I grew older and wiser, I discovered the tales to be true after all. This oral history gave me the reverence for the fabrics and woven materials that influenced my approach as a dressmaker later on in my life.

I observed the simplicity of my new attire and the crisp contrast of the white apron against the canvas of black fabric that consumed me. The material was a light kind of woven linen that kept me cold in the winter months. It did not bother me much at all, for I preferred the relief it gave me during the scorching heat during the summer months.

The attire was something I considered most proper at the time. However, I know now that this was a most degrading kind of distinction that marked me as a house slave.

"Thank you M'am. I promise to do my very best to take care of your baby." I said as the words barely escaped my mouth. I was downright unacquainted with the task at hand. *How would I know what to do? What if I cannot soothe her? How often will she need to be fed? Who will help me change her soiled clothes? What if she falls ill? Where is my mother? Am I not still a baby*

myself?

My mistress and her mother gave me clear instructions to watch the infant child well, to rock the cradle constantly, to keep the flies out of her face and to never let it cry. I was given the role of being the baby's 'little maid,' a title I was proud to maintain in my four-year-old mind.

I did find it unnaturally strange that my mistress barely attended to her own daughter (or the rest of her brood for that matter) and instead busied herself with other concerns such as throwing luncheons for the other mistresses in Dinwiddie County, often giving the inducement of her 'fatigue' and 'melancholy' on account of childbirth as her reason to justify such actions.

"Lizzy, you must promise me to never let the baby out of your sight. You have a very important responsibility and one I normally would have tackled myself had it not been for this unyielding feeling of downheartedness I am experiencing at this time. You understand don't you?" mistress Burwell asked as she looked into the carved vanity mirror combing her hair.

"Yes M'am." was all I could utter for I knew nothing of what she

was saying and assumed she was simply uninterested in taking care of her nearly dozen children since little maids like me were at her disposal on demand.

I suppose it was only a matter of time when my little inexperienced hands and body would find its fate at the hands of my mistress' overseer. The night before, baby had kept me up all night with a bout of colic that caused me no opportunity for rest or sleep.

When I finally got the poor child to calm down, I too, found myself dozing off whilst still rocking the cradle when lo and behold the baby had fallen out of the bassinet bouncing off onto the floor rendering me to cry out loud *"Oh no! The baby has fallen to the floor! Mother? Oh no, Mama help me!"*

Panicked, dazed and stricken with fear, I reached for the first thing I could find and grabbed the fire shovel to pick up the poor baby who was crying so loudly causing the entire household to run upstairs only to find me crying just like my poor baby. I was so frightened at the possibility that something terrible may have happened to her that I had accidentally soiled my black dress and apron. Drenched in sweat and tears, I shivered as I heard my mistress' footsteps ascending the stairs.

"You stupid useless fool! Get out! I knew somehow you would not keep up with this simple task!" my mistress bellowed a thunderous scream as she ordered me to let go of the baby. It was sheer chaos as the entire Burwell household awoke while my panic-stricken fellow slaves stood huddled in one corner as they watched in fear at the horror that was soon to unfold for me.

"But M'am, I did not know what to do. Please forgive me!" I cried and I begged until I was later taken to the pantry, to be lashed by my mistress' overseer despite my pleas for forgiveness. The baby's cries were drowned out by my own and my shrieks of agony dulled out the sounds of my mother's screams I could hear from a distance below.

It is difficult to forget the moment the whip hit my back and the realization that my black dress had begun to tear, exposing my skin to meet the sting that numbed me. This went on for what seemed like an eternity as I cried out loud for my mother to save me, but she never came. I was alone in that room, faced down as I saw the floor, the walls and everything around me smattered with blotches of red pigment and fragments of what I have come to realize was my own bloodied skin.

"You stupid unusable idiot!" followed up with several harder blows to my back. I cried to the point of losing my breath.

"It hurts! Mama help! Please Stop! Help me!" I cried so loudly I could barely breathe.

These were the only words I could manage to say, and it seemed the more I begged for the lashings to cease, the more my Mistress Burwell's overseer whipped me.

I was in and out of consciousness, praying it was all a bad dream only to come back to my own reality that in fact the lashings I was undergoing was a first-hand introduction to my fate for the next decade or so to come.

I cried. I begged for it to stop. At one point I prayed for God to end my life. I would have been fine with death for at least it was not enduring. It seemed I had lived a hundred years too long in a never-ending cycle of suffering, lest I forget that I was only four years old.

When I awoke, my dress and apron barely hung on to my frail bloody little body; the white apron turned into a crimson color and the dress was now indistinguishable. Inasmuch as I despise what the dress represented, I was grateful for the additional layer of overing it served against the lashing on my skin. The urine that soiled underpants caused an even greater sear against my mangled skin.

This was my first realization of the severity of the cruelty that was ahead for me. I was mistaken to think that somehow, I would be spared. A 'house slave' carried no such distinction. We were all the same in the eyes of our oppressors.

"Mama? I'm sorry Mama," I managed to speak upon seeing her beautiful face covered in tears as she carried me ever so gently into her strong arms towards our cabin where she attended to my wounds. She was breathing heavily and mumbling at the same time. I could not make out what she was saying but I knew my mother was dangerously on the brink of acting on on her rage.

The following morning I learned that mother was engaged in a confrontation with Master Burwell for she returned to our cabin with a bloody broken lip.

As years had passed, my little baby grew into a strong-willed, healthy, assertive young girl and for many years had been the source of much suffering for me. I cannot even count how many ill-fitting black dresses and white aprons have seen the fate of a lashing. Over time, a strange layer of thick raised discolored patches left permanent scars on my skin.

By now, I abhorred the thin airy linen fabric and often fantasized that the dress be made of a thick woolen material instead, because maybe - just maybe, the lashing would not hurt so badly. I took solace during the fleeting moments of quiet time when I had an opportunity to rest while helping mother knit socks, shawls and bonnets, along with the other household duties to get my mind distracted from the flashbacks occurring in my head. Sometimes, a simple sound can send a frightening sensation throughout my body causing me to shake uncontrollably.

As a child, living in self-abasing fear was a normal occurrence that being joyful was more unsettling at times.

Master Burwell had himself four legitimate daughters, six legitimate sons and a very large employ of slaves in his household. I mention the word 'legitimate' being that I was born from his stock against my mother's will and while there was much talk about whether other children were fathered by him, I shall not speak on that behalf and can only speak for myself.

My mistress was an unrelenting foreperson who demanded a

never-ending list of tasks for my mother to complete in a day notwithstanding the other duties already laid out for her by Master Burwell.

"Mother, I cannot bear to see you suffer so much. I promise to hasten myself so that I may be able to help you." She offered me a half-smile. The tears from her eyes welled up like a cloud looming above waiting to violently pour. Somehow, her cries never came because she was too proud to let her tormentors see her crouch in fear. Every day I hurried myself to complete my own responsibilities to help her.

By now, I was around eight years old but already had the soul of a woman. Being an only child, my mother tended to me even more; though she too, needed tending.

My father was a slave who belonged to another man in a nearby plantation. The distance between us limited my understanding and knowledge of him. Like my mother, my father had the benefit of knowing how to read and write. He was restricted to see us and was only allowed to visit on Christmas and Easter until finally Master Burwell arranged for my father's owner to agree for the separation to end. I am uncertain as to what led him to have a moment of kindness, but I was not consumed by that curiosity for I felt separating children from their parents and wives from their husbands was a cruel and unjust implementation designed to torture and inflict pain and mental anguish against my people.

It was a cheerful day especially for my mother, since finally my father was anticipated to come home. The loneliness and weariness in her face soon faded and she proceeded to perform her tasks with great vigor and enthusiasm as the days of his homecoming drew near. It was apparent to me and to everyone who knew them, knew that they both loved each other so dearly, and that love extended to me in a most profound way.

"Finally, our family will be together again Elizabeth," mother whispered in my ear with great excitement as we lay close to each other on the ground inside our cabin with nothing but a feedsack

to keep us warm. I prayed earnestly wishing for night to hurry and turn to day for my father's homecoming. To mark this day of keeping, my mother carefully plaited my hair using a mixture of honey and grease and decorated it with remnants of colorful string. Mother and I could not sleep a wink that night, barely capable of holding back our laughter. It was one of my fondest, most joyful memories and the first time I ever recalled laughing and singing out loud.

When father arrived, he cried saying: *"I do not know which is more pleasing to me, whether I can finally hold my daughter or whether I can hold my wife or both!"*

He was a tall man of rich glowing ebony skin and thick brown hair with bright reddish strands at the tips from spending countless hours under the sun. His eyes were round balls of earthen amber, and his teeth were white as snow. He was of muscular build, with arms that extended past his hips with solid hands that whenever he held me, made me feel safe. He was a strong, earnest, handsome, able man and my love and affection for him was boundless.

Inside our cabin, my mother and father sat quietly together in a warm embrace after enjoying a hot meal of rice and beans with bits of savory smoked meat that had been simmering slowly since the previous day. The only light that flickered was a candle father lit during our meal.

They were sharing stories of a light-hearted nature when a sharp ominous knock on the door stopped all of us from our reverie. Like a dark cloud of evil, stood Master Burwell at the threshold of our cabin and delivered to us news that hit us like a bolt of lightning. Nothing could be more blood curdling than the anguished shriek of a father and maddening desperation in a husband's cry. There he was, my big, strong, able-bodied father, who wept like a child was now relegated to his knees in the utmost bleakest sense of helplessness and pain.

"No! Oh, dear Lord! I beg you Master to please let us not be separated like this. I beg you please Master!" my father cried out, but Master Burwell's words would soon be drowned out by my mother's wails

that accompanied my father's cries as I stood there in disbelief at the cruel news of our separation.

"Immediately." he said to my father *"You must join your master to go with him to the West in the morning."*

Master Burwell turned to me and said: *"Because your father's master has decided to make the West his future home Lizzy."*

"I do not wish to speak to you. I want my father to stay! You are evil and God shall seek vengeance upon you! I want my father to stay!"

tI screamed as Master Burwell met my cold stare. His eyes fixed to the floor and as he proceeded to turn towards the cabin's door. My mother grabbed me and covered my mouth with her hands to prevent me from admonishing Master Burwell some more.

"Hush Lizzy, hush, say no more," she whispered as she held her breath.

With his back to us, he said *"I shall have a wagon ready to take you to your new dwelling in the morning Hobbs. Mind your tongue Lizzy."*

As he shut the door behind him, I threw my rag doll against the door as hard as I could, and it fell to the ground limp and lifeless like the rest of us. Not fully satisfied, I picked it up and threw it into the fire where it belonged.

My father held on to my mother's bosom like a frightened child sobbing tearful cries as he implored the heavens to hear his pleas. The rest of our night was spent holding on to each minute huddled together in a tight embrace, crying. All I could think of is regretting how I wished for day to quickly turn into night just a day ago. It was the last time I made a wish about anything ever again.

Morning came and in an instant, it was also the very last time I would see my father again, the very last time I felt his kiss, the very last time I held him close to me. I was suffering an insurmountable heartbreak and a kind of death that I would not wish upon an enemy. He was gone forever, and mother stood helpless in shock at the virulence, malignity and poison of slavery.

My mother did not deserve this. My father did not deserve this. Speechless and in shock, I stared at the black dress and white apron that I was once so very proud of while the wagon that carried the love of my life away became nothing but a small black hole in the middle of nowhere until eventually vanishing from my view.

This dress represented the cataclysmic ruinous life that seemed to pose no hope for me. Mother and I were both in mourning. That night, instead of a prayer, I vowed that I was to rid myself of these garments as swiftly as possible and plotted with great calculation and determination my eventual plan to become free.

CHAPTER 2

Little Joe's Sunday Clothes and a Dress from Scraps

Awakened from my sleep from the vivid image of my father's face and the resonance of his voice in my dreams. *"She has grown into a large fine girl,"* my father remarked as he beamed with delight upon seeing me again shortly before our tragic separation where the days ahead proved bleak.

How I wished for my dream of his homecoming to never end. I eventually woke up in a feverish kind of sweat. This dream stayed with me throughout most of my childhood and adult life.

Mother and I found respite while mending garments and sewing clothes for the mistress and the Burwell family. I asked my mistress if she would be amenable to me salvaging the scraps and remnants of fabrics, trims and notions to which she let out a laugh as if to mock me for such a ridiculous idea.

"Whatever you are thinking of doing will be ridiculous! Imagine a day coat made from scraps? You must be stupid Lizzy! You are stupid actually! Dumb nigger girl!" as she continued to ridicule me further with insults.

"Leave it up to you dumb good for nothing half-breed darkie!" Her eyes appeared to dilate like the devil himself as she vanished up the stairs to the upper floor of the house. How I wished she never

emerged from her room ever again. How I wished her heart would simply stop beating. How I wished the quilt mother made to keep her warm at night would stifle her breath forever. How I wished.

"Never her mind, you go on make yourself a pretty frock Lizzy. I reckon it will be most handsome once you are done with it," mother whispered as she nudged me to quietly leave the room, her beautiful smile offering me the assurance I needed.

"Yes Mama," was all I could say.

"Besides, the dress does not make the person. The person makes the dress my child," she added with an encouraging kiss on my forehead.

My strength was often challenged every time I witnessed mistress demeaning my mother at the slight sign of her feeling sad over the separation from my father.

"Stop your imaginary sorrow and misconduct! This is non-sense as there is no need for making pretensions! You are incapable of love Aggy. You are a slave no different from the pigs in the farm! A savage soul as insignificant as the dirt I see under that chair! Now clean that dirt!" she yelled and smiled simultaneously as if to miniscule my mother even more.

"He is not the only God damn darkie that was sold from his family nor are you the only ones who have been separated! Go find another boy out there- there are plenty of them if you want a husband that desperately, so stop this ridiculous crying and lamenting and get to work! Get!" were her words that drove a deeper cut into my mother's already bleeding heart.

Mother never uttered a word and offered no response. She exuded a stoic strength that bothered and angered my mistress further. Without saying it, my mistress knew how much my mother abhorred the Burwell family, but I detested them even more, though I never showed it. In earnest, I prayed they would all unceremoniously vanish into thin air, rabid mongrel dog included.

Mother and Father made correspondences with one another for many years, and mother found comfort and consolation in reading old, faded letters my father had written to her in between correspondences. They were always full of prayerful words of cheer, encouragement, love and hope for brighter days ahead. He would write, *"Please tell my little Lizzy to be a good girl, to read her books, to write of'n."* He would always end his letters with promises of coming to see me one day, though that day never came. In one of his letters to mother, he wrote:

Shelbyville,TN Sept. 6, 1833. Mrs. Agnes Hobbs

"Dear Wife:

My dear biloved wife I am more than glad to meet with opportunty writee thes few lines to you by my Mistress who ar now about starterng to virginia, and sevl others of my old friends are with her; in compeney Mrs. Ann Rus the wife of master Thos Rus and Dan Woodiard and his family and I am very sorry that I havn the chance to go with them as I feele Determid. to see you If life last again. I am now here and out at this pleace so I am not abble to get of at this time.

I am write well and hearty and all the rest of master's family. I heard this eveng by Mistress that ar just from theree all sends love to you and all my old frends. I am a living in a town called Shelbyville and I have wrote a greate many letters since I've beene here and almost been reeady to my selfe that its out of the question to write any more at tall: my dear wife I dont feeld no whys like giving out writing to you as yet and I hope when you get this letter that you be Inncougege to write me a letter.

I am well satisfied at my living at this place I am a making money for my own benifit and I hope that its to yours also If I live to see Nexct year I shall heve my own time from master by giving him 100 and twenty Dollars a year and I thinke I shall be doing good bisness at that and heve something more thean all that.

I hope with gods helpe that I may be abble to rejoys with you on the earth and In heaven lets meet when will I am detemnid to nuver stope praying, not in this earth and I hope to praise God in glory there weel meet to part no more forever.

So my dear wife I hope to meet you In paradase to prase god forever * * * * * I want Elizabeth to be a good girl and not to thinke that because I am bound so fare that gods not abble to open the way -

George Pleasant, Hobbs a servant of Grum."

The day came when the last letter my mother received from my father was dated on March 20, 1839 from Shelbyville, Tennessee. He wrote of hopes of seeing her again. There was an apparent sense of strain in his words. This was the last time we ever heard from my father.

That same year, I was a witness to the sale of a human being for the first time when we were living in Prince Edward, Virginia.

A young boy named Little Joe whose mother was instructed by Master Burwell to dress him in his Sunday clothes was ordered to report to my master in his house.

I watched Little Joe's mother carefully and attentively button his shirt while she spoke gently to her sweet little boy. I paid close attention to the loving way by which she dressed him. In ritual-like manner, she slowly buttoned his shirt and every time she held each button, it would catch a glint of light making it sparkle like a gem.

Little Joe's shirt was ironed to perfection, and its collar stood handsomely up. I observed how necessary and vital it was to properly iron clothes for it delivered a posture unlike garments left to look wrinkled and formless. It pleased me to see Little Joe looking properly appointed.

The straps that held his pants up were a beautiful shade of deep blue just like how I imagined the ocean to be. His boots although tattered and in near ruin were polished so nicely that it sprung new life to them, and the strings were perfectly crossed and ending in a neatly tied bow. I wondered if Little Joe knew how to tie his shoes for he was only approximately five years of age.

His mother spoke gently and slowly, and I noticed a pin held the tendrils of tight curls that gracefully fell from the crown of her head. She was almost as beautiful as my own mother. *"Joe, mind ya' manners when you is in Master Burwell's home. Don't you speak to nobody 'less you is spoken to, and keep yo' eyes low to the ground ya' hear? Oh Joe, you sho' growed up to be a fine young man just like yo' father. Remember what Mama say now... ya' hear me son?"* and Joe gave his mother a nod to acknowledge her instructions.

These words sounded all too familiar some years ago when my own mother's litany of rules and regulations were made clear to me.

A bad feeling in my gut started brewing and I prayed to be proven wrong. Unbeknownst to his mother, Little Joe was to be sold to free my master from the embarrassment and shame for unpaid debts he incurred for some hogs he had purchased previously but was unable to pay for its remaining dues.

Little Joe arrived at the house eager and bright-faced and was then placed on the scales, just like the hogs sold at a rate per pound. Little Joe's mother was kept in the dark about the sale of her young son but she soon realized that something was dangerously wrong when a wagon left with her son in tow. Pleading and begging for my master not to take her son away from her, Master Burwell ordered her to quiet herself as her son was simply *'taking a short leisurely ride to town in the wagon'* but that *'he would be back in the morning.'*

"Be quiet and get back to the house now, ain't nothing gonna happen to your son, I promise. Now get going before Mistress finds you out here wasting her time. Get! Skedaddle on outta here!" Master Burwell scoffed.

Morning turned into night as night turned into morning again and again and as the years passed and Little Joe's mother was eventually laid to her grave without ever seeing her son. I remember a time when Little Joe's mother was whipped severely for grieving the loss of her son because Master Burwell did not like to see his slaves looking sullen or sad. Master Burwell made it very clear to all of his slaves that if anyone were to offend him this way, that they would be severely punished. We were expected to behave and look 'happy.'

Master Burwell owned seventy slaves, all of whom were later sold; where wives were separated from their husbands and children torn away from their parents, siblings never to see each other again.

Another story that left a stain in my mind involved my uncle, who was my mother's older brother, Amos. Also a slave of Colonel Burwell's, my Uncle Amos had accidentally lost a pair of plough lines. Upon discovering the news, Master Burwell replaced it with a new pair but made it very clear to my uncle that if they were to come up missing again, that he would be severely punished as a result.

One morning, my uncle confided to my mother saying *"Oh Aggy! I done lost the secun set'uf lines again an' I don't wunna be lashed. Won't you please talk to master an' beg him to spare yo' bruther? I pruhmis I gon' try find it as best I can."*

"Yes, I will do my best to talk to Master Burwell, but for now try to steer clear of the overseer's way so as not to make him suspicious you hear?" Mother instructed as she hurried to the main house to request to speak with our master. I followed mother without her knowing and tried to listen intently through the crack of the window outside the pantry room where mother and Master Burwell where talking.

"You know better than to come to me making excuses for that useless fool! I have hogs worth more than that bag of bones! Aggy you know there is nothing you ask of me that I most likely will not deny, but No! I shall not be convinced otherwise. Leave my presence now before I slap the lights out of you!" he scolded despite my mother's tearful pleas.

Back at the cabin, my uncle was told of my master's response, and it frightened me to know what was to take place the next day. I ran to my uncle and gave him a long embrace and whispered into his ear, *"It helped me to think of a faraway place where nothing could harm me, and*

I imagine it to be a golden pasture where all of us were free to roam." I opened the palm of his right hand and gave him a pearl that my father gave me as a totem of protection.

My uncle smiled, *"Thank you 'Lizbeth. I'se sho would like to be in dat goldin pasture you is talkin' 'bout chile. I reckon it be sumthin' close to heaven. Dis sho is a purty lookin' pearl jus' like you."*

The following morning, my mother went to fetch some water in a nearby spring and looked up at the old oak tree to find the stiff cold body of her brother, hanging lifelessly beneath one of the branches.

"Massa! Massa! Oh God help! Help!" dropping the bucket, my mother screamed in horror as she ran to the house and eventually fell to her knees before reaching the gate.

My uncle had taken his own life rather than be punished and scourged to near death the way Colonel Burwell's overseers does to his slaves who offend him. His right fist was clenched shut and when we labored to pry it open and when we did, I discovered the pearl I had given that night. In a strange way, I envied my uncle for he no longer had to carry the weight of his suffering. Finally, he was at peace.

On the following day, Scipio found the plough lines inside one of the overseer's sacks and upon hearing this, my mother went into a fit of hysteria. Uncle Amos hadnt lost the ploughlines after all for it was the overseer who maliciously plotted to frame my uncle this whole time.

My mother was inconsolable by this news and remained incapacitated by grief. Aggravated and perturbed by this disruption, Master Burwell called upon the assistance of Dr. Cooper who administered a heavy dose of Laudanum, a tincture that rendered my poor mother sedated for a few hours. Aunt Evaline sat by my mother's bedside inside her cabin in constant prayer for her to awake.

"Oh God they done killed Aggy!" she cried. I did not believe her for I knew Master Burwell was too infatuated with my mother to kill her. It was a disturbing conflict of sorts in my mind.

I ran myself back to the site of my Uncle's lifeless body before anyone from the plantation got a hold of him. It was a common practice to immediately bury the bodies of slaves upon their passing which always took place at night in a designated area along the river by Master Burwell's plantation.

"I am sorry to see you pass Uncle. Please forgive me for taking something from you without asking, but I must keep you with me always," I said to the body hanging on the tree.

I took my father's knife hidden under the planks by the hennery and cut a piece of fabric from my uncle's pants. Later, I would include this remnant into a lovely quilt I later gave to my son on Christmas. Grieving our loved ones was disallowed, so I directed my sadness and sorrow on my sewing instead.

As I was developing into a young woman, so did my interest in sewing develop. One can only imagine the amount of scrap materials and fabrics I have collected over the years. I fantasized often about a day dress of a simple silhouette, with lines that gave me an air of dignified importance. I was exacting and scrupulous in my process and never hastened my method, thinking in due course the dress will be completed.

There never seemed to be enough time to work on it so before turning in for the night, I would neatly fold it and place it inside a woven basket that mother gave me to store my most cherished belongings which included the letters my father wrote to me, a lock of his hair, my needles and thread, a small pouch containing pearls from father, and a lucky feather a Pamunkey native girl gave me during one of my wanderings to plot my escape but never fully carried off.

In my early teenage years around the year of 1832, I was loaned out and sent to live with my master's son (whom I later learned was my half-brother) Mr. Robert Armistead Burwell, a minister of the Presbyterian order. He was of limited means with a small salary. His wife, Mrs. Margaret Anna Robertson Burwell was highly educated and well read. Despite this, she came from a needful background, was terribly insecure and assumed that I made judgments about her. I never held any grudge against her and sought to seek her favor to avoid any discourse that would jeopardize my safety.

I was sent by my master to serve them on the basis as a loan, as they did not have the money to purchase me and I performed the duties of not just one servant, but that of ten. Despite the service I rendered, I was treated with insults and distrust. I was spit on, slapped, scolded, starved, ridiculed and demeaned. I suffered the constant whippings that posed no promise to cease. It was a lonely existence having no one to talk to for I was the only servant working in the home. To this day, I fathom at my abilities of having performed the duties of ten slaves while enduring the abuse.

Some years had passed, and I had grown to be a strong and able woman at nearly 17 years of age. By now, I had grown to a height like my mother standing at a little over six feet tall and possessed a physical nature that was described by a distinguished Southern white businessman as more than satisfactory.

"That is one fine looking Negress," this white man said when he accidentally bumped into me while accompanying my mistress during one of our trips to the densely packed market in our township.

Beads of sweat formed on his forehead, his cheeks flustered pink, his eyes wide with bewilderment and his mouth agape, as he stood inches in front me appearing mesmerized and confused by his very own reaction when he unexpectedly uttered those words.

"You ought to be ashamed of yourself Sir! That is a Negro woman and MY slave you are fawning over! Scram Sir! Shame on you! Skidoo out of here and get in the wagon Lizzy, Now!" my mistress harrumphed as she squeezed my cheek and pinched me to the point where she drew blood from her sharp nails. To the embarrassment of the white man who was caught off-guard, my mistress spit out from the window of the carriage to further make her point. As the carriage drove away, I saw from the window that the man was still standing by the street lamp, frozen with his mouth still agape.

"Fool!" my mistress yelled out of the window. The ride home was no less unpleasant for mistress took it upon herself to accuse me of being a temptress among a slew of other words of debasement and degradation. She ordered me a barrage of household chores outside of my usual duties until it was almost sunrise.

Once back in my cabin, I sewed and focused myself to complete my dress of two years in the making made from scraps. It turned out to be quite lovely, in variegated shades of the forest in green, brown and the colors of autumn leaves.

I created the dress to fit my exact proportions but sensibly designed the bosom and torso area to be less figure forming and the skirt less womanly by creating a silhouette that resembled men's suiting. This was a calculated decision to blend in and not attract any attention to myself whatsoever. I saw the art of dress as a means of survival more than anything else.

Unlike the fashion of the times, the dress covered my entire personhood from the neck to the hemline with sleeves that concealed my golden-brown skin. Suffice it to say that I had fashioned a garment intended to serve as a deterrent from the lascivious stares and advances of Southern white men. To some degree, I succeeded. I had no idea how powerful and convincing the art of dress could be and only realized it during the many years later that followed.

Sometime around the year 1837, Young Mr. Burwell was appointed a new post and to take charge of a new church in Hillsborough, North Carolina. His salary was still small and thus unfortunately, my station as a slave on loan continued. During this time, young Master Burwell was exceedingly kind to me and although I felt this kindness to be duplicitous, it was still much better than being maltreated. There was a village schoolmaster of the town's church whose name was Mr. William Bingham. Mr. Bingham was known to be a cruel and cold-hearted man.

He was of medium build, his face unmemorable and he possessed the disposition of a destructive beast who enjoyed inflicting pain. His face was covered by a Garibaldi beard that started on one side of his face to the other, the only feature my memory allows me to remember of this miserably cruel man. He walked with a swift gait with footsteps that left an imprint on the ground.

Many school children were afraid of his temper and avoided him at all costs. Meanwhile, Mistress Burwell seemed to have a never-ending desire to inflict pain upon me. Her vitriol against me finally materialized when she convinced Master Robert to loan me out to Mr. Bingham to 'break' me. Mr. Bingham touted himself as a pious man, yet his agenda to break me defied all teachings of Christianity.

Breaking a slave meant tearing down their will to succumb them into obedience and facilitate the ease of a slave owner to control them. I never once thought that Master Robert would ever give in to his wife's demands and yet he did.

One night, her vindictive ways proved victorious when Mr. Bingham came to visit one evening. I was attending to the baby and as I bent over to put the infant down to bed, Mr. Bingham ordered me to meet him in the study.

Upon entering the room, he quickly shut the door and said, *"Lizzy, I am going to flog you."*

"Whip me? What for Mr. Bingham? Why? What have I done?" I asked.

Ignoring my questions, he ordered me to immediately remove my dress and demanded that I turn around to be flogged.

Although he knew that I was a fully developed woman at age eighteen, he nonetheless insisted on the removal of my dress and undergarments.

Refusing to disrobe, I said: *"I will not allow you to whip me!"*

This did not settle well with him, and he proceeded to tie me with a rope while ripping my dress off me. I fought and resisted for at least an hour until he succeeded to fully disrobe and bind me. He then grabbed a rawhide and proceeded to graze it over my shoulders as if to taunt me with what was ahead. Then with calculated measure, like a well-practiced expert, he raised the rawhide with a steady hand, gasped for air as if to gain a blessing and swiftly descended the instrument of torture with such sizable force to land on my skin sending me into momentary fragments of unconsciousness only to be awakened by yet another more serious blow.

My body shuddered and broke into a series of convulsions as my skin was cut open into instant welts of raw flesh - the blood violently exiting my being.

The poor infant baby was crying as she laid inside her crib and all I could think of now was the virulence and lack of human decency Mr. Bingham showed at that moment, exposing an innocent child to the malignancy of his ways.

Yet despite the severity of the agony and pain I was enduring, I did not scream, nor did I cry or beg for relief. I vowed to myself to never allow my tormentor to have the pleasure of knowing my suffering. I prevented myself from making any sounds, not even a whimper broke out of me as I stood there appearing unfazed by the immoral debauchery that was taking place.

Repeatedly, I could feel him gather more nerve to yield another blow, each one more forceful than the other. The more he whipped me, the easier it seemed for him to do so.

He was nearly out of breath once he was finished and he prayed as I collected my garment. I dressed myself quietly and hurriedly went back to the pastor and his wife, holding back the tears and the screams I yearned to express but withheld.

Prayers were supposed to be iterations of hope I thought. I discerned that night there were two kinds of Gods that people worship: The God of Good and The God of Evil. My intention to pray kept getting interrupted by the excruciating pain on my back and I could do was to cover my mouth with the dress I made from scraps to dull and mute out my screams. The dress was supposed to protect me and I realized nothing was safe from demons that plagued us slaves. Nothing.

Neither Master Robert nor Mistress Anna came to check on me or for that matter their infant baby whom I was still ordered to care for despite my condition. They were complicit in the near murder of me, and they allowed their child to be present in the room. By virtue of the presence of violence alone should have been enough to raise them to their feet to remove their child out of there. How does one become inculcated into the daily practice of such violence?

"Master Robert, why did you allow Mr. Bingham to whip me? Why are you punishing me?" I asked, thinking that maybe he would offer some empathy. Master Robert was reading a book whilst Mistress Anna was seated on a rocking chair pretending to busy herself with some needlepoint held by a hoop.

"Leave me be. Go away and stop bothering me Lizzy!" he said as he dismissed me away. I insisted to be given an answer and refused to leave. Flushed with anger, he picked up the heavy wooden chair he was sitting on and bashed it upon me so hard causing me to collapse to the floor. The chair's structure broke into segments no longer discernable from its original form. Several of its nails embedded upon my already mangled back causing me to howl from the pain of a quasi-kind of crucifixion.

I lay there, motionless, deadened and stifled from the pounding of my nerves. My ears were ringing in a momentary kind of deafness, and nothing was making sense to me anymore except for the cold floor that offered a soothing feeling against my half-naked body; my dress barely covering me as I painfully crawled myself slowly back into my room. I did not have any of mother's salve to tranquilize nor sedate my wounds, so I resorted to sitting upright instead. The salty sweat that trickled down my back stung the open flesh so violently in a kind of torture indescribable in words.

The affliction was so unbearable that I stayed up all night with eyes wide open from the agony until morning came. There was no one there to help me for I was the sole slave working for young Burwell. How I managed to tend to my wounds was nothing short of a miracle.

I prayed. All I could do was to pray. Before I knew it, I found myself stitching the rips and tears from my dress that Mr. Bingham had caused and pledged to behave as if nothing had happened to me the following morning. Praying and sewing became my only refuge. I was resolute in mending the damage he caused not only to my dress but also to my physical and spiritual welfare. I asked for my fear and anguish to be replaced with peace and courage instead.

Morning came and not a kind word was offered to me as I overheard Mr. Bingham telling Mrs. Burwell that he plighted himself to subjugate my stubborn pride.

The following Friday, a week after the incident, Mr. Bingham once again ordered me to the study where he was to perform another round flogging with a new rope to tie me and a freshly cut piece of rawhide of sizable measure to beat me with. By now, I understood him to be resolute in breaking and subjugating me.

I arrived to face him and said, *"I am prepared to die Mr. Bingham but you may never conquer me."* In the process of our struggle, I bit his finger to its bone giving him more reason to batter me for another hour or so until I lost consciousness and succumbed on the floor.

When I finally awoke, I felt his foot poking at my side to urge me to get up like a sleeping dog.

"Wake up Lizzy!" he said breathless and exhausted.

This was my cue that I had been given permission to go home. I managed to gather myself together and realized my wounds were still so raw that every small movement I made caused my body to jerk and convulse from the pain.

"Get out, you've exhausted me unnecessarily Lizzy." he said as the

sweat running profusely through his woolen coat left an offensive odor in the air.

The following Thursday, Mr. Bingham once again tried to vanquish me and repeatedly beat me. I remained pugnacious and resistant to capitulating into submission. Halfway through the beating, he let out a loud cry and asked for my forgiveness for he could no longer participate in the beatings.

"Vengeance is not mine, but the Lord's," I said as I left the study hobbling back to my room. The years that followed demonstrated Mr. Bingham to be an altered man and never again did he lay a hand on me or utter any words to degrade me.

He was known to never strike any of his servants again since that Thursday afternoon. I had deduced that my life would finally be somewhat lifted from the whippings, but I was wrong.

The young Master Burwell portrayed himself as a pious man who preached the word of the Lord at the pulpit thrice a week. When Mrs. Burwell found out that her husband had refused to whip me any further, the young Master Burwell was beckoned by his wife to do so himself.

I was attending to some household chores when Master Robert grabbed an oak broom that lay idly on the floor and snapped the handle off.

With the heavy end of the handle, he attempted to conquer me as I tried with all my might to fight him unsuccessfully. My body lay limp as he continued to pummel and beat me with the wooden broomstick. The force of the blows he drove to my body caused the broomstick itself to break into several pieces.

The sight of the deranged Master Robert depraving my bloodied body and lacerated flesh caused my mistress to order him to immediately cease and desist. Even her cold-blooded jealous heart could no longer take it.

"Oh God please stop! I cannot bear to see this anymore," she pleaded.

The beating was so heinous that I was rendered incapacitated in bed for five whole days. Not long after this, Master Burwell attempted once again to conquer me and at the sight of my unconsciousness vowed never to beat me again. My mental state of mind was bruised and bitter with anguish and despair, yet I stood proud knowing that the details of my suffering became the town's subject of scrutiny leaving my oppressors regarded in a bad light. At least I convinced myself of this understanding and whether it was true, found it necessary to lean on this sentiment for the sake of preserving my mental state of mind.

Young Master Burwell, as difficult as it is to swallow, was in fact my brother and yet nothing, not even the blood we both shared through our veins could convince him to treat me with even just an ounce of kindness.

This abuse was not the only source of my sufferings during my residency in Hillsborough. I would be someone best described as a Mulatto, a fair skinned blue-eyed Negro who became the object of attention of many white Southern men. Consequently, the white women in our township had so much contempt against me that I was often subjected to their ridicule and mockery. I was never spared from their rancorous inclinations and found it utterly incomprehensible that anyone of their stature and prominence would ever find reason to be resentful and begrudging of a slave girl like me.

There was highly respected prominent white man in our locality named Mr. Alexander McKenzie Kirkland. He maintained a good reputation as a businessman, husband and father.

One day on my way home from collecting Mr. and Mrs. Burwell's mail, Mr. Kirkland stopped me in my tracks and asked me to come into his office to ask me a question. Upon entering his study, he forced himself upon me and threatened to harm me if I said anything to anyone. The following day, Mr. Kirkland repeated to act out his fantasies of conquering a Negro woman and I was reminded once again of his threats.

"I will kill you Lizzy if you dare tell your Master Robert about this. Besides, no one would believe you. You'd be given the curse of a temptress by everyone," he said as he continued to terrorize me one night.

He and his wife were often seated at the dining table whenever my Master and Mistress hosted gatherings in their home. He assaulted and raped me on an almost daily basis for four agonizing years and the harm he caused upon me resulted in me becoming a mother. All my life, I never revealed who the father of my child was and dealt with the shame quietly on my own.

Born healthy and sound, I named him *'George Pleasant Hobbs'* after my father. I often wondered how I could absolve my son from the sufferings of a bleak future knowing that the life he was to embark on was a dark and dismal existence ahead. How I longed for the day when freedom was within our grasp.

These were the thoughts that ran through my mind. I felt an enormous sense of guilt and remorse for him for the humiliation, pain and scorn he would soon endure. At night I prayed that God spared him for I never wanted to bring him to this kind of existence, yet here I was about to undertake the long journey as a mother, inside this weary body was the son of Kirkland, who is to be born a slave no matter his father's station in life, no matter the blood that runs through him, no matter if one half of him was free.

I questioned whether or not I will ever rise from this deep chasm of suffering and the impending feeling of fear looming over me with each passing day as my belly grew; as my baby became more and more human, only for my child to arrive into this earth less base than the cattle that grazes the pastures beyond. *How on earth will I do this? How?*

CHAPTER 3

Dressing for a Betrothal

I t was Spring, on the month of March in the year 1838, when news of six weddings to be held in October were to take place in Hillsborough, North Carolina. A strange custom in the South allowed me the benefit of being a bridesmaid to these weddings even though I was the only Negro girl in the bridal party. According to this custom, this distinction was particularly common especially to Negro women who were considered attractive, well-mannered and poised.

I wrote a letter to my mother and asked her to send me a pretty frock as I was to be an attendant for two of these most auspicious events. I asked her to send it to Mrs. Robertson's servant Miss Bette who would then plan to send it to me.

With only a week left before Miss Sarah Cooke's wedding and seeing that I had not yet heard back from mother, I set out to make a dress of my own. By now, my figure had already fully developed, and I was aware of its implications and effect upon white men and their wandering eyes and libidinous desires.

Careful not to draw too much attention to myself, my goal was to create a dress that was both suitable and appropriate as well as modest.

For this undertaking, I used the taffeta fabric salvaged from the home of Master Burwell when my mistress had undergone a change of furniture and decorations in the sitting room facing the entryway. She considered the drapery of a *'washed out shade of coral'* though I fancied it very much.

Once again, my propensity to see the potential in things led me to ask if I could keep the material to which she replied *"For the love of God Lizzy, whatever for? That taffeta is as dull as sitting through Sunday service but go ahead and suit yourself."*

"Never her any mind," I thought to myself for surely something magnificent could be made from these volumes upon volumes of silk of excellent quality. I calculated that I would have enough material left over to assemble a few shawls for mother and myself, as well as yardage enough for another ball gown.

In the wee hours of the night, I frenzied and hurriedly assembled a dress of the utmost distinction. One would fathom at its prior station in life as the sitting room's drapery, but it bothered me none whatsoever.

I cut the fabric against the grain to allow the material to fall quietly against my form. My Uncle Solomon once taught me this technique when he demonstrated the importance of cutting a section of a cow he had butchered. Once it was cooked, it would render a most tender texture when cut on the bias or as he explained, *"Cut against the grain of the meat."*

Surely I concluded that the same principle applied in the same way to fabric given the similarity of the fibers.

With the warp and the weft of the material resembling a piece of meat, I discovered a technique in my garment construction. I applied this approach to practically every garment requiring a particular silhouette for so long as I had enough fabric to accommodate it. Sometimes in the past, if I did not have enough material, I would piece together remnants to make up for the missing yardage.

For this dress however, a rather simple silhouette with a Basque like waistline was the only element I desired to accentuate because the opulence of the silk itself was adequate enough to leave a lasting impression. I was wise not draw too much attention to myself given it is the bride's moment to shine. Simple delicate pearls my father bequeathed to me that I turned into buttons by painstakingly carving holes into them were sewn, located at the center of the bodice that served as stand-ins for jewelry I did not own.

I hastened against time to fashion a simple cape that fell to my waist in the event that I would catch a chill. It was a decision I was most grateful for, considering how cold the evening ended up being. To create a decorative element, I fashioned a 1/4" trim cut into the shape of petals and sewed it along the hemline made from the same taffeta. The result was a frock of absolute perfection. I was thrilled to attend the wedding in a dress of this beauty indeed.

Hot tea was served with an accompaniment of home baked sweets. To my surprise, Mrs. Adeline Sutton requested my services in having a dress made to her specifications. after finding out I sewed my own dress.

She asked, *"Oh Lizzy! Would you be amenable to making me a dress in that same shade of coral? I absolutely love the color and feel it would be suitable for a day dress and matching coat. What do you think?"*

It tickled me to hear this given how offensive the washed-out shade of coral seemed to be for my mistress. I gladly obliged to Mrs. Sutton's request especially since I had at least ten more yards of this coral silk drapery tucked away in my room.

How utterly fetching it was to have my first commissioned garment. I was most flattered at her faith and confidence in my abilities.

I decided from now on, I am to be my own walking bulletin and display. My mind spun into several directions on how to acquire materials and tools in order to accomplish this goal. I remember declaring to the Lord above that this was his will and thus it is done.

Mrs. Sutton asked that I meet her the following week to attend to her specifications and I was thrilled at the opportunity.

Mrs. Sutton was the bride's mistress and the wife of the man who owned the mercantile in Hillsborough. Talk around town was that the Sutton family footed the entire bill for Miss Sarah's betrothal, and it pleased me to know this, especially since my dear friend Sarah's father had recently met his maker in heaven after a terrible bout with the chills that brought him to his death.

Good old Mrs. Sutton advanced me a generous sum of money not only for the first commissioned dress and coat ensemble but also for several others she requested for her wardrobe.

She said, *"Lizzy, I assure you that from now on, provided that your work remains consistent, I shall inform all my lady friends of your services."*

I finally had enough earnings to start my very own 'secret' dressmaking services for hire. I began writing down my ideas on how to operate my little enterprise with the current inventory of materials I had on hand.

"I must command a fair price at the onset so as to help advance my future goals," I wrote on one of the first pages of my daybook where I also kept record of all ideas, client's specifications and accounting of supplies, fabric, as well as a log of how many hours I spent sewing each dress.

"I must roll over whatever income I make towards buying our freedom," was another entry I made. I was so focused on my dressmaking that I recited these notes often in my head.

For the wedding of Miss Anne Nash, I planned to wear a lovely blue cotton dress that Aunt Bella sent as a gift. It was a beautiful dress whose color matched my eyes. I was so particular with it that I had only worn it once and made every effort never to soil it.

I only had a week to get myself together and most of my time was spent sewing the coral-colored dress and coat for Mrs. Sutton.

My blue dress however needed a few modifications to make it appropriate enough to wear after sundown. A slight adjustment to the sleeves, the waist and bodice was all it needed.

I affixed a corsage that mimicked a small bouquet of miniature roses in various stages of bloom made from the left-over fabric from the sleeves and it served a most befitting final touch.

I must admit that Aunt Bella had a keen sense for beautiful things, especially dresses. She herself never looked disheveled or consumed, regardless if her days were spent laboring under the hot sun. I always fathomed at her composure and dignity and endeavored to mimic her self-possession.

I arrived to the wedding in what I would consider as the event's most well-dressed guest, from which more of my services were requested. By evening's end, I had acquired several patrons for custom orders, three of whom gave me generous payments in advance.

It was beginning to become more apparent that dressmaking was opening a new world of possibilities, centered on my yearning desire to buy my freedom along with my son's.

It became clear to me that my needle, thread and scissors were my most valuable weapons and the shield that would protect me in the years ahead were the dresses I would soon create. I was ready.

CHAPTER 4

Stitching My Freedom

O ne night, I found myself staring at my son as he slumbered in his sleep asking myself the question, *"Why should my son be bound into slavery?"*

Although my love for him is great, the truth remains that he sprung forth into this earth through no will of mine. What is certain is that I love him with such immensity that nothing deters me from doing everything in my power to ensure his freedom.

The two opposite worlds running through his veins represent an Anglo-Saxon entitled kind of freedom, while the other represented the African stain of despair. By the laws of God, one half of my son is free leaving me to ask the question, *"Why then does his birthright to be free be usurped by his other half that is shackled in a cursed lifetime of suffering?"*

In an unexpected turn of events, I returned to Virginia after some years of serving the young Master Burwell and his wife in North Carolina. I was relieved by this change in my servitude but later came to find out I was to support a family of seventeen.

Mr. Hugh Garland was an educated man whose law practice was not doing very well. Mr. Garland married one of my master's oldest daughters, Miss Ann Burwell and I was sent to them as a wedding gift.

Their life was unpropitious with one struggle after another eventually moving to St. Louis, Missouri with hopes of improving their fortune up West. Hard times and adversity followed Mr. Garland no matter what, to the extent that he was so poor that he could no longer even afford to pay for the small sum of dues for one mere letter in the post for him. Their condition was so dire that it was suggested for my mother to be placed in their service to be hired out as a dressmaker to help pay for Garland's bills.

The idea of my aging, gray and tired mother toiling away in servitude did not settle well with me. She dedicated her entire life to the Burwell family and though her time of servie there was grim and full of suffering, she knew nothing other than being a permanent part of their lives. To think that my mother would be ordered to serve strangers at her tired and aging disposition was an idea I vehemently opposed.

A thousand times, perhaps a million times is a resounding no, as I would much rather work myself to the marrow and to my last breath rather than witness my mother spend her last years in tireless labor. I implored Master Burwell to send me to work for the Garlands instead. Luckily they agreed and I was sent immediately to commence work for the Garlands. I vowed to pour myself into my sewing, until my fingers were rendered bloody, and my eyes blurred from the hours working at dusk to dawn in pursuit of completing a dress for my patrons.

I was responsible for an entire family to support and so I begged for work from every nook and cranny I found an opportunity and solicited my services as a dressmaker to anyone willing to take me on for my services.

No job was too small for me if it meant alleviating my mother from further hardship. I soon gained a small following and earned for myself a reputation as an able and reliable dressmaker. My patrons were some of the most respected ladies of St. Louis and my calendar quickly became full.

It became clearer to me to see to it that my son be spared the misfortune of his station in life and so with never-ending perseverance, I finally made some progress one day face to face with Master Garland, *"What will it take Master for me to purchase myself and my son's freedom? How much will you require for me to buy our freedom?"*

Staring towards the river, he sucked the tobacco collected inside his mouth, took a moment to pause to spit its essence on the ground hitting the tip of his shoe and said: *"Lizzy, why must you be a constant gnat trying to suck the blood out of me? Have you not been told not to pester me with such ridiculous questions and delusional hopes? You were a slave then, a slave now and a slave forever more!"* he barked.

"But Master, I have been good and loyal to you. I have served you and your children all these years. I have made you a very wealthy and comfortable man. What does one Negro slave woman and a useless boy do for you these days but an added burden of two more mouths to feed? With what is happening between the North and South, there are talks that the South will not prevail. And what now with two extra slaves to be responsible for? Let me buy our freedom now so you can profit before it is too late! Before the North prevails and you and all of this will be deemed a criminal act punishable by the laws of this land," as I repeated the dialogue I recited over and over in my head in the previous weeks that led to this moment.

I could not believe I uttered such confrontational words while at the same time begging him to agree. I shook in terror at the prospect of getting severely beaten for my boldness and audacity.

"The North shall not prevail. This nation is built on the business of slavery. It is rich because of it and there is no way the South will secede. But Oh God! Once and for all Lizzy, take this for I cannot listen to your constant whimpering anymore!" he said as he pulled out the shiniest silver quarter of a dollar I had ever seen from his right front pocket. I noticed my own handiwork with his initials embroidered upon the pocket of his trousers itself as he flung the shiny coin up in the air

towards me as I caught it with great dexterity. Master Garland offered a hearty laugh as if to compliment me on my keen ability. Still, I felt I could not trust him.

"Ha! If you are resolute in the purchase of your freedom and endeavor to leave me, take this silver quarter to pay for you and your son's journey by ferry and upon reaching the other side at the end of the river, you and your son will finally be free! Now leave as quickly as possible. I wish to no longer speak to you of this matter again, now go!"

In shock I stood there unsure how to respond but found myself saying the following words: *"The laws of this land define me as your slave. And I will choose to be free by the laws of this land in the process by which I need to abide by."* I knew that my son and I could suffer a great risk by not adhering to the law's process and I was unwilling to take the chance.

With The Fugitive Slave Act now strongly enforced, I knew that I could not live openly as a free woman without the proper emancipation papers. This was something that Master Garland understood all too well, having been one of the lawyers to argue the case on the behalf of Mrs. Irene Emerson, a woman who owned slaves named Dred and Harriet Scott, in the highly talked about lawsuits filed in the Missouri courts for the Scotts' freedom.

As time passed, Master Garland's health started to worsen and sinking into deeper financial hardship, reconsidered my request and offered to accept $1,200 as full payment in exchange for our freedom. Around this time, I met my future husband, Mr. James Keckley who presented himself to me as a free man.

I spent days without proper rest or sleep, sometimes skipping meals other than a small piece of bread and a hot cup of water indulged with a squeeze of lemon from a small batch given to me by Mrs. Carter. My life was consumed with the great burden of having to take care of 17 mouths feed, including my son and myself. I had to figure out a way to raise the money I needed sooner than ever for fear that Master Garland might change his mind.

The anxiety that came along with this undertaking led me to find respite in some of the most unexpected places. One afternoon, I discovered that lemons originated in Egypt; Africa's most civilized nation and learned that it had many wonderful qualities aside from being edible, heightening flavors in food and aiding in digestion and other ailments. I also discovered that it serves as a helpful and quick remedy in removing unwanted stains in fabrics.

Occasionally, I would be so exhausted that my eyes would be shut yet my hands would still be sewing. Sometimes, I would prick my fingers bloody while half-asleep. My first reaction was that of dismay when the silk of one of my most valuable patron's dresses became soiled with my blood.

Quickly, I reached for my cup of now cold water and lemon drink and gently dabbed a soft towel into the cup and proceeded to wipe off the bloodstain. I was relieved to discover that this was a solution to most of my future mishaps. I also discovered that when used in larger volumes, can serve as a lightening agent to change the hue or tint of a fabric from its original state. I enjoyed creating new colors and from this one fruit alone.

I avoided letting anything go to waste either; using the rind to serve as a liniment to my tired skin and perfuming myself with its citrus aroma on days when I needed a little refreshing especially when meeting my patrons for their fittings or consultations. Its fragrance permeated my makeshift workshop, but I never alluded to its origins every single time my clients would ask:

"Why Lizzy, whatever is that glorious perfume lingering in your workshop? It smells divine! Is it French?"

I realized then that as a dress shop, it was not only necessary to provide my clients a dwelling wherein they could not only escape from the rigors of their lives as women of high caliber and importance, but it was equally vital to create an environment that made them feel beautiful, desirable, effervescent and youthful. Creating an atmosphere of luxury, elegance and style was to be the backbone of my future dress shop, and the dresses were the final act of the experiences I would provide.

For now, I made it fashionable to sip hot water and lemon juice exclusive of tea, from a set of mismatched China hand-me-downs and thrown away pieces I've collected over the years. I learned that some of my clients had followed suit by serving the same drink in their own homes to their friends and family. It delighted me to know that my simple concoction was well received amongst the elite circles around town.

I eventually gained a small clientele of faithful patrons who by word of mouth garnered me a more than satisfactory reputation as a dressmaker of distinction. I was quickly becoming a sought-after skilled mantua maker offering dresses of utmost quality and style.

The well-to-do wives and their daughters subsidized an income that allowed me the advantage of a fully booked forecast of made-to-measure dresses as far as six months to three years in commitment.

My work enabled me to fully support my master's children's household comprised of 17 mouths to feed for almost three years in relative comfort and ease. This self-discovery of my ability, skill and endurance led me to become even more steadfast in pursuing my freedom.

I was enterprising enough to set aside a small portion of my earnings towards the sum of money required by my master to buy our freedom.

I often wondered how Mr. Garland felt, given his servant slave is the one putting bread on the table whilst his fortunes continued to take a downward declining pattern. I felt a strange sense of sympathy for him and often tried to console him even though my natural instincts felt disdain or sometimes wished to seek vengeance for the wrongs they committed against me and all of us for that matter.

"With every stitch, I envision a life I wished to have. In all of slavery's sham and drudgery, I find comfort in creating a secret world

immersed in beauty and an imaginary existence where nothing would hurt me. The dresses I make serve as an armor and protection against the cruel world out there. With dressmaking, I can be free to express myself as the inspiration begins in my mind, then transferring itself into my soul, and out through my hands. When I create, nothing matters but an existence surrounded in beauty and love. This is Freedom and I want to thank you my darling mother for teaching me your wisdom," written in a letter to my mother during one of my most desperate and weary times.

What dressmaking provided aside from earning an income to sustain the entire Garland family was a sense of freedom; perhaps not in the same context of its literal form but rather in some metaphor that allowed me the autonomy to express myself through my craft, which I considered an art form. I became one with the needle and thread just like my mother. I kept all her trade secrets and techniques alive and applied this knowledge with each dressmaking process.

I fantasized about establishing a school to teach young Negro women the art of dressmaking, the importance of looking your best not only in mode but also in manner for *'presentation is vital to one's success'* like mother used to read from a book on Etiquette.

I developed a particular sensibility about my designs that was unlike the mode of fashion of the times. These quirks and quiddities of mine were matters I was unwilling to break for I knew it is what would set me apart from the rest of the dressmakers of my time. My lines were simple, exacting, linear and definitively uncomplicated and minimal. The current styles called for elaborate, decorative designs, heavily adorned and embellished with voluminous skirts. Underpinnings and crinolines were all the rage that were meant to emphasize the woman's figure and establish an effect of grandeur and prominence. I endeavored to sway away from this trend.

My philosophy in 'dressing' was not only a matter of style and form, but a matter of function as well. In these times, a woman should not be so concerned with pomp and circumstance but rather with practicality, mobility, comfort and ease. It was a terrible time in the nation's political climate, and I was of the persuasion that some moderation in the choices made for fabrics, trims and decorations was a prudent approach.

The French doors that were designed to accommodate these skirts were to me, a thing of the past best left for conversations to study the technical and aesthetic provenance of such dress specimens and its influence in today's mode of dress.

Today's woman needed to look handsome, smart, yet feminine and of course, beautiful. Her ease to move with comfort and swiftness without putting any thought into it was essential. It was my utmost concern that my designs reflected a level of awareness and consideration to what our nation was facing and felt that fashion should go with the current times. I considered it '*déclassé*' to offer vestments that showed no such regard. After all, our evolution as a race of people is reliant on our ability to accept change, and with the circumstances between the North and South, I felt that change was soon coming and hence, my fashions should reflect this shift.

Mrs. Augustine Wilkins was the wife of Attorney Samuel Wilkins, whose plantation recently suffered a great loss on account of 34 runaway slaves who broke out in the middle of the night with the help of a Negro woman who facilitated their escape to freedom through the Underground Railroad.

Mrs. Wilkins heard about my abilities and requested me to produce a total of three dinner robes of 'utmost quality and style.'

"Now Lizzy, why on this God-given earth did you ever choose such a strange shade of brown. Clearly I told you that nothing should allude to the fact that my husband and I are still trying to recover from the loss of our slaves. This is a most unattractive color. I am very disappointed Lizzy! I demand my deposit back!" she scoffed at me.

"Mrs. Wilkins, with all due respect if I may say so myself, we are at the height of a civil unrest. The people of this nation are at odds against each other. Now is not the time to arrive in a public setting like a member

of Marie Antoinette's court. You must deliver and present yourself accordingly. This demonstrates your keen sense of your surroundings and awareness of our times that make you a woman of high regard, a woman sensitive to the struggle of the nation," I replied.

"I beg your pardon Lizzy, and might I remind you of your place when you address me?" she said.

"I am sorry Mrs. Wilkins please pardon my probity, but if you want your guests to suspect that you are hard up, then by all means allow me to fashion you a dress with everything but the wheel barrow with it, because when you flaunt your wealth this way, you are sending a direct message that you do not have it - wealth; whereas if you present yourself without much effort, you are sending a message that money is of no circumstance to you and that you have plenty of it. Would you like me to start over?" I asked.

Mrs. Wilkins looked out the window and stood there with eyes gazing far for what seemed like a long time. I proceeded to gather my things and started packing up thinking my services had been officially terminated when I heard the following words from Mrs. Wilkins' mouth: *"Never you mind about starting over. Let us move forward with my coffee-colored dress Lizzy. You are keen to offer me your honesty and perhaps you are right after all. I am pleased with what you have selected for the material and look forward to the next fitting in a week. I will fetch for you in due course, and meanwhile I trust you will keep on working as I intend to wear this at a dinner I am hosting for the upcoming Presidential election."*

"Of course, Mrs. Wilkins, please rest assured, I shall make you proud!" I replied with relief given the dress she commissioned me to create yielded a hefty sum of money.

The spring and summer months were quite pleasing with blossoming flowers and the sweet smell of their fragrance becoming more apparent at dusk. Perhaps it was the sunlight peeking through each blade of grass with hints of dew, or the promise of a new tomorrow with freedom in the horizon that offered a sense of consolation for once.

Everything around me seemed more vibrant and colorful, including the blue skies above and the slow breeze that blew at the same exact time mid-day every day. Even master and his family seemed less demanding, less abusive and more tolerable than most days.

Winter arrived and how I dreaded it for the chill it brought . The rigors of my work required my full attention in meeting the demands of my patrons, and I believed this winter chill eventually led to the stiffness and pain I felt in my hands. My eyesight became rather poor, and my bones begged for relief. As a child, I watched mother come to the aide of many a beaten slave where she applied a soothing balsam made from the essence of wildflowers and herbs. This mixture was placed in a mortar that she patiently proceeded to grind until became a thick paste.

This balsam would be gently rubbed on to the ailing, injured and painful bodies of slaves at the Burwell plantation, as well as myself before turning in at night. Bless my sweet Mother for the thoughtfulness she exuded.

My gratitude remains profound to her for her instincts in developing the remedies she derived from plants and herbs. I considered this to be a great form of intelligence and natural ability. She once told me that our forebears from Africa had a remedy for practically every ailment there was. Although our slave owners relied on these tinctures and extracts for their immediate needs, we were often mocked and ridiculed for concocting such herbal compounds for the practice was regarded as shamanic or 'savage' in nature with no proven medical merit. Mother said that not only were our forebears hunters, farmers, merchants, craftsmen and people of great innovation and skill, they were alchemists of the highest order who used plants and herbs as antidotes and cure-alls.

From Camphor and Horehound to soothe whooping cough and sore throat, Elderberry for open sores and wounds; Coneflower for intestinal pain, toothaches and burns; Cotton Root to regulate menstrual cycles and aide in childbirth pain; Sage for chills and fever (and to ward off evil spirits); Jimsonweed to ease headaches; these were just some of the remedies she gave not only to us slaves, but also many members of Master Burwell's family. Several instances when its use was implemented saved lives.

We were indoctrinated into Christianity early on and were forbidden to practice any of our ancestral traditions and so we became masters at improvising ways to make these practices and rituals hidden from our slave owners. We learned to speak in code, developed ways to communicate amongst one another and I must say with great pride that we often succeeded in this mastery of 'making do.'

Hypocrisy was nothing unusual for the Burwell clan. Many times, master would run to my mother's aide without hesitation upon each occurrence whenever the medicine Ipecac rendered no relief. He ran to my mother's rescue whenever he or someone from his family needed a more efficacious remedy from their illnesses and conditions.

"That Ipecac is nothing but a rapidly moving emetic Lizzy," mother once said while hurriedly preparing a dose of her herbal tincture for master's wife.

"Mother, what is an emetic?" I asked for the word was a new one to my ears.

"It is a vomit inducing syrup Lizzy. In higher doses, it can cause death, and truly would not be so bad if they would just accidentally take more of it. Now hush, don't you say anything about what I said you hear?" mother said as I briefly plotted a scheme I never actualized but wished I had.

One afternoon I told Master Burwell, *"Now drinking too much of mother's tincture might turn you into a goat, so best not to over-indulge yourself with this Master Burwell. Have you considered increasing the Ipecac?"* He looked at me in absolute horror and proceeded to gingerly pour mother's tincture onto the teaspoon without overfilling it.

Then he asked, *"Will this be sufficient to cure me but not indulgent enough to turn me into a goat Lizzy? You know too much Ipecac can be deadly too,"* he said with a goat-like timber in his voice. I was disappointed to know he knew of the risks involving the Ipecac overdose and considered this revelation an act of God to keep me in line with a sound moral conscience.

"Ah, yes, that seems adequate though I never know with these things Master, it is a risk one takes you see. We never know what will happen until it happens," I said as I hastened my steps to leave his bedroom to let out a most satisfying laugh inside the pantry where Himself, the tabby cat meowed in agreement.

During my time with the Garland family, I met my husband Mr. James Keckley. I would remiss if I did not share the details of how our union came to be. While working for the Garlands, I grew quite fond of Mr. Keckley however not in the context of a romantic affiliation, but rather along the lines of an older brother or friend. By and by, our friendship advanced into somewhat of a more serious nature where he eventually moved to St. Louis to be closer to me. For several times, I turned down his proposal in marriage because the idea of bringing children into this world to be enslaved was a cruel reality I wanted to take no part in. My son was enough.

Eventually after considering that I would soon be granted the opportunity to buy my freedom and my son's, I capitulated to meet him at the altar to be his wife with the help of some convincing from my mother and relatives. He was a kind-hearted man and pleasing to my eyes. It was also an excuse to break away from the monotony of laboring day in and day out, and a chance for friends and family to grow bonds and strengthen relationships. I was hopeful at the idea that I could slow some of the work down as his contribution could offer me some ease.

Mother feverishly began sewing a quilt she planned to give us for a wedding gift. Uncle Isaac would serve as our minister, while my cousin Alice and her husband James offered their cabin for two nights and thoughtfully planned with Master to take on the work for me on those two days. I was pleasantly surprised to know that my master agreed without hesitance.

My wedding dress was a borrowed dress that I once fashioned for the wedding of a white lady patron's daughter. It was a simple dress of cotton muslin with a silhouette that I easily altered to fit my waist. The skirt gently flared into a semi-full skirt and edged at the hemline with hand embroidered baby roses. I recall how long it took me to finally finish the embroidery for each one and from what I remember, counted 89 flowers (not including the branches, leaves and doves) all in a row by the time it was finished. I remember being so tired that I would find myself fast asleep on top of the dress from sheer exhaustion. I regretted why I had endeavored on such a lofty idea to add more embroidery to the already beautiful gown but I was too far along to quit and had no other recourse than to keep going until the last and final bloom was stitched.

Morning turned into night and night turned into day and I remained steadfast in completing the alterations of this borrowed wedding dress. I secretly regretted having to undo all the beautiful handiwork when it was time to return it to its rightful owner.

"Mother, have you any further suggestions for this dress before I put a hot iron to it?" I asked.

"It is perfect Lizzy, there is nothing further required my child. I only wish your father was here to see you," she said staring at me from the reflection of the mirror and then held me in a long embrace.

Mother was a master at ironing garments with such detail. She taught me the importance of this process in dressmaking.

"The beauty of a dress not only rests on its silhouette, the material, and the way it was made, but its outcome relies heavily on the way it is ironed and smoothened with heat. You must always consider this in all your dressmaking pursuits Lizzy," as she demonstrated to me the

exactness of her method sometimes pressing gently and sometimes strongly against the garment using a sadiron; a thick slab of cast iron that had a handle, and then heated in a fire.

"Sometimes, you can heat it on the stove like this Lizzy," mother said as she laid a thin piece of cotton muslin over the wedding dress for those *"sensitive areas"* that required *"only a whisper of heat,"* she would explain. I watched and observed with great attention and detail how she brought the dress to life. It was truly impressive to me.

I recall the spark in my mother's eyes when she opened a box to reveal the opalescent tiny treasures she had been safekeeping for many years. How proud she was to be able to finally offer them to me.

"Lizzy my dear, these shells once belonged to your father's mother whose origins were from Congo in Africa, where the ocean was bountiful and abundant with treasures," she explained.

Each represented my grandmother's sons and daughters, all of whom were stolen and separated from each other and sent to travel by ship in the gruesome journey to America.   None of them ever reunited.

"Your father was the youngest child at only age six and his mother, your grandmother- gave him these shells which he kept inside his mouth under his tongue during the entire journey. On our wedding day, your father offered these shells to me, and I wore it as a necklace. The night of the news of our separation, your father asked that I give them to you on your wedding so you can be reminded how much he is always with you in spirit," she continued to say as she held back the tears that quickly welled up in her eyes.

'"Thank you Mother. I shall cherish them like you have and keep father close," I said pointing to my heart.

That afternoon, I re-strung the shells and placed fresh flowers in between each one to wear as a coronet on my head for the following morning's wedding rites. I felt my father's spirit so strongly that it was almost as if he was there with me.

The wedding was a much-anticipated event amongst us slaves. A simple, modest arrangement of wildflowers graced the entryway of the small parlor as Mr. Keckley and I exchanged vows officiated by Bishop Hawks (who had also solemnized the nuptial ceremony of Mr. Garland's own children.)

In honoring our ancestral traditions, my groom and I jumped the broom to officially seal our fate as husband and wife. Master Burwell did not make an appearance during our celebration but sent a sack of rice and a small trough of fermented molasses that tasted like rum; a generous gift that was quickly consumed and enjoyed by our guests.

We were entertained by a never-ending repertory of music played by my cousin Amari, a handsome young man, fair complexioned with eyes that glistened like gems. When he was born, his father gave him the name because it meant *"One who possesses great strength and courage."* If a name epitomized one's personhood, he exemplified this indeed.

"Lizzy, you are as beautiful as the Sun and as deep as the Moon," as he sang to me like a lark while he played the Banjo, an instrument from the motherland.

My cousin whom I considered my fondest little brother escaped with the help of the same woman who led the Underground Railroad a year after my wedding day, and the last news we heard was that he was living as a free man working as a groom for a livery somewhere in the North. I also imagined that he was still playing his Banjo wherever he may be.

Mother retired early and kissed me goodnight on my forehead offering us her apologies for not partaking any further as she had an early morning duty to travel back to town with the mistress at sunrise the next day. It was a rare moment to see everyone in a state of merry making.

Amari's banjo played all evening long and eventually, intoxicating feeling (both physical and emotional) that the evening offered, kept our guests in a state merriment and stupor until it was time to retire back to their respective cabins to bid us goodnight.

Everyone left with full bellies, memories of joy and laughter, and a sense of temporary relief from the physical rigor of their labor and the absence of living in fear for but a few fleeting hours.

That night, we were all we were human again as I slumbered in the warm embrace of my new groom, while Amari continued his lullaby filled with hope and a promise for a new dawn to come.

Tomorrow, I shall have a new name, Mrs. Elizabeth Keckley.

CHAPTER 5

A Veil of Lies

The wedding day was a happy day of reverie and celebration, but that too came to a quick end. My husband, whom I thought would offer me strength and support proved to be less favorable in these areas. More importantly, I soon discovered that he was not a free man as he presented himself to be, but rather a slave himself. For eight years, I honored the vows I declared to be my truth despite the unveiling of the lies that left a dark cloud in our eight-year pact as husband and wife. Eventually, a mutual decision to part ways was agreed upon and lest I say that I was not proud of this conclusion but deemed it necessary.

I labored and endured in order to purchase my freedom and each year seemed longer than the one that just passed, yet I continued diligently never releasing my focus on my plans. Each year, I remained a slave, older, less agile, weaker and more painful. My days were spent working for Mr. Garland and his family reached a point where it was nearly impossible for me to save any money towards the purchase of our freedom.

Eventually, Mr. Garland passed away and Mr. Burwell soon arrived in St. Louis to attend to the business of Mr. Garland's estate (or rather what remained of it.)

I was under the assumption that upon seeing my dedication and earnest work, Mr. Burwell would feel some sympathy for me and agree that I should be set free and offer his assistance in raising the required amount to pay for my freedom. He was in fact less abrasive towards me, yet I wondered if this was on account of his age and weaker constitution. Either way, I felt it to be the most opportune time to go forward with my plans.

Over and over, I ruminated during many sleepless nights to devise a way and strategize the process of acquiring my freedom. I hastened without delay and great timing to proceed with my intentions. As I was close to heading Northward, Mrs. Garland informed me that she would need a minimum of at least six respectable men willing to guarantee and vouch for my immediate return. Fortunately for me, my lady patrons agreed to assist me in convincing their husbands to act on my behalf.

"They must all vouch for you Lizzy, and certainly pledge for the price of your full value, along with your son's because otherwise you may not leave this property," Mrs. Garland demanded. I almost wanted to give up for such a daunting expectation to fulfill for my resources were limited, if not scarce. It was clear to me that Mrs. Garland knew this was an impossible feat to accomplish and she was set on my failure.

That evening, branches of the oak tree that wrapped me like a warm blanket, I prayed to God and asked him for guidance and strength. It seemed only fair for my petition to be heard and granted for we have suffered enough.

"Oh Lord, hear my prayers. Give me the fortitude and will to survive this impossible task. I beg you Father Almighty to help me and my son!" and I fell asleep until morning came.

I was awakened by the sound of Mr. Burwell's carriage arriving. I hastily readied myself to meet him and planned to use this opportunity to explain to him the demands Mrs. Garland required given his recent show of kindness towards me.

"Do what you must Lizzy, and do it quickly," he hurriedly and emphatically snapped.

"But how shall I attend to this demand when I am stationed here in the never-ending task of attending to the Garland family's needs? How can I possibly…." I attempted to say as Mr. Burwell quickly interrupted.

"I have ordered Samuel to take you town in my carriage so that you may attend to this matter today, and only today. If anyone questions why you are in town, present them this note signed by me. I shall have Sarah take your place in the meantime. Let me handle Mrs. Garland myself. Go now!" he said adamantly as he pulled a handwritten note from his pocket and stepped out of his carriage to let me in.

"Thank you Master Burwell. I shall move without delay," I said as I entered the carriage with Samuel and the horses leading the way.

From one patron's husband to another, I was able to collect the names of five men. The sixth and final one I reserved to be the last, as I knew my chances on acquiring his commitment was close to impossible for I had not once spoken to him, other than the one brief time when he appeared at my cabin to retrieve a garment his wife needed for an event.

I calmly stated my case and explained the terms by which Mrs. Garland held me to task for. I expressed to him, just as I did to the others, that with his help, I would be allowed to state my case to the courts in New York through the assistance of the Abolitionist party and pray they advance me the $1,200 that was required in order to purchase our freedom. I apologized for my lack of consideration by not requesting the honor of his time with advance notice but explained to him the urgency of my need.

He said, *"Yes Lizzy, your scheme is a fair one and you shall have my name, but on behalf of Mrs. Farrow who is unfortunately not here as she is with her cousin on the other side of town, I shall bid you forever goodbye now."*

"Goodbye for a short time," I responded.

"No Lizzy, goodbye forever," Mr. Farrow said looking down on the cobblestone street we were both standing on.

"Mr. Farroow, surely you don't think I will not come back?" I asked.

"No Lizzy, you will not come back. While I know you mean to come back, you shall not. Once you reach New York, the Abolitionists will tell you how cruel we are, what wrong-doers we are, and that will cause you to never wish to see us again," he stated.

"Oh Mr. Farrow, I assure you that my gratitude prevails. I promise I will come back," I said.

I felt sick to my stomach that this man would willingly pledge on my behalf, yet he had no faith in me. These were people I held with the highest esteem and as contradicting as that might sound, it was the truth.

"Lizzy, I am not mistaken as we have seen this many times before. Goodbye and be safe," handing me the document with his signature neatly folded inside an envelope with the handwritten words *"Elizabeth Keckley / Signatory: Farrow"* in front of it.

A deep sense of sadness swept over me. My heart grew heavier as I neared home. I could see Samuel, the carriage driver, turning his head ever so slightly to steal a glimpse of my face for many times and over, he has seen the same face of loneliness from the slaves that came before me. I wondered if Samuel ever desired to hop off the carriage and petition signatures himself and it made me sad to think that perhaps he had resigned to the understanding that his life was forever designated to remain a slave.

Upon arriving the house, everyone was moving with the same weary feeling in the atmosphere. No words were spoken for all of them knew I was successful in acquiring Mrs. Garland's demands. Even the rabid mongrel dog stayed quiet.

I threw myself on my wooden cot, weeping in sorrow. What I had imagined to be a jubilant moment was on the contrary. Mother had lovingly packed me a luncheon and organized my bags in advance for my journey North to New York for she too knew ahead that I would be successful in reaching my goals. Mother was never wrong and proved once again how correct she was.

I hugged her goodbye for now and waved my hand through the carriage's window for I did not want anyone to see me cry. Inside the carriage, I felt the breath I inhaled transition from shackled air into inhaling the air of freedom.

I imagined the contrasting difference between drinking the water inside my jug collected from the wells of persecuted soil in comparison to the sweet taste of crystal-clear water from the rivers from which freedom prevailed.

Merely yards away from the house, instead I felt there was no rainbow's end, nor the sweet whisper of the roses presenting their fragrance in the early stages of the sun's rising. I did not hear the humming sounds of hymns sung by my elders anymore during the height of a labor-intensive morning's work, nor were there barefoot naked babies running in the plantation ignorant of their misfortunes and void of any understanding of their stations as slaves in the making.

These were the thoughts that meant 'home' to me and as morose and dismal this setting might be, these were the familiar echoes I was accustomed to. For once in my life, freedom appeared to me as the enemy.

As we turned the corner at the end of the road, I crossed paths with Mrs. Le Bourgois' carriage, who appeared harried and bothered by almost missing me. Ordering the carriage to come to a screeching halt, Mrs. Le Bourgois stepped out of her carriage, her bonnet slightly askew and demanded to speak to me.

"Lizzy my dear, I hear that you are needing assistance to gain your freedom and bound for New York to beg for money. How utterly gauche and humiliating! I have been thinking about this and spoke to Mama

about it and feel that rather than having you beg for the money, that we should give you the money rightfully owed to you for the work you have done for us still left unpaid. Might I add how gracious you have been by not even uttering a suggestion to collect these arrears from us all these years? I mean really Elizzzzzzzzzubeth," she said as she struggled very hard to catch her breath.

I was dumbfounded and staggered by what she said. I asked very slowly to make sure she understood what she herself had just said to me, *"Whatever do you mean Mrs. Le Bourgois?"*

Just then, a little, white-crowned sparrow landed on the branch of the same old oak tree where I fell asleep just the evening before. Mrs. Le Bourgois continued to speak with such exuberance and pride. She was sincerely happy for me and perhaps I was imagining it, but so happy too was the little white-crowned sparrow chirping in agreement.

She said, *"You have many friends who wish to help you Lizzy and I shall promise to raise the twelve hundred dollars required amongst all of them, my dear. Now, I have two hundred dollars set aside for a present and oh yes, an additional one hundred dollars that I owe you. Yes, yes that's right. Mother owes you fifty dollars, and pledged to add another fifty dollars to it, isn't that swell? Oh, and another thing, I shall also no longer wish to save money towards a present for myself, and instead shall make that money my present you. So essentially what I am saying is go back home and do not waste your time going to New York, because Lizzy my dear, you will do no such begging and I shall have this money raised for you amongst all your friends in St. Louis! If you'll excuse me Lizzy, I have got to get back home for I cannot be out this long under this heat. That is all, and for crying out loud Lizzy, go on home!"* she said.

And with that declaration, she jumped back into her carriage and was whisked away to the end of the road until she disappeared before I could even utter another word. I sat inside the carriage befuddled and in shock while Samuel laughed in disbelief.

Grief was replaced with Joy. Fear replaced with Courage. Pain replaced with Peace. I was stunned. I was stupefied. I was astonished and overwhelmed. *What did I do to deserve this magnanimous act of kindness?*

Like a ray of sunshine, Mrs. Le Bourgois delivered her promise and was able to raise the twelve hundred dollars within a short period of time.

At last, my son and I were finally free. The bitterness of slavery has come to an end. By the laws of the land, I was free, no longer manacled by the stigma of the dark evil that terrorized me all the days of my life.

I began to imagine the first frock signifying the sovereign woman I was destined to be, and looked forward with bated breath at the kind of dress I would soon fashion; a dress that exuded a resounding statement embodying all that I am.

I smiled as Samuel turned around and drove the carriage headed for home; his laughter echoing down the path while the little sparrow flapped its wings as if to symbolize the freedom that was soon to unfold in tandem, synchronizing beautifully with the song that escaped from Samuel's lungs:

"When the Sun comes back
And the first quail calls
Follow the Drinking Gourd.
For the old man is a-waiting for to carry you to freedom
If you follow the Drinking Gourd.

The riverbank makes a very good road.
The dead trees will show you the way.
Left foot, peg foot, traveling on,
Follow the Drinking Gourd.

The river ends between two hills
Follow the Drinking Gourd.
There's another river on the other side

Follow the Drinking Gourd.

When the great big river meets the little river
Follow the Drinking Gourd.
For the old man is a-waiting for to carry you to freedom
If you follow the drinking gourd."

I arrived back at the Burwell property with Mother standing right around the bend, her arms outstretched, smiling ear to ear to welcome me back as if she knew, as if she knew all along.

CHAPTER 6

A Wardrobe for Mrs. Jefferson Davis

I made sure that the twelve hundred dollars I was given by my loyal lady patrons to purchase our freedom was contingent on the understanding that each of my patrons agreed to the condition that I would only accept these monies on the basis of a loan. I wanted to ensure my reputation be cleared from any discrepancies that could potentially arise in the future, and while my gratitude to each of them cannot be replaced by any monetary value, I did not want to feel beholden for the rest of our lives nor wish that feeling of uncertainty to loom over me in the event my status as a free woman were ever to be questioned or challenged. I acted with a firm resolve to use every ounce of my common sense, wisdom and critical thinking to properly abide by the stipulations set forth by the law. I could not afford to be careless nor be consumed with the thrill and excitement of freedom. The risks were too high, and I was not willing to take them, especially not while my son was still under my guardianship.

I committed myself to working diligently and within a period of time, was able to satisfy the loan in full with every cent paid back to each of my most esteemed patrons in St. Louis.

As I commenced plans for our journey North, my estranged husband Mr. Keckley, suddenly returned into our lives and became a strain that consumed my days.

While it sounds insensitive to say, he was for a good majority of the time, simply a downright burden. Constantly having to account for my whereabouts, finances and business matters, he became a source of aggravation and worry for me; compounded by the fact that I was working at the beginning of sunrise until the next sunrise came, where my health eventually started to be a matter of great concern.

I had to do something quickly and made the decision to have nn honest conversation with Mr. Keckley. I explained that since he was set on causing much discord and havoc in my life, the only recourse was to officially separate and that I had planned to make the North my permanent home, determined never to see him again until such time when he proved himself worthy of my affection and companionship.

He was a troubled soul and of no fault of his own having endured the wrath of slavery causing a damning emotional and psychological toll on his personhood. He took to the bottle and spent his days and nights in a self-loathing quandary that eventually led to his premature death. I often prayed for his peaceful repose and eternal rest.

In the spring of 1860, I left St. Louis headed to the North where I had the idea to attempt making a modest sum of money. I planned to teach young colored women the techniques of cutting, sewing and fitting custom-made dresses of high design, quality and craftsmanship while in transition in Baltimore, Maryland.

After much effort and time expended, my plans to earn an income proved to be unsuccessful with barely enough money to leave Baltimore to pay for our fare to Washington.

By the grace of God, through small sewing jobs here and there, my son and I arrived in Washington safely. I was exhausted, hungry and unsure of myself. With what little earnings I made, I focused on my son's immediate needs; mainly comprised of food and shelter. My sweet young son barely uttered a word of displeasure or complaint throughout our journey. He was by my side most of the time patiently waiting for our fortunes to rise.

"It will be alright Mama. Don't you worry about a thing Mama," my son would often say when he observed me during my times of deep thought and distress. Holding my hand tightly all the time, he'd give it a squeeze every so often to remind me to remain strong and steadfast.

By the grace of God, I obtained work at the rate of two and a half dollars a day. While this was not the kind of income I was hoping to garner, it was an opportunity I was deeply grateful for. However, my sense of optimism posed to be threatened when I learned of a law Washington imposed upon recently freed slaves like me. I was mandated to provide a license to work within ten days upon arrival to the city. Unless this requirement was met, my son and I would be taken back to our owner and forced back into slavery.

Add to this regulation, I was required to provide a voucher to attest and confirm that I was a free woman. Essentially, the paperwork indicating that my son and I had been released from bondage by purchasing our freedom was not sufficient.

Not knowing how to obtain this license, I became increasingly consumed in worry. Time was running out and I had to act swiftly.

Desperate to furnish these documents, I called on a lady client whose dresses I was working on and asked her to assist me.

Mrs. Ringold was a relative of General Mason, whose family hailed from Virginia. She was a woman of strong influence and possessed the disposition of a commander of an army. Nothing can go past her for she was that astute and discerning.

"Mrs. Ringold, I humbly seek your assistance in acquiring the following requirements in the next few days or my son and I risk being sent back to my previous Master. Can you help me?" as I showed her the list of documentation required and stated my case in the most desperate way.

"Oh my! Don't you worry Lizzy. I shall assist you and do everything in my power to see to it that you are safe. Without sounding self-

important, I will help you but please promise and make sure my dress is beautiful as I cannot attend this event in anything less than magnificent," she said as the wrinkles on her forehead caused her brows to meet in the middle.

"She needs a proper bonnet," I thought to myself; to ward off the sun from her face causing the grooves and ridges to rumple and become more prominent and deeper.

Calling upon the influence of Mayor Burritt, Mrs. Ringold kept her promise in ensuring that I remain in Washington with the proper documentations in place and absolved me from having to pay the large sum of money for obtaining them. In addition to this stipulation, Mrs. Ringold sought to ensure in writing that I was not to be molested or abused.

I am forever in gratitude to her and hence, sought to make sure that every time she requested my services, to go above and beyond the call of my duty by always making myself available to fit her into my busy schedule and delivering to her dresses (and bonnets) that stood out in a crowd that garnered her much admiration from her husband and peers. It was the least I could do given the magnitude of her kindness, trust and belief in my abilities and character.

I was fortunate enough to have the favor of some kind lady friends, one of whom was my landlady and was able to secure a modest dwelling at a boarding house on 13th street for a reasonable monthly rent, where I eventually operated my dressmaking business.

Summer came and went and by the winter season, many of my patrons eagerly anticipated the arrival of their friend Mrs. Varina Davis, wife of the formidable Southern Senator Mr. Jefferson Davis.

One afternoon, after having walked all over town to circulate my business cards, my landlady said, *"Elizabeth, word is out that Mrs. Varina Davis is actively seeking a qualified modiste and I know your lady patrons could surely give a good word for you."*

Just as soon as I heard this, I hastened my steps to Mrs. Hetsill's house just four blocks down my workshop to ask her for a referral. I was determined.

"Elizabeth, what brings you here? I don't believe I am scheduled for a fitting am I?" she inquired.

I apologized for such an intrusion and requested to speak to Mrs. Hetsill in private as some members of her ladies club were in the room. I informed her of my desire to be considered for the position as Mrs. Davis' personal dressmaker. Mrs. Hetsill gave me the assurance that she would put in the good word for me and shortly thereafter, I was pleased to know that I was selected.

Now serving as her official dressmaker, Mrs. Davis often confided in me about personal matters along with subjects of a trivial nature. One night she said, *"Mrs. Bell and Mrs. Breckenridge and I were at luncheon the other day and couldn't help ourselves from hysterics over that lawyer from Illinois. Dear God, yet another abolitionist who has this audacious idea to free all the slaves. What do you think of this Elizabeth?"*

I immediately knew Mrs. Davis was speaking of the tall Senator with the beard and was startled not by the question she posed, but rather by the loud noise coming from a crowd across the street from the Davis home.

A small group of young men had gathered outside. They appeared to be a group of college-aged young men who were of the Abolitionist movement, two of whom were Negroes.

I thought of my own son, George who was in his first year of college at Wilberforce University in Ohio. He was diligent not only in his studies, but wrote to me often to share his experiences, newfound friendships and outings when not immersed in his schoolwork. He was curious about the state of affairs in Washington and asked what bit of information I knew of through my dealings with my patrons.

I was always forthcoming in my response and though some matters were strictly confidential, felt assured that my son would never compromise anyone, including myself within those dialogues.

This young group of men held signs that read *"Fellow Citizens: An Abolitionist Lecture is to be delivered this evening at 7 o'clock at the Presbyterian Church! Union Forever!"*

"Oh, those young Abolitionists have no idea what they speak of. How it troubles me so," Mrs. Davis said under her breath.

Another time some weeks later, Mrs. Davis confided hat she always felt like she was living in the shadow of Sarah and for all accounts described her marriage a matter of transactional convenience.

Mrs. Sarah Knox Taylor was the daughter of General Zachary Taylor who became the 12th President of the United States from the years 1849-1850. Sometime in 1835, Mr. Davis met Sarah when he was only 27 years old and fell in love. They were both stricken with malaria, and after only three months of marriage, Sarah died while Mr. Davis recovered slowly. At age 36, Mr. Davis married again to a then 18-year-old Varina Howell, a native of Natchez, Mississippi.

Mrs. Davis described herself as a 'half-breed' with dark features, ebony eyes and soft wavy dark hair. She was tall and slender and had a bosom that was abundant with a posterior that likened mine. She was considered unattractive at the time - though I vehemently beg to differ for she had a unique quality to her beauty. She had an olive hue to her complexion that glistened like the sun. This posed many curious minds to question her parentage, which caused her to have very few Southern suitors so much so that when Mr. Davis requested to court her, she quickly obliged when he asked for her hand in marriage.

As a child, she was not raised with the traditional Southern upbringing and was rather assertive with her opinions. Unlike many of her peers, she was a highly educated scholar and often challenged Mr. Davis in heated debates about matters pertaining to the North and South.

To maintain her marriage, Mrs. Davis capitulated to most of her husband's wishes leaving him to have the final word on most matters. She was a patron of the Arts and made good friends with the painter James McNeil Whistler. This relationship caused discomfort in the eyes of her husband, who was considered one of the richest plantation owners in Mississippi owning a total of seventy slaves.

Mr. Davis was known to provide adequate food, clothing and shelter to his slaves, while Mrs. Davis tackled the responsibility of sewing their clothes and provided medical care to those that required her attention. Mr. Davis' overseers took charge of the plantation's overall management. Unlike her husband, Mrs. Davis learned all the names of their bondsmen whereas Mr. Davis did not.

While they both supported slavery, they differed in the way they viewed the issues of race. Mrs. Davis was often on the verge of threatening to break her promise of marriage to him especially when Mr. Davis once compared slaves to animals during a publicly held speech. This gave cause for Mrs. Davis's embarrassment according to several witness accounts.

He loved the countryside and thought it to be most idyllic whereas she found it much too rural and preferred living in the Capitol instead.

She was mostly responsible for hosting bi-partisan gatherings in their rented home in Washington where she maintained conversations with heads of state. Her commanding presence and wit was something she was known for and all those within the inner circle knew that her husband was lacking in this area.

A brilliant conversationalist, she held equal ground with the likes of former Secretaries of State Mr. Henry Clay and Mr. Daniel Webster, Abolitionist leader Mr. Charles Summer, as well as former Presidents Zachary Taylor, James Buchanan and Franklin Pierce.

Mrs. Davis continued to maintain relationships with key figures as tensions about the issues of slavery rose; the Blairs of Maryland, the Bache family of Pennsylvania, First Lady Jane Pierce and many other influential people of the time like the Democrat from Illinois Mr. Stephen Douglas known to hold strong views on supporting slavery. Many of their wives became my clients as a result of Mrs. Davis' endorsement and faith in my work as a dressmaker.

The two husbands whom Mrs. Davis previously spoke of were the Kentucky Democrat Mr. John Breckenridge, who believed that secession was an *'inherent right of the States,'* and a friend from Tennessee, a former Whig; Mr. John Bell who felt that all issues including slavery should be resolved in the Union. She also spoke of the Republican from Illinois, who argued and insisted that the expansion and implementation of slavery to the West needed to stop without further delay. He was a tall brooding, highly intelligent bearded man named Mr. Abraham Lincoln, the lawyer and Senator from Illinois.

Mrs. Davis was said to believe that her husband was ill-fitted to hold the position as head of state because **"he simply did not possess the ability to compromise,"** a characteristic that in her view, was vital to the success of a politician and leader.

She did not hold back when she said that she felt the South simply did not have the resources, adequate population and manufacturing prowess to defeat the North; nor did she feel the Southerners had the mental capability to win a war. She called the whole thing **"a disaster"** although she continued to appear in support of her husband whilst among his colleagues and counterparts.

Her dark skin always became the subject of scrutiny where she was more than several times called a *'mulatto,'* a word used to describe someone of African and European ancestry with its root word derived from the Latin word, 'mulus' meaning 'mule,' the hybrid offspring of a horse and donkey. Mrs. Davis was unfazed by such scrutiny and idle talk and made no apologies for her appearance nor her existence.

Unquestionably educated, her quick–witted retorts and remarks would often be received with baffled blank stares, most of whom were men in politics. She was clear that she was not in full support of the

Confederacy and offered no hostility to the Northerners within her circle whatsoever.

In the beginning, I did all my work in Mrs. Davis' house although eventually relegated half of my day inside my workshop instead on account of the Davis family's propensity to be late risers. Given that I had to conduct fittings for her, I requested to attend to my other lady patrons for the first half of the day until she awoke later to make good use of my time.

She was kind enough to accommodate me and so it was agreed that I reported to Mrs. Davis' house after twelve o'clock in the afternoon daily instead. I was relieved by this arrangement for I was still quite unfamiliar with the Davis family's regular daily patterns.

This schedule was maintained even during the winter months before the onset of the impending war. Mr. Davis was gaining traction with a large following and the their home soon became a watering hole of many prominent leaders from the South. Being around their family as intimately as I have been, and hearing the strategic plans of the Southern leaders, I became privy to many closed door conversations and confidential meetings that took place in the house. These meetings sometimes carried on until the sunrise the following day. I learned and listened attentively to everything they conversed about.

Talk about the likelihood of a war to break out was openly discussed with various members of Washington's political circles in my presence. I was not sure whether they considered me to be someone not intelligent enough to understand matters pertaining to politics or that they trusted me implicitly that ventilating such matters so freely was safe around me or whether they were simply careless and unassuming.

Even more concerning was the fact that Mrs. Davis's circle of wives shared their husbands' confidential affairs and the roles they played in government so freely without giving it a second thought.

I found this to be dangerous and quite risky to say the least. I listened nevertheless and continued to quietly do my work in their shadows. These conversations presented a learning platform for me in many ways and gave me the advantage to form my own understanding about the institution of slavery from the white man's perspective. Crucial was this exposure to my future. I learned everything from the inside.

The Christmas season arrived quickly and Mrs. Davis planned to give her husband a well-made dressing robe. With very little time left, she instructed me to purchase the materials and I began working on it right away as time was of the essence.

On the afternoon of Christmas Eve, I found Mrs. Davis standing on a ladder while decorating the Christmas tree in the adjoining room where I was feverishly working to finish the robe. My head was enduring a pulsating kind of pain, my back felt bruised from hours of sitting in one spot and my hands stiffened further with each passing minute.

I was reminded of the same familiarity of foregone days in the Burwell plantation. It was an uneasy and eerie feeling, and I thought maybe perhaps, it was just how the holidays always sent me in a state of unsettling emotional strain and a deep sense of melancholy. I missed my mother, my family and friends especially during the holidays and prayed for them often. At least I had my son which was the only thing that kept me going.

As I finished Mr. Davis' robe, I found it difficult not to drift in recollections of my experiences as a slave, bringing back a vivid recounting of my past.

In his memoirs, the great Abolitionist Mr. Frederick Douglass described his experiences as a slave himself. These events were eerily like my own experiences when I read the transcript from his book shown to me by my son while visiting me from Wilberforce University.

Mr. Douglass wrote that around June through July, the first

picking of cotton would be done mostly by the young children ages eight to twelve years old. Usually accompanied by either their mothers or surrogates known as 'sucklers,' the little ones and these women would be relegated to long hours of picking the first bale; a time consuming and arduous undertaking for the cotton was usually not yet in full bloom. Nevertheless, this task was to be completed rapidly as it was a custom among the planters to be the first to send their bale of picking off to the market. This first picking would then be put inside a large basket usually accompanied by a bottle of champagne.

The sight of little children crying to their mothers from the pain they endured picking the fields was gruesome to say the least, yet slave masters despite the understanding of such conditions, proceeded to celebrate the first picking's long tradition by ordering their slaves to work until sundown without fail.

As nature would have it, the cotton matured and flourished quickly, its beautiful buds turning into full bloom until winter's end. Slave-owning families became exuberant over the year's crop and continued to push their slaves to work even harder to yield a successful harvest.

Everyone was expected to deliver a minimum of two hundred fifty pounds of cotton to avoid the implementation of a severe whipping. There were various methods by which this punishment was administered and though I wish never to recall of its barbaric ways, one incident left permanent impairment to my emotional and mental state of mind.

A terrible incident occurred when Julius, a man no more than thirty years of age, fell ill one morning with the chills. Fearing he would be punished should he remain rested inside his cabin, had decided to join the rest of his group. When it was time for his picking to be weighed, it rendered a mere seventy-three pounds.

Imploring the overseer, he explained to him how weak felt and asked if he could be pardoned for it was not his usual manner to deliver such a paltry result. No matter how hard Julius sought for leniency, he was still ordered to the back of the stable where his lashing was to take place. Poor Julius was so sick, frightened and inconsolable yet nothing could change the minds of the overseer and his assistants who undressed him completely and proceeded to tie him by both ankles and both hands onto four wooden stakes where they laid his face down on the ground.

This time, the overseer pulled out a large wooden paddle of which he began to beat Julius with throughout his back, legs and the soles of his feet until blood was drawn in the most violent way. This went on for about two and a half hours until the overseer finally said, *"This lazy bones good for nuthin' got me so damn tired. I need me something to eat. Here, why don't you take that switch and finish him off for me while I head to the house for some food."*

Using a more pliable limber switch from a tree, the overseer's helper continued to whip Julius until he was rendered listless and unconscious. The overseer's assistant then bent down to the ground, spat on Julius' face and gave instructions for Uncle Willie to douse his body with a bucket filled with warm water and salt. This brine was an added form of punishment not only to Julius but also to Uncle Willie and to all of us witnessing the atrocity. The idea of furthering your fellow slave's suffering was in and of itself barbaric and downright cruel.

After the cacodemons left, Mother gently removed the rope that bound Julis' feet and hands, and carefully placed a folded rag on all four corners where his feet and hands lay, to offer a little ease after each corner was untied. Quietly, so as not to further agitate the overseer and his men, we all helped carry Julius slowly and quietly back to his cabin where mother administered a liniment made from slippery elm, alumroot and herbs that helped heal the wounds.

Mr. Frederick Douglass spoke of a similar account in his memoirs that further confirmed the frequency of these heinous practices throughout the South.

Christmas usually marked the last season of the cotton harvest and it also meant that the picking season was finally over, which in turn meant a brief respite for the slaves.

Back inside the Davis home, the chime of the clock struck at exactly eleven o'clock in the evening as I snapped out of my thoughts of days gone by. It was Christmas Eve and I worried for the dressing robe was still unfinished. A long line of cold sweat had formed on my brow bone. I was quivering and was on the verge of going into hysterics when I realized it was an after-effect from reliving my memories of Julius and the past. It was a traumatic memory that stayed in my consciousness.

As I wiped my face with a handkerchief to dry myself off, a knock on the door startled me sending a sudden gush of energy and a much-needed diversion to bring me back to the present time.

"Oh, Thank God," I thought to myself as I noticed Mr. Davis was standing at the doorway with his head leaning against the wall admiring the Christmas tree in the adjoining room. His face looked weary, his eyes tired and he appeared sapped and run-down.

It was clear to me that the Senator had a lot on his mind when he said, *"Is that you there, Lizzy? Why on earth are you still here Lizzy? It is so late, and I certainly hope that Mrs. Davis is not too demanding with her requests?"*

I explained *"Oh No, everything is as planned. Mrs. Davis is eager for this to be finished tonight and I agreed to stay to complete it."*

"What color is it? My old eyes cannot decipher its hue especially with this candle you have here Lizzy. How can you work in such limited light? I suppose Mrs. Davis considers this urgent if she has you here working this late," he asked as he slowly walked up towards where I was seated.

"It is a dull muted champagne silk Mr. Davis," I said. I could

have said it was a rich and saturated silk but refrained from offering mistruths to not disappoint him in the morning.

Selecting the proper material and color for this undertaking was a calculated decision on my part for I felt it only appropriate to select colors that are not too celebratory in theme. Given the Senator's position and the uncertainty of the nation, it behooved me to remain particularly sensitive to the kind of message my work was delivering. Unlike most dressmakers of my time, I considered my work not only to serve form, but thought of its function to translate what the wearer of the garment represented. Dressmaking essentially, was also a statement of action wherein I had the freedom to stir emotions, heighten joy, honor the dead, celebrate birth and marriages, establish confidence, gain trust, convince decisions, and forge friendships and bonds. Unique was my ability to transform and materialize.

The Senator smiled and proceeded to walk in the other direction without asking another question. A part of me felt that he appreciated my response and was in full understanding of the subtle implication I made.

He hinted that the gown was in fact a gift to him from his wife but that he did not want to ruin the anticipated glee and pleasure that Mrs. Davis would experience for this special surprise. This was a tender moment that I was fortunate enough to witness and for this alone, I considered Mr. Davis to be a man full of sensitivity and consideration relating to the matter of his wife and his marriage.

Midnight came and I had just finished the last stitch to the robe. Mrs. Davis presented the gift to her husband the following morning on Christmas day. I watched the Davis family open gifts with excitement as the ornaments that hung upon the beautifully adorned tree swayed back and forth from all the activity going on. What a joy to witness a family together this way, simply enjoying one another's company without any limitations.

Even limber Jimmie, an olive-skinned Negro little boy whom Mr. and Mrs. Davis treated as their own, was excitedly opening his present along with the Davis children. Over the years, rumors of his parentage milled around the inner circles of both the North and South, that Jimmie, whose real name was James Henry Brooks was the child of the Davis' and that his complexion was on account of the suspicion that Mrs. Varina Davis was of some Negro parentage. Again, I did not consume myself with such idle talk for all that I witnessed during this time was a loving family who did not allow the discord that gossip caused to affect their way of life.

Watching them gather under the tree sent memories of the last night I ever saw my own father and the night we were forever separated. I couldn't help but think of my very own son who was on a brief holiday from Wilberforce University. I was eager to come home and give him his first gift as a free young man; a handmade quilt with his name embroidered upon it and a remnant from Uncle Amos' trousers sewn in his honor.

Mr. Davis offered a well-played out surprised response upon opening his gift. He turned his gaze quickly in my direction and offered me a wink. With this simple acknowledgement, I knew that he was pleased with my handiwork. Later, I learned that the robe was oftentimes worn during the dark and uncertain years while Mr. Davis served as the President of the Confederacy.

When I finally arrived home, I was welcomed with the warmth of the fireplace. My son prepared a hot cup of tea served with the leftover holiday meat pie our kind neighbor gave us a few days before. I gave him his gift and together we wrapped ourselves in the warmth of the quilt gazing at the fire. It was our very first Christmas as free people.

Not long after the holiday season passed, we approached the New Year with talk about the inevitable war. This subject was openly discussed in the Davis home on an almost daily basis. Mrs. Davis was not keen on uprooting herself to move to the South for Washington was very close to her heart. She often expressed her disappointment in having to end her friendships and acquaintances in exchange for a life of hardship and turmoil once settled in the South.

During a fitting one day, in the presence of a few of Washington's finest ladies, Mrs. Davis lamented, *"I prefer to remain here in Washington and suffer the humiliation of being thrown out forcibly than head to the humid South and hold title as Mrs. President of the Confederate States! Oh Lizzy, how I envy you!"*

I did not think Mrs. Davis truly understood the weight of what she said. One of her friends remarked, *"I have NEVER heard of a more off-putting statement especially coming from a woman whose role as the wife of the future leader of this nation deems it necessary to advocate for the Confederacy! I should like to be exempt from these conversations and wish to no longer be privy to such ideas. Varina, please mind what you say to us. I mean really Varina, it's enough for me to walk out of this door!"* Mrs. Davis' friend admonished.

"Darling, suit yourself. I was raised to speak my truths and I shall take these self-evident facts to my grave whether anyone likes it or not. While it is my promise to be a dutiful wife, the fact remains that the South needs to prepare for the coming of this imminent war. Now Lizzy, what will it take for me to convince you to come with me?"

"Oh, but when do you intend to head South Mrs. Davis?" I asked.

Mrs. Davis alluded to the fact that this would be taking place soon, followed up with a resolute *"There will be war Ladies."*

"Who will be engaged in war Mrs. Davis?" I was afraid to ask.

"Whatever do you mean Lizzy? Have you not been in this house long enough to know that the war shall be between the North and the South? And might I add that the South will never agree nor retreat to the ultimatum of the Abolitionists. Oh, ladies I am telling you the South will fight and die first whether or not it is worth the lives of thousands dare I say? Fix this hemline will you Lizzy?" she said.

"Yes, Mrs. Davis, would you kindly stay still while I pin the hemline to mark it? May I ask then why is it that you long to stay in Washington if your sentiments agree with the Confederacy?" I was curious to know.

"My dear Lizzy, Washington is far more comfortable than anywhere in the South. Don't all you ladies know that Washington affords me the time not to be involved in the incessant need to maintain 'appearances' for the sake of supporting my husband's desire to uphold the Confederacy? Simply put, the South will be victorious because they are impulsive and driven by their emotions whereas the North is exacting and frankly simply too thoughtful.

In the end the North will yield after realizing how passionate the South will be and rather than risking the loss of thousands of lives in a war anticipated to be this nation's bloodiest, the North with all their practical sense and thought, will retreat before any blood is drawn, at least that is what I should like to believe and at least that is what should happen." Mrs. Davis said as I hemmed the final stitch of her dress. I observed her beautiful figure as he she proceeded to undress and handed me the gown. Motioning me to give her the day dress she previously had on prior to my arrival, I noticed how evenly distributed her brown her skin appeared throughout her arms, legs, and chest areas.

"I pray it is not long enduring if war is near." I said with a pin inside my mouth, pretending not to notice the melanin she possessed.

"Oh Lizzy! As for me, I wish to remain fashionable in all your delicious creations. God forbid I am to head south looking like last year's fashions, Ha! Never!" letting out a hearty laugh.

Not able to fully grasp the seriousness of her statement about the war quite yet, I asked another question to confirm, *"Are you absolutely certain beyond the shadow of a doubt Mrs. Davis that there will be war?"*

"Absolutely! Positively! Yes Lizzy and so you ought to go south with me because once this war breaks out, all slaves will suffer the wrath in the North whether freed. You will be targeted and highly blamed as the reason for this bloody war and will surely be maltreated worse than ever before. You must come with me, and I shall take good care of you. In fact, it is most likely that I shall return to Washington soon after the war. Mr. Davis is likely to be appointed by the South as its new President, and we

will all march with our army to Washington and move into the White House. And of course, I shall need gowns of utmost style as the First Lady Lizzy, the utmost of all!" she said with exacting words.

Perhaps I imagined this, but I could have sworn Mrs. Davis rolled her eyes in what looked like an attempt to mock the South under the façade of her advocacy and support for the Confederacy.

Shocked, scared and flummoxed by what she said, I was almost tempted to go with her especially after having served as her loyal dressmaker for some time. After all, she treated me with much dignity and respect, paid me well and had plenty of work to keep me busy for a long time. Her predictions seemed highly likeable to happen in my eyes. I expressed to her that I would thoughtfully consider her offer and would give her my final decision sooner than later.

That evening, my heart grew weary and confused. I prayed in earnest for God to give me clarity in my thoughts and actions. The more I prayed, the more I was less willing to accept Mrs. Davis' offer. My people have endured too much to give up now and my thought was to align myself with the North especially since most recently, they had just gained victory and traction from an intense campaign. I also suspect that no one from the Republican party would easily surrender to the South after all they had gained in the recent campaign.

I deduced that should the South posture for war against the North, there would be a response that would not deliver retreat but rather an onward kind of charge to fight profusely. I also heard that the man named 'Lincoln' was being positioned to lead the North to victory and my confidence for this so-called capable leader was bolstered by the fact that he was in good favor with Mr. Frederick Douglass himself. That was alone was convincing enough for me.

I decided that night to wage my bets on the North and chose to respectfully decline Mrs. Davis' kind and generous offer with a promise to perhaps join her in the event I had a change of heart and mind. In my heart, I knew I was never going to work for her again but felt it only prudent to offer her some form of assurance.

Mrs. Davis expressed her disappointment and added that she would have to give up certain luxuries for a while, including expensive dresses and coats after I delivered two chintz wraps she requested. She explained that she, along with her Southern counterparts would have to practice modest living since the war was soon to erupt and to send her the remaining needlework while in transition to Montgomery, Alabama with the help of Mrs. Emory, her closest friend.

From 1860 to 1865, I never saw the Davis family again. I often thought of them in the fondest of ways. Many years of bloodshed, turmoil and havoc ensued as all the words Mrs. Davis uttered unfolded into the bloody war she had described right before our very eyes. She was however, proven wrong about who would rise victorious as history would later account.

Suffice it to say that despite all that I have endured as a slave, I bore no resentment towards her. How strange it is a feeling, to bear no ill will against the very ones inciting and leading the oppression and molestation of my people for hundreds of years. I have no rational explanation for this and leave these mysteries of my human experience to God instead.

Sometime in the year of 1865, while visiting a patron in Chicago, I set myself to attend a charity event benefitting the wives, children, parents and families of all the soldiers who were either wounded or killed in the war, an excited crowd grew fixated towards one area of the hall.

Curious to see what the commotion was about, I walked towards the large crowd to look at the area of everyone's interest.

There I saw a human-like wax figure of Mr. Jefferson Davis, wearing over his actual garments the dress in which it was said he was captured in. As I walked closer to the figure, I was taken aback to discover that the garment displayed was one of the two chintz wraps that I had made for Mrs. Davis shortly before she departed Washington to make her journey to the South.

I shall never forget the moment when she said, *"Oh it is beautiful Lizzy, and shall keep me handsomely warm in the winter months. Thank you darling Lizzy. How very kind of you,"* as she wrapped herself in the chintz I had painstakingly made for her in earnest.

"I was Mrs. Davis' personal dressmaker, and this wrap was one of the last garments I made for her before she left Washington," I uttered to the crowd without realizing it.

That simple statement caused a raucous of sorts and the crowd cheered with much admiration and curiosity. The crowd started following me within the building and I soon managed to escape from that embarrassing situation with stealth quickness.

The reports first described that Mr. Davis had on a waterproof cloak instead of a dress at the time of his capture that did not support any of the details in my story. The dress replicated on the wax figure in Chicago was without a doubt a wrap made of chintz in the exact details as the one I had made for Mrs. Davis in the month of January in 1860. I paid close attention to the fact that since the reports indicated that the wrap was not found on the body of Mr. Davis, who was now a fugitive, I deduced that it had to have been taken from the trunks belonging to Mrs. Davis. The resemblance of the chintz I made in comparison to what was shown at the gallery was uncanny, striking and far too coincidental to me.

I later discovered that Mrs. Davis eventually moved to New York sometime around 1890 where she devoted most of her time as a writer for a newspaper owned by Mr. Joseph Pulitzer. In her later years, her writings developed into deeper subject matters and in her usual outspoken manner, she spoke about the need for reconciliation between the North and South suggesting that each party had more in common than conflict with one another.

While there was much controversy concerning Mr. Davis's

business and political affairs after his capture, I wish to remember the good moments that surrounded my time with the Davis family.

While the tittle-tattle of the controversies pertaining to Mrs. Davis' ancestry continued, and the constant chatter about the temerity of her character, I choose instead to etch the memory of Mrs. Davis as the wonderful, kind and generous woman she was to me.

She possessed a stellar sense of style and grace; blessed with an undeniable keen mind and a wit that would silence even the brightest of male (and female) scholars. She was a woman of immense clarity in purpose, confident posture and possessed a vast kind of strength. I felt great delight knowing that the last two garments I made as she journeyed her way to the South brought her a great sense of comfort, pleasure, satisfaction and most of all, warmth.

CHAPTER 7

Dressing the First Lady, Mrs. Mary Todd Lincoln

I always hoped to create dresses for the ladies of the White House and vowed to myself that I would do almost anything in order to reach this accomplishment. In the beginning, work was scarce for I had not yet established a reputation as an expert Mantua maker and dressmaker of 'High Fashion,' also known to the French and throughout Europe as the 'Haute Couture.' Mother always said these words with great facility and flair.

A new apparatus called a 'Sewing Machine' became all the rage though I neither had the time nor the interest to learn its use for I felt it would pose an added measure of time just to learn its mechanics. I felt it could potentially cause a tremendous risk to the work I was already committed to complete. Besides, the price of one such contraption would have set me back a great sum of money of which I was prepared to squander nor risk.

My goal was to present myself as a skilled Modiste specializing in custom-made dresses of utmost distinction with designs that were not yet introduced to the public at large.

Oftentimes, my inspirations were derived from visions that came to me in the form a dream. Sometimes ideas came along during my observations of women in their day-to-day lives.

During one of my visits to the home of distinguished lady

patron, (whose identity I promised to withhold for she preferred to remain unknown especially in matters pertaining to her extravagant lifestyle) I witnessed the delivery of an important nature wherein the entire household was called to gather in the main dining room where this important package was to be unveiled.

There, I saw the one of the most beautiful images my eyes had ever seen. It was a painting that came all the way from Paris, France rendered by a man with a name that sounded strangely peculiar and unusual to me.

Everyone in the household stood in disbelief as it slowly emerged from its meticulously wrapped package. It was an impressive work of art that sent a barrage of feelings through every cell in my body. It was sizeable and wide taking up the entire span of the main dining room's wall.

"Magnificent! It is a true work of art in the Impressionist movement. Oh, please do come closer - look at the colors and the brush strokes," my lady patron announced as each one of us took turns carefully examining this masterpiece. I left that afternoon thinking about the word my lady patron used to describe the new object of her affection, 'Impressionist.'

The following day, I made my way to the library to inquire about this expression and technique that was quickly becoming the 'de rigueur.' In newspaper articles, I read of its large following throughout Europe. I also learned many things from my lady patrons and took inspiration from this newfound knowledge and registered everything I learned in a handy logbook with precise detail. I wondered whether these faraway places in Europe knew of our conditions in America, particularly the institution of slavery. Someone reliable told me that slavery was considered a crime in some townships in Europe, and I wondered about the life I could have had, had I lived there instead.

The political climate between the North and South directed my tendencies towards simple silhouettes. By reducing the volume of a woman's skirt to nearly half its typical size and selecting colors leaning on less vibrant saturated hues, I constructed dresses that could soon be easily identified as one of my creations.

"That looks like an Elizabeth Keckley design," a lady passerby once said when they saw a woman disembarking the carriage in one of my originals. I offered my patrons more subtle shades but still appealing to the eyes. Adornments and embellishments were also kept at a minimum if anything at all, and textile options reflected less pomp and circumstance such as cotton, light silks and weaves, and sometimes materials from beddings and draperies no longer in use – damask being a favorite fabric to work with.

This design approach affected my ability to impress a following at first – posing a hardship upon me for I had debts to pay. While my debts were considered small to many members of the elite clientele I served, they were worrisome and direful to a person like me, nonetheless.

Through the assistance of one of my lady patrons who journeyed to the South almost on a bi-monthly basis, I was able to send my mother a stipend from my earnings. My son who was maturing into a young man was also dependent solely on my ability to provide his basic needs. Add to this, my son's matriculation fees while in college, of which I was proudly dedicated to support. What a good son I had for never once did he utter a remark of discontent or complaint during our transition as free people.

Nonetheless, many nights I ruminated on how I was to secure the next meal. I was not accustomed to fending for myself for I lived in constant servitude to my previous owners. While our meals were never enough to satiate our hunger after working tirelessly as slaves, I never had to concern myself about the next meal for ours was rationed on a daily basis. Eventually, our stomachs were reduced to a smaller size, and we grew accustomed to the paltry portions. Our meals were of the simplest nature mostly comprised of cabbage cooked in grease from the rendered fat of the meat and accompanied with one to two small pieces of the same meat.

On some days depending on what was available, a meal of peas and scraps of left-over meat from the master's family's food would be palatable enough for all to enjoy. Auntie Jane, highly skilled in the kitchen usually worked alongside my mother, would make a delicious meal of freshly made cornmeal dumplings thrown into a huge pot of boiling water seasoned with salt and fat.

I enjoyed watching the men as they drove two thick wooden sticks and affix them to the ground, and a long pole would be placed on top of the sticks that were carved like large forks. The kettle would hang in the middle of the pole directly above the fire that was usually placed under a shady tree. All would gather after a long day's work, share stories and sometimes, if hearty enough to continue, singing and dancing would ensue. This ritual was practiced religiously and gave blessing to the food that nourished us.

In the winter season, our victuals offered a change in the familiarity and this time, most of the cooking would be prepared inside the cabins. A combination of dried peas, sweet potatoes and a small piece of meat was the usual afternoon meal, and dinner was comprised mostly of corn meal made into thick pieces of bread with one or two small pieces of meat.

From a very young age, children were taught to save a portion of their dinner for the following morning's meal, for breakfast was only served to master and his family members. The overseers and others would be fed something similar. Slaves were not allowed to partake. This small meal was the previous night's leftover meal and was savored sometime before lunch during a moment, (usually five minutes) to catch a breath and drink water. Many slaves would not have the opportunity to have this small meal for they had consumed all their food the night before. I was methodical about my rations and always set aside a reserve for myself or for anyone needing a small bite to eat. Sometimes if we were lucky, Master Burwell would indulge us with a treat of Molasses and Hominy which all of us enjoyed. It would pose as a rare occasion in my memory however, yet somehow has been etched in my mind as a pleasing occurrence of my past.

All my life, I was accustomed to taking care of my slave owners and absorbed their financial obligations through my sewing. How ironic it was that I could not even find the means to adequately care for my son and myself as a free woman. I was for the first time in my life fully responsible for my own existence, and often it would stop me amid my day and terrify me.

I had no other recourse than to call upon Mrs. Ringold, who then made the kind introduction to Mrs. Mary Anna Lee, who was the step-granddaughter of former President George Washington and the wife of a military man named Mr. General Robert E. Lee.

Mrs. Lee, who had already purchased the silk material for her yet to be constructed dress, was on the fringe of sheer thrill in anticipation for the one of the most important events of the season. It was a grand formal ball and dinner given in honor of none other than the Prince of Wales! Even I was delighted beyond measure to learn of this news, because in my mind, how is it possible that I should be considered to conjure a dress suitable enough for such an occasion, let alone a guest in attendance whom I would soon be serving to meet a real-life Prince in our midst?

The recommendation made by Mrs. Ringold to retain my services proved convincing enough to Mrs. Lee that I was immediately hired to begin the process. The following day I arrived at Mrs. Lee's home and was received by General Lee himself who then handed me a large sum of neatly folded bills amounting to one hundred dollars.

He instructed, *"Please purchase all the necessary trimmings, ribbons, and all needed decorations for this dress and spare no expense in making your selections. I trust you will make a dress for my wife that shall leave a lasting impression to all in attendance. These are my instructions, and I am confident you shall live up to my expectations. Thank you, Mrs. Keckley."*

I put the money inside the secret pocket of my coat along with my license to operate and documented proof as a free woman and hastened to begin my walk towards Harper and Mitchell, a store with some of the most exquisite supplies for a dressmaker to work with. On the way there, as I neared Harper and Mitchell, my heart was beating so rapidly that I nearly lost my balance and had to find a place to sit for a few minutes before resuming my walk.

"Gather yourself Elizabeth," I mumbled to myself as the door flung open when a bell hung above the door's entrance announced my entry.

"Hello and welcome Ms.?" the man behind the counter asked.

"Mrs. Elizabeth Keckley. I have been retained by Mrs. Lee to fashion a gown for an upcoming ball. Good Morning Sir," I said with a crack in my voice. Walking away from the counter, the man offered me a soft smile and extended his hand for me to shake it.

I explained to him my initial plans and provided him with a simple outline in pencil of the silhouette I had in mind. After briefly studying it, he guided me to a room to see their finest assortment of Belgian and French laces.

I felt especially important when the shop's proprietor himself, Mr. Harper, attended to my every need. He was a polite man, soft-spoken and patient with his time and generous with his attention. Realizing that I was unable to make a committed decision on which lace Mrs. Lee would prefer, he agreed without an ounce of doubt to allow me to bring the assortment of choices to Mrs. Lee for her final approval.

"Are you sure Mr. Harper? These laces are of extreme value, and I am a mere stranger to you," I said.

"I have no doubt you will return them to me once Mrs. Lee makes her selection. You have the face of an honest heart," Mr. Harper said with a look of implicit trust in me.

This was a rare feeling I did not often get from a white person.

I realized what I had been missing in my life--to be regarded with mutual respect as a human being on equal terms. I will never forget Mr. Harper's kind words and throughout my life, would often imagine traveling back in time to that moment especially during times when I felt the struggle was too great to bear.

I was excited in purchasing the materials for Mrs. Lee's dress and Mr. Harper extended a twenty-five-dollar commission on the purchase. In the coming weeks leading up to the grand ball, I worked diligently with great focus and unstoppable momentum.

I made an exception this time and chose to slightly deviate from my design philosophy on simplicity and subtlety given the magnitude of this occasion and the necessity for me to use this opportunity to showcase my talent as a skilled dressmaker whose fashions have not yet been seen by members of society. Mrs. Lee's dress would be my first public introduction as an expert dressmaker to the most discerning women of Washington. I was thrilled that an original Elizabeth Keckley design was days from its official debut.

For this endeavor, I decided to go above and beyond in conjuring the most divine gown for Mrs. Lee. It was also my intention to make Mrs. Ringold proud and satisfied in making the recommendation. I was grateful for her gesture of kindness and confidence in my skills.

Mrs. Lee purchased a lovely shade of light pink in the most exquisite silk moiré. This fabric mimicked the appearance of water with beautifully variegated impressions from its weave that left a watermarked appearance upon the textile. Depending on where the light hit and landed, the colors changed in hues from a silver-like sparkle to one that resembled a damask pink rose.

Considering Mrs. Lee's soft features, her alabaster skin, dark hair and petite build, it was important for me to fashion a gown that did not consume her, but rather highlighted her natural assets and beauty. I borrowed inspiration from paintings depicting scenes and landscapes of the impressionist works of the day.

The gown had an Empire waistline that held her torso and bosom in a most upright position, with a lace overlay that modestly draped over the keyhole neckline. I hand-sewed delicate gold passementerie trim with silk hand knotted bouillons and galloons throughout the edges of the neckline for a finished and rich look. The torso's silhouette transitioned at the waist into a soft outline with the layer of soft gossamer above the silk textile to create a beautiful illusion.

Each flower and leaf on the lace was adorned with hand embroidery using silk thread for a life-like effect. At the center of each flower, I installed freshwater pearls to create realistic looking flowers in a garden-like backdrop much like the painting in the main dining room of my unnamed lady patron's house not too long ago. I fashioned a pair of satin opera length gloves in a soft white shade customized to fit each of her delicate fingers. Mr. Harper was kind enough to introduce me to Mr. Durand, a Frenchman whose lovely atelier specialized in custom-made women's shoes. I explained my vision to him in detail, to which he created a pair of satin evening shoes in a shade of pale blue to match the color of her eyes.

I recommended her attendant to comb her hair in an upswept style to emphasize her swan-like neck. She wore a pair of pearl drop earrings surrounded by small blue sapphires all around. This was accompanied with a beautiful necklace that had a pearl pendant to complete her evening attire.

Mrs. Lee looked utterly divine and resplendent. To my relief, she expressed her satisfaction with exuberance at the outcome. The General appeared to stand taller that evening as they made their way into the horse-driven cart that led them to the ball.

The following morning, Mrs. Lee requested my presence to meet her at her home for tea, to which I gladly obliged. She thanked me profusely for my services and ordered a few more dresses for me to make. She informed me that several other lady friends who attended the dinner party already inquired about my services and should be calling upon me soon.

One of those ladies was Mrs. Mary Louise McClean, the daughter of Major General Sumner of the Union Army and the wife of Brigadier General Nathaniel McClean, also of the Union Army. She arrived at my apartment unannounced during a time when I was extremely busy with deadlines.

"I apologize for this intrusion Lizzy, but I have been invited to a dinner party at Willard Hotel this coming Sunday, and positively absolutely have I not one singular outstanding dress to wear on such an occasion. Please I beg you to commence work right away as I have since purchased all the materials, please Lizzy won't you please?" with imploring eyes she pleaded, both hands in prayer-like stance.

"Oh but Mrs. McClean, I have so much more work that I promised to do as it is, and there is only several hours in a day. It is not possible for me to make you a dress with such little notice, I am terribly sorry to decline," I responded with all honesty.

"Oh, hush and woe shall not be you! Lizzy, with you nothing is impossible! I heard of your quickness and abilities. I must have this dress by Sunday, and I promise to pay you generously. Thank you Lizzy, here is the fabric and everything you will need," and with that she handed me a large basket with the supplies and a sum of two hundred dollars.

I proceeded to say *"Oh No, Mrs. McClean - I do not think you understand that I..."* as she interrupted me mid-sentence to say:

"Oh stop it Lizzy now, and please do not say no to me again. I am telling you to make this dress. I heard Mrs. Lee say that you would love to make dresses for the ladies of the White House, yes? I will have you know now that I have that power to get you in the door. You see, I know Mrs. Lincoln very well and I promise that you shall be making her a dress soon after you finish mine to wear on Sunday. Make haste Lizzy, I have every faith in you! Oh, thank you, thank you, a million more times Lizzy, thank you Lizzzeee!"

As if a sudden bolt of electricity hit me, I agreed to Mrs. McClean's proposal even if it meant staying up all night to the following morning to repeat the process until the dress was delivered on time.

For this nearly impossible undertaking, I employed two spry Negro female dressmakers who assisted me with the handiwork and the construction of the gown. I relegated one to assist in assembling the sleeves, while the other focused on the skirt.

I attended to the more tedious work of the underpinnings of the gown's bodice. Given the challenge I was faced with respect to time, I fashioned a gown with a silhouette that offered an understated kind of elegance using a fitted bodice as the focal feature of the gown since Mrs. McClean possessed a figure that was slim and curvy at the same time. To her great satisfaction, the gown was completed and delivered a day ahead of time. I look back at that moment and can only attribute it to something close to an act of God, a miracle.

(As time went on, I became one of Harper and Mitchell's most loyal customers and eventually, was given the accommodation to be the first client to review their latest and newest inventory imported from Europe never seen by the general public before. I was given exclusivity of certain laces and materials to be reserved for my clients' custom orders. It was something I was most particular about whenever my patrons retained my services because having a "one-of-a-kind" Elizabeth Keckley design was vital to my business strategy. Since then, Mr. Harper would 'reserve' items he felt would resonate with me, and he was never wrong about his choices for he knew me well.)

A few days after Mrs. McClean's event at the Willard Hotel, I was informed that Mrs. Lincoln had the misfortune of soiling a gown she designed and had planned on wearing on the night of the reception following Mr. Abraham Lincoln's inaugural ceremony as President of the United States.

The troubled Mrs. Lincoln asked Mrs. McClean, *"Who is the dressmaker that made the lovely dress you wore at the Willard's dinner event last Sunday?"*

"Why thank you, and might I add she is swift and professional. Her name is Lizzy Keckley, Elizabeth Keckley to some. She is a Negro woman," Mrs. McClean said knowing this was the moment her promise to me would be realized.

"Lizzy Keckley? That name sounds awfully familiar. I believe she worked for one of my lady friends in St. Louis and she spoke so highly of her dressmaker named Lizzy. Surely it must be the same Negro woman because I have never met another Lizzy in my life. Would you be kind enough to recommend her to see me?" Mrs. Lincoln asked.

I received a message for me to report to Mrs. Mclean's house the following afternoon. However, since I was inundated with work and considering Mrs. Mclean did not state the nature of her request, I thought to wait until the next morning to pay her a visit instead.

On my way there, the streets heading towards the Capital were swarming with people preparing for Inauguration Day to arrive. Mr. Abraham Lincoln would soon be sworn in as the President of the United States; regarded as the man who was of the people and for the people and would soon assume the most important responsibility as the nation's Chief Commander in charge. No one has ever witnessed anything in the nation's history with this level of interest and magnitude. Threats of his assassination loomed over the Capital and the South pressed on with talks of war.

One hundred and thirty-one politicians gathered at the Willard Hotel located on Pennsylvania Avenue in what was to be a conference of the nation's greatest leaders. Former President turned private citizen of Virginia, Mr. John Tyler thought that a cumulative and concerted meeting to preserve the Union and resolve the sectional split between the free and slave states needed urgent attention. Mr. John Lechter, Governor of Virginia agreed to sponsor the convention.

The conference's objective was to avoid the secession of the eight slave states from the upper and border areas of the South that had not done so yet. Meanwhile, the seven Southern states of Alabama, Florida, Georgia, Louisiana, Mississippi, South Carolina and Texas had already passed ordinances of secession and were actively preparing to form a new government in Montgomery, Alabama.

In an act of defiance, they did not attend the conference believing that it would not accomplish any significant role in changing their minds.

The Willard Hotel's surrounding perimeter was laden with a large and excited crowd that extended into the residential areas. I found myself stuck between Pennsylvania Avenue and Fourteenth Street nearly suffocating from the throngs of people quickly growing and expanding around me. An electrifying energy prevailed throughout the city while the faces of its residents were more worried than the next; each movement more urgent than the other's, and every breath taken so deep that once released to exhale, collected in the atmosphere like a dark heavy cloud above.

Across the way, I could see Mrs. McClean's house populated with a staff of aides appointed by the General himself to dissuade passersby to step beyond their property line.

Mrs. McClean was coming in and out of her house with a concerned look on her face as I tried to call out her name in the hopes that perhaps one of her assistants would help get me out of the impassioned and dangerously growing assembly. The noise merely drowned out my cries as I continued to make my way to her.

Finally, she spotted me from the crowd and yelled *"Lizzy! Why did you not come when I called for you? Mrs. Lincoln wanted to see you desperately, but I am afraid that it might be too late for her request is of an urgent nature,"* she said as she motioned for her aides to come and lift me from the swelling deluge of people.

"I am so sorry Mrs. McClean. You did not state why you needed me so I assumed it could wait until now," I responded with my voice cracking as I finally entered her home safely.

"You should never assume anything Lizzy. Go up to Mrs. Lincoln immediately and pray she may still find some use for you. Hurry! She

awaits you on the second floor," she instructed.

With that, she handed me Mrs. Lincoln's room number handwritten on a piece of paper and I hastened my steps to the hotel with the help of one of Mrs. McClean's footmen who cleared our path by warding people off with a cane.

Upon arrival, I knocked on her door three times. A high-pitched cheerful voice beckoned me to come in and a rather short and round lady stood before me. I estimated her to be in her middle forties as I wiped the sweat quickly collecting on my forehead with a handkerchief embroidered with the letter "E" that mother made for me.

"Might you be Mrs. Elizabeth Keckley, the dressmaker known as Lizzy whom my dear friend Mrs. McClean recommended?" she asked as I bowed my head in acknowledgement.

"Very good. Well, I have no time to discuss things with you right now but if you would please report to the White House tomorrow at eight o'clock in the morning that would be most convenient for me, Lizzy. Thank you."

In a daze, I walked back home to my apartment unfazed by the maddening crowd and noise around me. As I walked further, my thoughts recollected the ease by which I was able to make my way to Mrs. Lincoln's hotel room after meeting Mrs. McClean in her home and considered that rather strange. With no instructions from her, the footman simply took charge of the undertaking with effortless calm depsite the confusion and excitement that surrounded us. I felt protected in a sense; an unusual foreign feeling. I was not quite sure myself if I was dreaming about it. *Is this what Divine Providence meant?*

Brushing the thought out of my mind, I walked further. I was shaking throughout my body in a kind of convulsion difficult to contain. In child-like manner, I released a giggle out loud as I made my way closer to home. My long-awaited dream was about to materialize, and I was restless with excitement throughout the remainder of the night. I felt mad, crying and laughing at the same time. Sometimes as if I was about to jump out of my own skin.

The following morning at exactly eight o'clock, I entered the White House for the very first time. As I neared the North front of the building, I stumbled at the graveled path set in a flat-rolled lawn that caused the heels of my shoes to sink deep into the fresh gravel.

A guard dressed in uniform noticed and began to walk towards me with one eyebrow held in the most suspicious manner.

"Pardon me, Sir. I have an appointment with Mrs. Lincoln this morning and I am afraid I am running late," extending my hand that held my license to work and proof as a free woman.

Without a word, he turned himself around and walked towards the iron fences and railing located directly in front of the North front of the building which were clearly designed to control the public's access to the grounds.

The beautiful green lawn that encircled a statue of Mr. Thomas Jefferson by the sculptor Jean Pierre David d'Angers was still fresh from the morning's dew.

This spectacular replica of Mr. Jefferson's image was designated its placement by President James K. Polk in 1847. I stood in front of it for a few seconds to log the memory of the experience in my mind.

Taking a slight right turn from the house, I neared the Conservatory, which was built atop the West Terrace. It was apparent to me that Mrs. Lincoln had commissioned for renovations and improvements to be made as evidenced by the current work that was taking place. Everything was in a state of reform. Everything was being revamped.

"How apropos," I thought mumbling to myself.

On the other side of the Conservatory, I noticed a throng of people entering and exiting the house, comprised of mostly men from all walks of life carrying about in all directions.

I asked a nearby gentleman, *"What, may I ask are all these people doing here, Sir?"* to which he replied, *"Business, politics, war."*

This man told me that he was a student hailing from Harvard who made the trip to Washington to witness Mr. Abraham Lincoln's Inaugural ceremony.

"One aspect of Mr. and Mrs. Lincoln's open-door-policy," further stating that since the Lincolns had taken residence at the White House, there has been a deluge of visitors and curious folks who make every effort to avail themselves of this equal access to the extent of climbing the walls, entering through windows at levees, sneaking in through the corridors and camping directly outside of the President's office door on all conceivable errands, for all imaginable purposes and that despite all preventative measures for the President and his family's security, his demanding and unquenchable following of office seekers, bureaucratic aspirants and probing public were the biggest drain on the Lincolns' time, energy and resources.

These people were verbose about their reasons for being there making every desperate effort to persist and harass the President for a remunerative appointment in government. I was appalled at the rapacious exhibition that was taking place before me.

"What kind of people are these?" I mumbled to myself again. Like a large swarm of bees, these men in all their pomp and circumstance were nothing but future extortionists and mercenaries driven with one sole purpose to advance their goals for personal gains. I couldn't help but reconsider whether to turn around and go home. This setting in the atmosphere was incompatible to what I had envisioned for myself as the future Modiste to the First Lady. How could I possibly work in these disruptive and debasing conditions?

Soon before I knew it, I had made my way through the maddening crowd of loud boisterous self-important men and by the off chance that my eyes met the gaze of another woman, she was usually too busy and concerned with controlling her children, who too, were just as ravenous for the opportunity to meet the President. While it is not my custom, (nor am I proud to admit) to think lowly of innocent children, I could not refrain from thinking that these tots were little opportunists in the making too.

Somewhere along the way, a toothless aged man holding a sign with the hand-written words *"NO TO THE EMANCIPATION OF SLAVES! GOD SAVE THE CONFEDERACY*!" stopped me in my tracks. Appalled and terrified, I quickened my pace to get as far away from him and the rest of these people as soon as possible.

My heart was racing and at last, I was at the designated room where I was to report for duty. A well-dressed pleasant looking Negro man introduced himself as Mr. William Henry Johnson greeted me at the door.

"Good morning Mrs. Keckley, thank you for your promptitude. Mrs. Lincoln will call upon you shortly. If there is anything you mighneed, please kindly ring the bell and I shall come up to see to it," he smiled.

My mind swelled with the highest spirits and pride upon making Mr. Johnson's acquaintance for it affirmed to me that my decision not to turn around and go home was a wise one. Mr. Johnson was a white-haired man, with dark brown skin. His round black eyes were deeply sunken with a softness that made you feel safe. He was a tall man with long legs and arms that were hardy and strong. A full set of perfectly lined teeth glistened as he smiled at me.

He was the President's personal valet, brought to Washington by Mr. Lincoln from Illinois where he previously worked for then Senator Lincoln prior to his appointment into the Presidency.

Mr. Johnson was a meticulously groomed man with shoes polished so perfectly that I could almost see my own reflection upon them. His shirt was gleaming white and starched with great detail He walked with an erect posture and his voice was of a deep baritone timbre.

Impeccable in every possible way, Mr. Johnson carried himself with a composure that commanded and demanded respect. My mother would have been proud to meet him.

Reverberating through the newly installed blue silk damask wallpapered walls, I heard a voice utter, *"I am beginning to feel at home and enjoy everything very much. Every evening, our blue room is filled with the elite of the land, the grounds of the garden by the Conservatory is turning out to be exquisite, with so many fragrant flowers and fruit bearing trees. Just delightful."* I deduced this was the voice of Mrs. Mary Todd Lincoln.

It was intimidating to be inside this magnificent building when not too long ago, I was toiling away at the Burwell plantation sometimes wishing for my life to end. I remembered how my mother Aggy painstakingly sewed clothes day in and day out for 82 people; 12 of whom were members of the Burwell family and the remaining were 70 slaves for the entirety of her lifetime.

My thoughts of my past life were interrupted by Mr. Johnson who then directed me to enter a waiting room where three other Mantua makers were also waiting for an interview with the wife of the newly appointed President. I was the only Negro woman in the room and was received with undeniable scrutiny and study.

"Are you here to be considered as Mrs. Lincoln's personal dressmaker?" asked an older lady whom I knew was far more experienced than me given her age. Around her neck was a lovely necklace from which a small pair of embroidery scissors hung.

"Yes, and you?" I asked.

"Indeed I am. I am here upon the recommendation of Mrs. Brown who informed me that Mrs. Lincoln called upon all her lady friends to send their personal dressmakers here this morning," and then she whispered into my ear *"because apparently, Mrs. Lincoln has been throwing fits and tantrums."*

Hearing this, my excitement turned dull, as I wondered whether I stood a chance amongst these highly experienced white dressmakers. With a formidable line of rivals ahead of me, my hopes for success became increasingly dubious.

As it turned out, I misunderstood Mrs. Lincoln the previous day and interpreted her to mean that I was already hired to do the work and to report promptly in the morning. Instead, what she meant was that I would be considered for the position amongst many others hoping for the privilege. A teachable moment for me in the importance of paying attention, I ruminated as I waited for my turn.

Looking at the women in the room, one's attention is immediately directed to their mode, manner and dress. Most of them were older and that meant more experience in my mind. All of them were white and had an air of confidence about them. My mind was racing in all directions as my fears started to consume me. I closed my eyes and prayed instead.

Before each candidate entered the room, Mr. Johnson would announce their names to Mrs. Lincoln in preparation for their introduction. One on by one, each of my rivals entered the room in what seemed to be an eternity while I waited. Through the thick wooden hand-carved door, I faintly heard Mrs. Lincoln speak in agreement with one of the candidates as if they were already discussing the work to be performed for her.

"Do you know Mr. Johnson?" one dressmaker asked me.

"I am afraid I do not. He seems to be acquainted in the White House quite well," I replied.

"Oh, so you have not heard? It is said that he is a very important part of the Lincoln family, having come all the way from Illinois where he previously worked for Mr. Lincoln while he was a Senator. And did you know that during that dreadful train trip from Baltimore, Mr. Johnson was observed to have been very attentive to Mr. Lincoln. I was told that not only is he Mr. Lincoln's personal valet, but his untiring vigilance and guardedness for Mr. Lincoln has gained him the position of his personal bodyguard and for that, I am told he is handsomely paid. I reckon had it not been for his safeguarding, we may not be sitting here today!

Oh, and some chatter about how the President took an alternate route to Washington to evade an assassination plot against him. Can you imagine? I think it is with utmost respect that I say this to you, Slavery must end, and I shall do everything in my power to stand with this administration to see to it. My husband stands with the Abolitionists," said the white lady who gently put her hand over mine in a gesture of assurance. I offered her a smile and pulled my hand away for I was taken aback by what she said. These words coming from a white woman are a stark difference from the venomous utterings of my previous Mistresses and I could not figure out for myself whether to be happy or sad.

The next one took even longer to finish. I overheard Mrs. Lincoln speaking to her in French. By the time the last candidate exited the room, I was exhausted.

Mrs. Lincoln offered the French speaking woman a warm hug and said *"Merci Madame Dufort. Je ferai bientot appel a vous."*

Mrs. Dupfort who appeared pleased, offered me the following parting words, *"There is no room for people like you in the White House."*

"I am sure Mrs. Lincoln would not be happy to hear you say that," I quipped without looking at her, my eyes transfixed to the ground in strict defiance. In my mind, she did not deserve the courtesy of my attention. I thought the French were against slavery and that morning I learned a little more about the French.

What a contrasting set of words I heard from the previous recitation of the kind lady earlier. I offered her the same smile as I did the other for the gesture was sufficient to shoo away all feelings of self-doubt and timidity. I abandoned all thoughts rickety, all thoughts frail, and all thoughts unsteady. Instead, I called upon the spirits of my ancestors in one outright go, I was ready.

I was the final dressmaker left in the waiting room for Mrs. Lincoln to meet and by this time, I presumed surely she must have been exhausted from this arduous task. I was proven wrong for as I entered after my name was announced by the kind valet, she appeared gleaming and alert.

"Ah, yes. Please be seated. You are Lizzy, correct?" she asked as I tucked my skirt from underneath me to sit down. Mr. Johnson after slowly closing the door behind me paused for a half second to meet my gaze and offered me an unforgettable glorious smile that lit the room up even brighter.

Mrs. Lincoln briefly left the room but quickly returned holding a silk fan which she proceeded to open with nimble proficiency. My attention was averted as I admired the beautiful scenery the fan beheld. Cherry Blossom trees beautifully hand-painted in hues of pink, white and red spanned its width with figures of women dressed in a most unusual kind of robe, donning elaborate hairstyles held by jeweled pins and tassels of silk. Golden birds were depicted in flight throughout its landscape, and I sat there mesmerized by the beauty of such a simple personal ventilator of an object.

Add to this, a waft of fragrance filled the room with a floral kind of perfume that permeated every nook and cranny of the space. Mrs. Lincoln was rapidly fanning herself in a flurry, the fragrance traveling across the room each time her fan flapped.

Noticing my gaze, she said: *"Chinoiserie, the scenery of this fan is called Chinoiserie. It is the French's attempt to imitate Chinese motifs."*

I listened to Mrs. Lincoln digress about France and its relationship to Far Eastern art and design, wherein she expounded on one of the nation's founding fathers Mr. Thomas Jefferson as a self-admitted Francophile.

The drapery surrounding the room was a rich silk blue and white toile which was intentionally drawn to block out the sun and perhaps to avoid the confusion and chaos going on outside.

Mrs. Lincoln stood next to the side table by their bed. I couldn't believe my eyes when I saw the stovepipe hat the President just recently wore at the Willard Hotel. It was unceremoniously sitting on top of the table, the Holy Bible directly underneath it.

Here was I, a former slave standing inside the bedroom of the future President of the United States just two feet away from his wife. If I were not to be hired for my services, this moment alone was well worth the effort because never in my mind did I fathom ever being inside the most private room in the White House let alone stand face to face with the First Lady whose husband's hat seemed to have a spirit of its own.

Taking a sip of her tea, Mrs. Lincoln walked over to sit on a chair upholstered in a rich red damask silk with carved wooden legs.

"Ahh, at last Lizzy, you are here. Tell me something, who have you worked for in the city?" she asked with upturned lips.

"I had several patrons in the city, but my main patron was Senator Jefferson Davis' wife, Mrs. Varina Davis," I said.

"Ah yes. Varina. This is good to know for I have always admired her wardrobe and often wondered, notwithstanding her husband, how she acquired such lovely gowns from Europe. Tell me something Lizzy, was it you behind the seams?" the First Lady asked as she slowly took another sip of tea from the beautiful porcelain cup she held so daintily with one palm holding the bottom of the saucer, whilst the other hand slowly guiding the cup to her lips.

"I am humbled for such kind words, Mrs. Lincoln. Yes in fact I created a wardrobe for her, a total of 15 or so gowns, not including the wraps and overcoats over the short period I was under her employ. Dare I say that they were often mistaken for gowns imported from the fashion houses in Europe Mrs. Davis delighted in this assumption of course. It was a pleasure to create dresses for Mrs. Davis. I am forever indebted to her," I answered.

"Then it is settled! I shall be your most loyal patron hereon. You shall no longer work for Mrs. Senator of the Confederacy ever again, not even if she writes to request for a dress for any reason for I am sure they have plenty of dressmakers in the dreadful South suitable enough

for her. You shall instead be the official Modiste to the First Lady of the United States. Let us begin and commence work, shall we?" putting her teacup down and rising from her seat, clapping her hands and then ringing the bell to summons Mr. Johnson to the door.

In shock, I gasped for air and was overcome by her remark. *"Thank you. Yes Mrs. Lincoln. I am available to begin as early as tomorrow if you wish. May I ask what your terms might be?"*

Mr. Johnson begins to collect the teapot, cup, saucer and accoutrements and gently placed them on a silver tray.

"Thank you William. Mr. Lincoln shall be returning in a short while. Please give him a haircut before he starts to look like a mad mongrel, and would you be kind enough to deliver this sum of money to my sister at the post?"

"Yes Mrs. Lincoln, I shall. Is there anything else?" Mr. Johnson asked.

"Yes William, meet Lizzy. Mrs. Elizabeth Keckley shall be commencing work for me very soon and I should like for you to show her around the White House, especially familiarize her with the rooms where she will frequent, including the reception room and anywhere where the President and I will be often. Please also kindly inform the staff and the guards. Also, kindly plan to introduce her to all the merchants in town as Mrs. Lincoln's dressmaker. I will host a special announcement at the White House Rose Garden regarding her official employment followed up by a ladies' luncheon once things start to settle down as it is still a madhouse around here. Thank you William." Mr. Johnson offered her a nod of acknowledgement, turned to me to do the same and politely excused himself from the room.

"Ah yes, terms. Terms are contingent on your prices for unlike Mrs. Davis, I cannot afford to be extravagant. I expect your rates to be reasonable Lizzy, for if you do not charge too much, I shall give you all the work and no one else," she assertively responded.

"I very much understand, Mrs. Lincoln. I think it most prudent of

you to be mindful of your expenses especially since there is talk of war. If I may say so, what I envision for your wardrobe reflects an image that the people will relate to – dresses that evoke modesty without compromising beauty and style."

"Hmmm…Lizzy, would you kindly elaborate further what you mean by modesty? That is not in partnership with my personal style- this concept of modesty," Mrs. Lincoln said as she emphasized the latter word and moved the drapes slightly to peek at the crowd outside.

"Yes, Mrs. President, if I may suggest using less volume on the skirt, selecting colors of more subdued nature, consider minimal ornamentation, cleaner lines and silhouettes, wear less jewelry or at least jewelry that is more simple…small increments that show the people how you understand the hard times we are undergoing and that you are the First Lady of the people and for the people. The art of dress is one way to say something without saying anything at all. Clothing when utilized beyond function can be a strong tool in earning respect and at the same time, build power for the President as you are most vital in that role," I explained.

"Why Lizzy, I had no idea you were a scholar of Psychology! How profoundly intriguing your life must have been before making your acquaintance. Tell me, how did you become so learned in the matter of clothing in relation to politics and the human experience altogether?" she asked.

"Mrs. Lincoln, from as early as I can remember, I have always considered clothing as the armor of my life. Clothes, however soiled and damaged they may have been served as a shield to lessen the pain of the lashings. It offered protection from the white man's disrobing eyes. It created a wall that disallowed others to be too close to me. At night, it not only served as the much-needed warmth from lack of proper protection, but it served as an impostor layer against the chill of the wet dirt we laid on. The mere idea of having something to cover you was enough to create the illusion that it was real. Making a quilt, I sewed the pieces of blocks and patterns envisioning a roadmap to my

escape and how I wished for my story to unfold. On cold nights, I'd be wrapped in the quilt of my own dreams. I regard making dresses as my refuge from the cruelty of slavery. It drowned out my cries and muffled the amplification of my fears. It is what bought me my freedom too. Dressmaking is the reason why I am here today. I am free because of it and now I stand before the wife of the leader who promises the nation of slavery's eradication once and for all. I owe my life to this humble needle," lowering my head to avoid Mrs. Lincoln's significant stare.

"I am deeply moved by your words. I promise you all the work to keep you busy for a very long time," Mrs. Lincoln said as she put her hand on my shoulder and gave it a soft and assuring squeeze.

As I gathered my things and readied to leave the room, Mrs. Lincoln said: *"Lizzy? One more thing, you are safe, I promise you."*

With that, I walked home. As I neared my apartment, a young fair-skinned Negro man handed me a piece of paper that read:

"Abolitionist Mass Meeting to be held at United Methodist Hall at eight o'clock in the ev'ning sharp this Wednesday on the urgency of abolishing slavery. A transcript from the words of the greatest living colored orator, the Honorable Frederick Douglass entitled 'What to the Slave is the Fourth of July' shall be handed out to all attendees and orally recited on the stage by a trained actor to be witnessed by those in attendance. Seating is limited and may require standing outside the hall on the courtyard by the roundabout."

"Tell me Sir, will I be safe should I like to attend?" I asked. The young man offered no response, and I understood the silence. As if in one fell swoop, I was taken back to my childhood all the way to the last moment when I left the Burwell plantation. A nauseating gut-wrenching chill ran down my spine causing me to struggle as I tried to catch my breath.

"M'am? May I offer you some assistance?" the young man asked as I quickly gathered my composure to hasten my way back home.

He had no inkling of my past life as a slave of thirty-seven years for in his mind, surely I had been a free woman all my life.

I was relieved to finally make it back home. The anticipation of my new set of circumstances as Mrs. Lincoln's Modiste was a miraculous turn of events. I immediately began drafting ideas on paper for a wardrobe suitable for the First Lady. I developed a few silhouettes with accompanying coats and hats with detailed notes and swatches for Mrs. Lincoln to review. The ideas came to me like lightning bolts from all directions and if they arrived any quicker, I wouldn't make good sense of it all. The expediency and ease by which the concepts for her designs came to me were inexplicably miraculous in a way. Something greater than me was taking charge, and I was its vessel.

At the same time, I kept thinking about how much I yearned to meet Mr. Douglass in the flesh one day. With great determination, I concluded I was to attend not only to join the Abolitionists, but also to find a way to make Mr. Douglass' acquaintance as soon as possible.

I prayed until the sweat from my forehead trickled down to the corners of my eyes causing a sting that rendered me uncomfortable. Eventually, the sweat made its way throughout my body that turned into thick-brined layer. I prayed in earnest until I could no longer.

Little did I know that soon, I would become emblazoned and determined to help my people and utilize my dressmaking as the instrument to accomplish this goal. Soundly I slept until the morning awakened me with illuminated vigor and I stepped out of my apartment in absolute pursuit of excellence; in thought, in speech, and in action.

CHAPTER 8

A Fashionable Friendship

The following morning, I arrived at Mrs. Lincoln's room ready to attend to the first order of business with the finished rose-colored silk moiré dress she had given for me to adjust and modify the day prior. Inside the room were several women along with Mrs. Lincoln's sisters, Mrs. Kellogg and Mrs. Edwards and her two nieces Misses Julia Baker and Elizabeth Edwards.

The ladies were all dressed handsomely in morning attire, while Mrs. Lincoln was wrapped in a lovely cashmere day dress with quilted stitching at the center of the bodice and an unassuming hair ornament atop her head.

As I proceeded to fit the rose colored-gown on her, all talk of preparations for the levee to come off on Friday night ensued. Doing my best not to be distracted by this good news for I wanted the gown to fit her perfectly well, my attention shifted when Mrs. Lincoln requested that I fashion a waist-belt sash of blue watered silk for her friend Mrs. Grimsley.

I considered this request reasonable enough since the work for the rose-colored gown was minimal in scope.

That evening, I received a message that the levee for Friday had been postponed to Tuesday instead, giving more time to work on Mrs. Lincoln's alterations and Mrs. Grimsley's sash. I decided to take my time and deliver the garment on Tuesday.

The day arrived and all the alterations for Mrs. Lincoln's dress were finalized. Mrs. Grimsley's sash resulted in a beautifully executed outcome as well. Carefully packing Mrs. Lincoln's gown and the sash in tissue, I made my way to the White House where I was greeted with great anxiety and concern.

To my surprise, I found Mrs. Lincoln in a state of dismay stating that she refused to receive her guests at this late stage of the reception. I was not certain as to why she was in a state of panic for the event hadn't yet begun.

Bewildered by what she said, I asked; *"Mrs. Lincoln, I have come to present your dress to you as I have been hard at work on it."*

"Mrs. Keckley, how bereft and disappointed I am that I cannot face my guests for I have nothing to wear," she said as she wiped the tears from her eyes.

"But Mrs. Lincoln, I do not understand why you are disappointed, though I am terribly sorry; however, I am here now and shall be more than happy to dress you," I implored.

"I am afraid that there is not enough time Lizzy. I simply won't be dressed in time and shall stay in my room instead," crossing her arms in protest.

Mrs. Lincoln continued, *"The President can go down to meet the guests with the other ladies without me."*

"Mrs. Lincoln, let me dress you. There is plenty of time if we do not waste any of it further. Allow me to dress you please?" I said trying to console her.

Mrs. Grimsley and Mrs. Edwards offered words of assurance as well, *"There is certainly plenty of time Mary. Do not fret."*

Finally, after several minutes of coaxing and convincing, the First Lady obliged. Inside the dressing room, I lit a candle, opened a window to allow some of the cool breeze to enter, creating a calm and soothing environment. I directed Mrs. Lincoln to sit down in front of the mirror while I gently combed her thick beautiful hair. I proceeded to perfume it with a light spritzing of one of the bottles of French perfume from her collection in the corner of her vanity. I gently hummed to encourage the First Lady to calm herself down. Then I realized, Mrs. Lincoln had a case of the jitters.

At this time, the President entered the room, threw himself on a nearby sofa and playfully engaged with the children, Tad and Willie. It was my first time meeting them and I was so pleased to know what fine, lovely boys they were. Mr. Lincoln whom I was introduced to earlier that week stood up and proceeded to remove his gloves. To our surprise, the President delivered several excerpts from a series of beloved poems while Mrs. Lincoln and I attended to finish the task of getting her dressed.

There inside the dressing room, I selected a pearl necklace, matching bracelet and earrings. I adorned her hair with fresh fragrant red roses harvested from the White House garden to accompany her rose-colored gown. She looked resplendent, impressive and well poised.

"You seem to be in a most poetic mood this evening darling husband," the First Lady said as she stepped out of her dressing room.

The President gasped and smiled. *"Mary my darling, you are as beautiful as the roses on your hair. Shall we?"* Mr. Lincoln's eyes glimmered as he offered his arm to his wife while they made their way to the foyer leading to the lobby where the guests awaited.

I peeked to discover that Mrs. Kellogg was dressed in a rather dull ashy colored dress; Miss Elizabeth Edwards in garnet red; Mrs. Edwards in a black and brown silk; Mrs. Baker in a pastel yellow silk and of course Mrs. Grimsley in a blue water colored silk with the waist-belt that I made.

Just as they were to step into the foyer from the bedroom,

Mrs. Lincoln realized she had misplaced her lace handkerchief on account of little Tad playing with it and hiding it earlier in the day somewhere in the most inconspicuous place by the fireplace. After much commotion for its search, everything calmed down when it was finally found.

Mrs. Lincoln's poise, confidence and utter composure impressed me to say the least. She dispelled all misconceptions of her supposed malicious, disorderly, ignorant vulgarity going around in all the social circles in Washington and beyond.

Tonight, I saw a woman of sheer grace, maturity and distinction. She had the self-assurance of an educated woman who spoke French fluently and presented herself alongside the President of the United States with aplomb.

She was regal like a Queen and exuded an air of royalty about her. It was an incredible sight to see, and I was most definitely proud of the woman in command of her audience.

The President too, appeared to be proud of his wife and held his chin up as they greeted their guests.

From the corner of my eye, I noticed how Mrs. Lincoln shifted her body to turn to my direction to smile at me. Immediately, I felt the blood run down my spine and a feeling of love grew inside me. I saw a friendship beginning to grow that night and I was so proud to be included in her most intimate circle.

The levee was a huge success and my work for Mrs. Lincoln continued to become more involved with an approximate 20 dresses during the spring and summer months, while Mr. Lincoln journeyed throughout Saratoga, Long Branch and many other places as the Chief of the Nation.

I fathomed at her vast reserve of energy and will power; a characteristic that she and I both shared. In the interim, Mrs. Senator Douglas, Mrs. Secretary Stanton and Mrs. Secretary Wells among several other ladies of Washington retained my services for custom gowns. I was especially thrilled to create new fashions for Mrs. Senator Douglas whose discriminating taste was of the highest caliber sparing no expense where her wardrobe was concerned.

Often the subject of everyone's scrutiny, suffice it to say that Mrs. Douglas was the center of criticism and jealousy amongst Washington's most elite women, and in huge part was on account of my own doing having sewn show-stopping dresses for her so far. Secretly, this thrilled me so and I would not be surprised if Mrs. Senator Douglas shared the same sentiment.

Winter came and the cold wind had an unusual feeling to it. The days seemed to last longer than usual, and the evenings had an eeriness in the air. It was November when Mrs. Lincoln finally returned from her long journey and my services were once again requested at the White House.

Washington was exceedingly tense and ill at ease as war was already underway throughout the nation. With each passing day, news of the war brought further anxiety and fear. New graves were being dug every day, the wailing cries of mothers receiving news of a son's demise echoed the atmosphere and the smell of death was in every fiber of everyone's existence. This was a dark time in our nation's history that left an unsettling feeling in my gut.

The life of our country was at stake, and nothing could bring cheer to the nation's Capital. Not even our President could offer to crack a smile. Mrs. Lincoln offered her unwavering support and strength, *"The North will succeed! We are positioned to win this war Mr. President!"* she often said.

I focused my attention on the work at hand to keep my mind free of anxiety and worry. Mrs. Lincoln's dresses gained the admiration and adulation of her peers and my appointment as the "Official Modiste to the First Lady of the United States" was soon announced at a luncheon gathering hosted by Mrs. Lincoln amongst her prized roses. It was a well-attended event, and I was deeply honored by this distinction.

Soon, I was included in many social engagements as Mrs. Lincoln's friend and fashion attendant. These parties and gatherings would sometimes put me in the most uncomfortable predicaments when certain women whose names I choose to withhold would try to persuade me to divulge personal and confidential information regarding the 'domestic' nature of the Lincoln family's affairs. Of course, I never acquiesced to such a betrayal of trust and considered Mrs. Lincoln my very best friend.

An incident occurred when a woman, not deserving of the term 'lady,' called upon me to make her a dress. She was extremely generous and was of a friendly-natured type in the beginning.

"Mrs. Keckley, I understand that you are in good favor with Mrs. Lincoln correct?"

"Yes Mrs. _____" I said.

"I understand you are her personal modiste and that you know her very well. In fact, some women have told me you have become somewhat of a confidante to her, is that correct?"

"I spend quite a bit of time with the First Lady, yes that is correct."

"Very good. I assume you have some influence on her then. Do you?" she asked with such intrusive posturing.

I remained quiet. I felt the malice of her delivery and hence, I opted not to respond. What was evident to me was that this woman posing as a patron but was really a spy!

"I asked you a question Mrs. Keckley. I deserve a response," she demanded.

Hesitantly I said, *"I am uncertain as to how to properly respond because I am not sure what bearing this has on retaining my services to make you a dress? I suppose that Mrs. Lincoln would listen to me if I offered her suggestions or advice, though considering she is in absolute control of herself, I am afraid that I cannot offer you any guarantees that would ensure your satisfaction to whatever it is you wish to accomplish."*

By this time, the woman's face had turned into a flustered sallow shade of gray. Her piercing blue eyes looked into mine intently.

"Malarkey! What non-sense! I am certain you can influence her. Here is my request. I have longed to be an inmate of the White House and you can help me get near Mr. Lincoln for I have heard so much of his goodness. If you can facilitate me entering the White House, even in the most menial capacity, I shall not be offended. If the role is that of a maid, then so be it. Just get me in there!"

I was infuriated while this woman carried on. I prefer to abstain of speaking ill of anyone however could not remove my attention from her dirty, ill-fitting dress, unkempt hair and bosom spilling out of her stomacher that appeared to be made for a slenderer woman.

"Please Mrs. Keckley, kindly recommend me as your personal friend seeking employment as a maid or servant and if you do this for me, I shall pay you several thousand dollars which I know will be of most good use to someone like you," she said as she turned around to pick up a remnant of fabric from the table and then scanning my workshop with great scrutiny.

I was disgusted by such an audacious bribe and the proposition to betray the trust and confidence of my beloved First Lady and her husband.

I retorted at the offensiveness of her inducement and said *"Absolutely not ever! I would much rather throw my body into the Potomac River and drown than have the gall to disavow the trust of a friend. You have me misunderstood Mrs. _____ and please make your way out of this room. There is the door and I request that you never enter my workshop again."*

Discombobulated and frenzied by my response, the woman hurriedly grabbed her belongings, sprung from her seat and left the room stumbling as she grumbled, *"Ha! You will regret you ever denied me my proposition, mark my words you half-Negresse Mulatto heathen!"*

"Oh, spare me your non-sense and get out of here immediately," as I briskly slammed the door behind her with a loud and intentional bang.

Sure enough, some days later, I discovered that this woman was an aspiring actress who wished to enter the White House as a chambermaid, seek the 'attention' of the President, divulge secrets and publish a concocted scandal to the press. I chose not to release her identity for she is associated with many of my lady patrons who for all intents and purposes, might suffer the damaging ramifications through their associations with her.

This is just one example of the kind of unprincipled people who have attempted to ruin the President's and the First Lady's reputation, but no avail with me. I've refused every single proposition with vehement disapproval.

On New Year's Day, Mrs. Lincoln was in preparation to make her first public appearance after a long time. A reception was held and later followed by a brilliant levee. The following day, I returned to the White House where the First Lady had been patiently waiting.

"I am so sorry for my delay in getting to you Mrs. Lincoln. Mrs. Anderson kept me from being on time when I ran into her at the mercantile this morning. She has a request for her daughter's upcoming dinner party to which I obliged. Here are your hatpins Mrs. Lincoln. Mr. Bedford suggested a few other options and I am happy to return those you decide not to keep."

"A hard decision Lizabeth," dropping the "E" to my name which I thought to be quite endearing.

"Yes indeed Mrs. Lincoln. Now let me see how these look with your hats," as I proceeded to examine her collection.

"Lizabeth…we are amid a war. I have been thinking…"

"Let me guess. You are thinking of being economical am I right?"

"In fact, Lizabeth, I am. Mr. Lincoln is scheduled to host several state

dinners every winter, and you realize how costly these dinners will be?"

"Yes Mrs. Lincoln, I understand and agree."

"Yes, of course the dinners are necessary, however I was thinking to perhaps host three fairly large receptions instead of the state dinners."

"What do you think Lizabeth?" as she turned to face me and in child-like manner, put the Gainsborough lavender colored hat with matching hatpin from Mr. Bedford's jewelry shop on her head.

"I think the hat should be reserved for the spring season- perhaps for the anticipated Easter egg hunt, Mrs. Lincoln. I should like you to consider fashioning a lightweight day dress for the occasion, don't you think?"

"Oh Lizabeth, I am talking about the three receptions instead of the state dinners, silly! But yes, an Easter dress to match this hat would be wonderful, just make sure I don't end up looking like the Easter Bunny!"

In unison we fell to the floor laughing in an outrageous manner that one of the armed staff designated for securing the safety of the First Family came to the room thinking something had gone wrong.

"We are fine Sir. I am just here with my very best friend Lizabeth having a good laugh. You may go...Oh and thank you for coming to the rescue," crossing both eyes, tongue exposed and with a mocking look in her face that induced further hysterics from both of us.

Once we calmed down, I concurred - *"Mrs. Lincoln, I think your plan to minimize expense is not only a wise decision but a thoughtful one considering the resources you need to reserve. This war has no guarantees."*

I proceeded to gather my things and neatly tucked them inside my sewing basket to make my way out when Mr. Lincoln entered the room. Before I could leave Mrs. Lincoln said, *"Oh Mr. President, Lizabeth and I were just discussing my plan to scratch the state dinners from the program and instead economize and throw three big receptions instead."*

The President took a long and thoughtful pause and then he removed his stovepipe hat, sat down on his chair and said: *"I am afraid that plan is not going to work, Mother."*

Despite the frequency and intimacy of my relationship with the First Family, I couldn't help but fathom at the sheer magnitude of the President's presence, towering at six feet and four inches tall, his hat further heightened his personhood by another foot or so. As he set the hat down on its side on his desk, I noticed the label to read: *"J.Y. Davis."* I decided that I too, should have my own name on the label of every dress I make.

"Oh Father, it will work if you are determined to make it work," she said.

"Mrs. Lincoln, my darling wife, it is breaking against the custom of the White House's tradition," Mr. Lincoln said as if to tease his wife further.

"Oh, but my thoughts lead me to believe that we are amid a war, and now is not the time to be spending on state dinners when we can be more economical. Tradition can be broken at least once, especially while we are at war?" she reasoned.

The President was again in deep thought as Mrs. Lincoln continued to say, *"Quite honestly Father, I do think of other things other than running this enormous household of yours with staff whose names I committed myself to know by heart...which by the way, is the absolute least I can say for you. Public receptions are more representative of our current situation than these pretentious stuffy silly state dinners. Those long-winded boring speeches of self-importance put me to sleep. Imagine all the great and interesting people that we can invite to a reception whom we cannot invite at state dinners?"*

Mr. Lincoln smiled and uttered a chuckle. *"I see your point. Once again, you present a most convincing argument. Oh Mother, proceed as you see fit Mrs. Lincoln."*

The First Lady's plan was approved and arrangements for the

reception were underway. In February, the official invitations were hand-delivered and some mailed, and Mrs. Lincoln once again had every say in the matter.

CHAPTER 9

Draped in Mourning

T he children were still receiving presents even after the Christmas season had already passed.   Mr. and Mrs. Lincoln purchased a little pony for Willie who delighted in riding it every morning. The weather was unpredictable and little Willie developed a severe cold that progressed into a horrible fever.

Little Mister Lincoln was so sick that I was summoned to stop all dressmaking and remain attached to the young boy's bedside. No amount of medical aid was sufficient to relieve him of his suffering. Already delicate in nature, Willie was in a constant state of discomfort due to his weak constitution.

As the days grew closer to the reception, Willie grew weaker, and his skin began to turn sallow and gray. Willie was Mrs. Lincoln favorite child and it pained her to see her son suffer. Constantly by her side especially at times when he felt stronger, it was clear that he found relief from his mother's loving comfort.

I remembered seeing him inside his room, curled up in a corner reading a book. Sometimes I would catch him on the floor, with his pencil and paper, quietly scribbling. Like his father, he had a strong interest in poetry and storytelling. He was intelligent, studious and always curious.

He once wrote a poem dated October 30, 1861:

"Dear Sir: -- I enclose you my first attempt at poetry.

Yours Truly,

WM. W. Lincoln"

To the Editor of the National Republican:

<u>LINES ON THE DEATH OF COLONEL EDWARD BAKER</u>

"There was no patriot like Baker,

So noble and so true,

He fell as a soldier on the field,

His face to the sky of blue,

His voice is silent in the hall.

Which oft his presence graced;

No more he'll hear the loud acclaim

Which rang from place to place.

No squeamish notions filled his breast,

The Union was his theme;

'No surrender and No compromise,'

His day-thought and night's dream.

His country has his part to pa

To'rds those he has left behind;

His widow and his children all,

She must always keep in mind."

Mrs. Lincoln decided to cancel her engagements and suggested to announce the withdrawal of all invitations to the upcoming reception after realizing that Willie's health had taken a turn for the worse. Upon hearing this, Mr. Lincoln sought the advice of their family doctor for he wanted to ensure that this was a wise decision before any actions were to be taken.

Dr. Stone arrived promptly and performed a thorough examination of Willie who was given a promising prognosis with an anticipated speedy recovery. News of Willie's condition brought a huge sense of relief for Mrs. Lincoln as plans to continue with the reception were underway.

The evening of the reception came like a dark and ominous beast. Little Willie had suddenly fallen ill as the guests started to arrive as the reception was about to commence.

Willie's fever spiked to an alarming temperature and his breathing became more pronounced and labored. Mrs. Lincoln was doing her best to stay strong and not show Willie any signs of worry, although I knew that she was unsettled.

"Lizabeth, please help my sweet darling Willie," she cried.

"Yes Mrs. Lincoln, I shall stay with him," I assured her.

In a large bowl of boiled hot herb-infused water, I asked Willie to slowly inhale the steam from the eucalyptus leaves, camphor and lavender essence I prepared, *"If you breathe in the steam slowly Willie, I promise it will help ease your discomfort and offer you some relief."*

Sweet and thoughtful as he could ever be, he managed to utter the following words to me: *"Thank you Ms. Lizzy for being so kind to me and Mother. Will you please stay and never leave my side?"*

"I wouldn't dream of doing anything else. In fact, I have some lovely stories to read to you tonight Willie," Willie managed to smile.

His blue eyes looked into mine and although they appeared sunken and weary, they were nonetheless beautiful. I was brought back to my childhood in the South where I often fell asleep on the grassy fields with a half-eaten apple dangling from the side of my mouth. Like clockwork, I became so adept at the practice of pilfering an apple from the wagon as Master Burwell's footman unloaded the goods every Tuesday morning upon their return from town.

Sprawled on the grass, and fast asleep an hour would pass and I'd be awakened in terror from the burning sting on my cheek resulting from the harrassment of uninvited picnic guests called 'Fire Ants.' A fight would ensue between me and them for I refused to surrender my half-eaten fruit to these troublesome pests. One by one, I would fling them as far away from me as possible and curse them to never return. To alleviate myself from the painful aftermath of their assault, a good amount of eucalyptus and lavender oil rubbed on my cheek always proved to be a quick and effective remedy. Mother would give me a sermon about how I deserved the attack since stealing was not ever to be condoned and thus my punishment was well-deserved.

I could only hope for a more long-lasting remedy for Willie, but my mother's concoction only provided temporary comfort as his condition continued to worsen through the night. I was concerned for Mrs. Lincoln's growing worry and anxiety.

Like a true First Lady of the people, she commenced to make an appearance at the reception and asked for my assistance in combing her hair into a simple, yet elegant style. For this event, I created a gown of white satin with an elegant trim of lace. I chose black lace for a color contrast to accentuate the richness of the white satin. The effect was a style that had never yet been seen before.

The gown had a long train that fell behind and followed her as she made her way towards the fireplace to warm herself up before proceeding to the reception. It made a bit of a rustling sound that caught the President's attention.

"Well I see that our cat has a long tail tonight."

Staring into the fireplace with an empty look in her face, Mrs. Lincoln offered no reply as the President continued to speak: ***"Mrs. Lincoln, I am of the persuasion that if that tail was closer to the head, it*** *would be more appealing."*

Glancing at his wife's bare arms and exposed neck, the President appeared to have met his wife for the first time. Mrs. Lincoln on the other hand, was too concerned about her son's condition and couldn't quite focus on the reception that was about to take place.

With the quickness of lightning, Mrs. Lincoln turned away, grabbed her husband's arm in annoyance and said *"Oh for the love of God, let's get this darned reception over with,"* as they both met their guests downstairs, with full smiles, showing no signs of the urgency they were both facing, leaving me alone in the room with the ailing boy.

Immediately, I ran back to tend to little Willie, who by now had broken into a violent sweat.

The Marine Band's music resonated through the walls of the White House causing my teacup to rattle in place. It echoed through each possible entryway in the building including the sick room where Willie and I stayed.

I overheard some guests wanting to dance to which the President denied the request. He too, was not in the proper frame of mind to partake of the gaiety and celebrations.

The White House was beaming in full regalia, but no amount of cheer could take away the worry and anxiety the Lincolns were experiencing that evening. Not once did Mrs. Lincoln show a sign of excitement or pleasure. Her mind was solely focused on her son.

Several times during the evening, Mrs. Lincoln came upstairs to sit with Willie. She must have climbed those stairs at least two dozen times and back that it began to cause me anxiety for the gown was quite voluminous. I feared that Mrs. Lincoln would accidentally mismanage her hurried steps as she made her way to her son, each time thrusting me to say a prayer for the good Lord to watch over her that she not fall down the stairs and get hurt in the process and also to spare little Willie's life.

Gently wiping the sweat throughout his failing body, she kept telling her son how much she loved him and how much he meant to her; how much joy he brought to her heart.

This may have been the longest night I have ever known during my status as a free woman perhaps largely because I loathed having to witness Willie's suffering. As a mother myself, this is something you do not wish upon your child and for all that I have been to this family, consider myself Willie's kin.

Morning came and Willie was not improving. His condition rapidly declined and poor little Willie died. The White House had not even been fully cleaned and organized from the reception from a few nights past, yet the atmosphere that now surrounded us was that of the deepest kind of sorrow. The First Family was in mourning.

I was called upon to immediately assist with bathing and dressing Willie's body. I attended to my little Willie with utmost love and care doing my very best to withhold my tears for fear that it might trigger Mrs. Lincoln's emotions to flare. No amount of effort prevented me from crying however, as I carried his limp and lifeless body in my arms after bathing him to lay him down on his bed.

Then, like the still oak tree, Mr. Lincoln stood for a few seconds at the doorway staring into the room. Moments later, the President took a step forward moving slowly towards his son with his hands clasped together and over his lips. Upon seeing the lifeless body of his son, the President fell to his knees and wept. His cries reminded me of the time when my father was sent away and forcibly separated from us. It was the same kind of grief that gutted me to my very core.

When he came to Willie's bedside, he carefully lifted the blanket off his son's face and stared at it with what seemed like time lapsing in a long and enduring kind of pain.

"My son, my poor beloved boy. God has called him home. He was too good for this earth and although I know he is better off in heaven in the arms of the Almighty, it is simply too hard! It is too painful and too hard

to see my son die!"

President Lincoln sobbed loudly and choked on his own words. His massive frame convulsed like a moth caught in a flame, slowly burning to its death, secretly wishing he too, was dead like his son. The leader of the nation bowed his head and buried his face into his shaking cold hands. His emotions shattered in the deepest form of anguish even I cannot articulate into words.

I stood at the end of Willie's bed and witnessed before me a strong and powerful man diminished into a sorrowful, weak and vulnerable child himself. If cries could break the glass windows into thousands of pieces, the President's lamentations would. He sat there for a long time, wailing and groaning in the most sorrowful way. Every member of staff stopped midway in their tracks, unable to further move upon hearing the President's grief-stricken pleas and cries for the heavens to bring his son back.

"Dear God, please I beg of you. Bring me back my son. I beg you Almighty God, please?" he sobbed.

I tried hard to stand as still as possible but the river of tears coming from my eyes gushed out uncontrollably. I was enduring a pain doubled- for not long before Willie's untimely passing, my son, George Kirkland left Wilberforce University and enlisted himself to fight for the North.

Considering the Negroes were not allowed to enlist, my George declared himself as a white man in order to join the Union Army. He was tragically killed in the battlefield of Missouri. His grave placed on the same spot where the great General Lyon fell.

I received a most consoling letter from Mrs. Lincoln upon hearing the news of my son's death that offered me a sense of deep comfort and gratitude. I prayed to my son, that he may take Willie's hands as he entered the gates of heaven, that he watched over him like a big brother. The pain of this grief was numbing.

Mrs. Lincoln, who was in the adjoining room, was hysterical and inconsolable. She fainted several times causing her body to convulse and grew increasingly more feeble. She mourned like the slave women whose children were violently taken away from them, and oftentimes killed.

I realized that there was no difference in distinction of a mother's grief whether she is White or Negro over the loss of a child. I discerned that Mrs. Lincoln was no different than my Negro counterparts for we were all of the same flesh, marrow and blood; and our grief is the same as all mothers.

She did not relent and showed no signs of calming down. At one point during her grief, Mr. Lincoln took his wife by the arm, and slowly directed her to the window.

"Mother, do you see that building in the distance past that hill? Please Mother, with all my love, try and control yourself for I fear that if you don't, may end up driving yourself mad and we shall be left with no recourse than take you to that asylum."

The White House was fully draped in black crepe fabric to signify the nation was in a state of mourning. The flag was at half-mast and all signs of gaiety were to be immediately removed per Mrs. Lincoln's orders.

Evening gowns and all-party dresses were stored away expeditiously and if a flower was anything other than white, was ordered to be removed from being seen. Members of the White House staff spoke in soft, quiet whisper-like tones so as not to trigger Mrs. Lincoln from further hysteria.

"Under the sod and the dew," said one member of Washington as they neared the threshold of the White House.

The funeral was arranged, and Willie was laid to his final resting place in the cemetery. Too grief-stricken, Mrs. Lincoln was unable to attend the funeral and stayed behind with a nurse by her side.

Mrs. Lincoln and I were both mourning the losses of our sons and

I questioned whether she and I would eventually get through this. For now, I promised Mrs. Lincoln that I would stay by her side for so long as she needed me, and to my comfort, she offered me the same promise.

A beautiful statement honoring the life of little Willie written by a poet named Nathaniel Parker Willis read:

"I am honored to say that I am one of this little fellow's acquaintances. Willie always looked for me in a crowd. He was curious about the world and always had something interesting to share with me. At the young age of 10, he was extraordinarily smart and could carry on a conversation with his father's friends with great confidence, sense, logic and wit.

With all the splendor of his new home at the White House, Willie was authentically and bravely himself, and that ONLY. He was like a wildflower from the meadows and then transplanted into the greenhouse yet and still, remained a wildflower, simple and genuine until the day he died. The news of his death came to me like a hard blow to my chest rendering me gasping for air, hoping for my little fellow to come back so that at least I could offer him a proper goodbye.

His most endearing trait, that which was of his kindness and frankness remained evident and intact, as I stood before his lifeless body one last time. Everyone had just left the room before I arrived, all the nurses, members of staff and servants confounded to a state of unrestrained sorrow for they loved him like their very own. His brown hair was parted to one side in the usual manner and his eyes were shut as if he was just in a temporary slumber.

He held in his little hands a small bouquet of exquisite flowers his mother who was unable to attend the funeral requested to have preserved for her safekeeping.

At the East Wing of the White House, members of President Lincoln's administration, senators, ambassadors, generals, soldiers and heads of State gathered inside one room, tearful and emotional, struggling to remain strong with aching hearts mourning in unison with the President as their grief-torn friend and brother. I ask and beseech the Almighty God to give him strength for all his sorrow and at this time the most heartfelt prayer of a nation."

Mrs. Lincoln was deeply touched by this statement that she kept a copy of the poet's writing and tearfully pasted the clipping in a scrapbook I kept for safekeeping. These moments brought us closer to one another and forever bonded us as friends.

Shortly after the funeral, I was instructed to make a few dresses of mourning for Mrs. Lincoln. I hastened my process for Mrs. Lincoln was growing more and more impatient with having at least one mourning dress made within a few days. Considering that it was all in black, I decided to install little reminders to comfort her; her son's name sewn in the inner lining of the dress, a small bouquet of embroidered flowers inconspicuously placed at the hemline with a verse from the Bible that read: *'Blessed are those who mourn, for they shall be comforted.'*

Finally, I sewed a remnant of fabric from Willie's jacket pocket and kept a small lock of his hair inside it. I surprised myself when I realized I had sewn a total of four mourning gowns in less than two weeks, each one of them so beautiful and dignified.

And then I realized that I had been so consumed in attending to Mrs. Lincoln's needs, that not even I had my very own gown for mourning my son.

CHAPTER 10

An Advocacy by Design

Washington saw a great migration of freed slaves from Virginia and Maryland. In the summer of 1862, thousands upon thousands of buoyant spirits, despite their long and arduous journey towards sovereign soil, arrived at the nation's capital.

Every freed man, woman and child, young and old, rejoiced upon entering the capital, leaving behind the evil and painful darkness of slavery, abandoning the conditions of the past with the bright promise of liberty and a life promised to be void of oppression forever – at least that is what they thought.

Instead of a warm and assuring reception, it pained me to see how they were welcomed instead with neglect, abandonment and disrespect. Mothers were desperate to feed their hungry children, and fathers grew increasingly hopeless in securing employment to provide for their families. My people were getting sicker by the minute, and without any assistance from government, they laid suffering on the streets and eventually dying in the squalor of temporary refugee encampments, begging in the alleys, hopeless and lost on the sidewalks throughout the nation's Capital.

The blood that ran through my veins shared theirs and our souls intertwined no matter how many ways one reasons around it. Hence, it was undeniably clear to me that I had to act swiftly and without further delay to help my people. I proceeded to write out a plan with great focus.

It was a balmy summer night when I was taking a stroll through the streets with a friend when I noticed Mrs. Farnham's home brightly lit with the sound of music amplifying the neighborhood. Curious to know what the celebration was about, I made my way towards Mrs. Farnham's home and asked the gentleman standing by the property's gate, who was clearly appointed to stand guard on duty, *"Good evening Sir, may I kindly ask what is the occasion that calls for such a joyful commemoration?"*

"Ah yes, Mr. and Mrs. Farnham have invited Washington's finest to gather in the festivities this evening to help raise funds benefitting the sick and wounded military officials and soldiers in the city. Heroes if you ask me."

Hastily, I walked back to my apartment that evening and when I arrived, threw my coat on the chair and set all sewing aside for one night. My chest expanded and I felt a surge of determination come over me.

I was steadfast to finish writing my plan which was to recruit all the wealthy members of the Negro class of Washington, including the Abolitionists, the President and Mrs. Lincoln to do the same with a single objective to help all freed slaves arriving in the city.

My stomach was roaring and a fire inside me was beginning to rage. I stayed awake all night planning all the details of my plan. This was my chance to be of good use to my people.

The following morning, I attended Sunday service at Union Bethel Church and realized that I had not slept a wink. Trying very hard to stay alert, I made my way towards the congregation that was quickly forming from my view. In an unexpected force of sheer determination, I found myself speaking to every church member about the need for an organized group whose single mission was to assist all freed slaves. I explained that those fleeing from slavery to Union-occupied areas and to these makeshift Union encampments are now considered 'Contraband.'

"What do you mean?" asked a fellow church member.

I responded: *"It means that slaves who fled from the rebel states crossing Union army lines are now classified as property of the war and all enemy property that falls into Union hands are considered Contraband. Hence, they cannot be returned to their masters. It means that as our brothers and sisters are arriving by the thousands, most of them are tired, hungry, sick and afraid. It means these encampments are overcrowded, filled with disease and lacking in proper sanitation. It means that they require medical attention and adequate nourishment. It means they are in dire need of medical supplies and medicine. It means we have men, women and children desperately needing shelter, clean, dry, warm clothing, shoes and supplies. Beyond that and just as importantly, it means we urgently need to educate and employ them so that they can become productive citizens as they assimilate into their new lives as free people. It means it is our duty."*

I delivered a most convincing speech that caught the approval of many well-to-do Negro business owners, educators, doctors, Abolitionists and more. I made sure to include the wives of these leaders and offered my services at a slightly reduced rate as an incentive for their participation and support. My plan was received with great applause and a vast majority of the congregation offered their generous financial support that very same morning.

Within two weeks, I formed *The Contraband Relief Association* with the help of forty brave Negro women from my congregation who were each assigned a duty and goal to accomplish. I became committed to the organization's cause and did not take no for an answer. We received donations of food and clothing and acquired financial contributions from donors in order to purchase much needed supplies such as medicine for the sick, clean water, more food and clothing as well as facilitate safe, adequate and clean housing.

Several doctors offered their services for free and business owners provided transport of donated goods to and from.

Members of our church opened their doors for those needing emotional support and counseling. Freed slaves were able to learn how to read and write taught by many volunteers. We offered employment training and facilitated jobs to those who met certain qualifications whilst others were given guidance on how to advance in their search for employment.

Things were beginning to develop at a rapid pace. I knew all along that God held my hand throughout this time as I endeavored to take the next big step towards advancing the CRA's objectives.

Mrs. Lincoln was destined to journey to New York and my presence was requested to meet her shortly after her arrival at the Metropolitan Hotel. Seeing that this was a good opportunity to state my case, I confirmed that I would join her and packed my bags along with my CRA manifesto. During the train ride to New York, I read my proposal many times over and eventually memorized it in my head.

I arrived at the Metropolitan Hotel and was pleased by the accommodations Mrs. Lincoln had generously arranged for me. The room was richly decorated in tapestry curtains held together by silken cords. Above the mantle of the fireplace, hung an Impressionist painting of a beautiful woman dressed in a gown that reminded me of my own designs. She was portrayed with an upswept hairstyle that accentuated her thin neck. Her gown was made from silk that was held at the waist with a floral themed waist sash. I tried to read the artist's signature, but I could not decipher the name of the painting's creator. Surely it was a painting of importance for it reminded me of my lady patron whose name she asked to remain anonymous.

Inside my hotel room, the bed was made of a rich mahogany wood, with four carved posts that depicted a scene from the story of Bacchus; the bed's covering was made from a luxurious silk reminiscent of the Far-Eastern worlds and mystical places. I removed my shoes for my feet were tired and swollen from my long train ride and noticed how they had sunk so comfortably unto the thick woolen rug on the floor. I remembered my mother and the days she toiled cleaning Mistress' Jacquard rugs. If not for her, I would not have been standing in this room as the free woman that I now am.

How did I end up here? Was it not only a few years ago when I felt the sting of the whip against my skin? How did my fortunes raise so drastically whilst the rest of my people continue to suffer? These thoughts brought memories of my dark past and I was even more determined to bolster the CRA with Mrs. Lincoln's support.

I freshened up and headed to the sitting room to meet Mrs. Lincoln at the scheduled time for afternoon tea.

"Lizabeth, how lovely to finally see you! How was your train ride?" Mrs. Lincoln stood from her seat to give me a kiss and an embrace.

It was clear that the sitting room's guests in the hotel were curious about the Negro woman that caused the First Lady to stand from her seat in the middle of the afternoon.

"Oh Mrs. Lincoln, thank you for the accommodations. The room is lovely, and the train ride offered me some much needed rest," I fibbed for I did not want her to worry nor think that I had been incessantly ruminating over the proposal from the time I entered the train's cabin to the moment she met me with an embrace.

"Very good, shall we request for a pot of tea? I understand they have a most delightful tea from an exotic part of the Far East. Will you be daring enough to oblige and partake with me, Lizabeth? I have been curious about this tea for months. I shall request for some savories to go along, and sweets of course!"

Mrs. Lincoln was to me my dearest friend and that afternoon; I saw a childlike side to her I had not seen for a long time since the death of her son. I was relieved and pleased to see her somewhat expressing even the mildest form of joy. It was especially nice to be together in a setting outside of the White House for a change.

I thought not to impede on her time of relaxation and resigned to the understanding that perhaps this was not the moment to present her with my petition.

"Yes, allow yourself to indulge a little Mrs. Lincoln, for you truly deserve some respite away from the busy world in Washington. How was your train ride?"

"It was bumpy, dear heavens...my headaches have become more frequent I'm afraid and my goodness, my posterior has suffered greatly from the bumpiest train ride. In fact, I shall place a pillow and sit on it," she said as she grabbed a pillow from the sofa and positioned it under her buttocks to sit directly on it. We laughed a hearty laugh and nearly spit out our tea. What a wonderful friendship I had with her and one unlike any friendship I have ever had in my lifetime.

"Lizabeth, something is wrong. Tell me, what is bothering you my dear?" Mrs. President asked earnestly. Unable to withhold it any longer, I confided my woes to Mrs. Lincoln and asked for her support in advancing my cause for the CRA. Without hesitation, she immediately drafted a letter to her husband with a demand for the sum of $200 and at her behest, asked that he call upon his counterparts in support of my organization. She handed the letter to the gentleman manager of the Metropolitan Hotel and instructed that he *"...personally drop this very important letter to The President of the United States in the post office immediately,"* and that he *"not allow himself to be distracted by anything else for lives are on the balance and the letter needs to be delivered without delay."*

The manager vanished and I later came to know that the letter arrived to the White House some days later.

While in New York, I busied myself with meeting Negro citizens and shared with them the objectives of the CRA. I was received with much enthusiasm and support. I later joined Mrs. Lincoln in Boston during her trip to visit her son, Robert who was enrolled at Harvard University. I had the distinct pleasure of meeting Bostonian philanthropists, including the esteemed Mr. Wendell Phillips who made strong promises to support the CRA.

Upon my return from New York, during a luncheon after church service, the Abolitionist Reverend Leonard Grimes of the Colored Baptist Church assisted in gathering his members together to listen to me speak. I was honored to have someone of his composure in support of my purpose for he was a man of particular importance.

Born a free man, Reverend Grimes operated his own coach as a Hackney driver carrying passengers around Washington. Dedicating his life to helping slaves, he served as a conductor for the Underground Railroad using his coach business to transport fugitive slaves to and from Virginia to Washington. He was so good at what he did that no one suspected his participation in the effort to assist slaves in gaining their freedom. He was later caught and imprisoned for two years and released sometime in 1840. Still committed to helping slaves, he was a key figure in helping one such man in particular named Mr. Anthony Burns, a fugitive slave who escaped Virginia sometime around 1854.

Burns became a member of Reverend Grimes' church and when word got out of his whereabouts, he was captured under The Fugitive Slave Act of 1850 and was tried in a court in Boston. Reverend Grimes petitioned all his congregation and those who opposed the Fugitive Slave Act to raise enough money to assist Burns' case in court. The Reverend continued to share his story with me as I listened intently, *"Good old Burns. He was eventually ransomed from slavery, with his freedom purchased by some of our Boston sympathizers. Then Burns went on to Oberlin College and became a Man of God just like many of us here tonight. He made his way to Canada was the last I heard, helping refugee slaves and free Negroes start new lives in a place called Ontario. Ah yes, yes indeed. Good ol' Burns,"* he said with a smile.

"I am honored to be in the same room with you Sir," I said.

"I understand you had a son who fought for the Union. I am deeply sorry for your loss. I have many friends who perished, but the pain a

mother endures over the loss of a son is not something I would ever wish on anyone. Again, I am sorry."

After the Civil War began, Reverend Grimes petitioned for Negro enlistment. He then recruited soldiers for the 54th Regiment Massachussetts Volunteer Infantry, a regiment of Negro men where he joined his regiment and fought valiantly.

That same afternoon, I was able to collect a large sum of money and organized a branch of the CRA to hold its headquarters in Boston.

Mrs. Grimes and the wife of the esteemed Reverend John Sella Martin, Mrs. Sarah Ann Lattimore Martin was of great assistance to me in securing over 80 very large boxes of supplies from the generous contributions of the Colored Baptist Church members. I learned that afternoon that Mrs. Martin's husband also escaped slavery by way of Alabama. Born into slavery in 1832, his mother was a slave, and his father was her white master. Under the principle of Partus Sequitur Ventrem, adopted by Virginia in 1662 and later other colonies in slave law, children of slave mothers took her status and were born into slavery, regardless of whom their father was and what proportion of European ancestry they had. Reverend Martin continued his work as an Abolitionist and traveled to England to lecture about slavery and the urgency of its abolishment. I was pleased to make his acquaintance briefly and thanked him for his generous support.

Upon my return to New York, Reverend Henry Highland Garnet of the Shiloh Church opened his congregation for a meeting I conducted to discuss the next steps of the CRA. Reverend Garnet himself was a man of great influence. As a child, he escaped slavery along with his family from Maryland to later move to New York. He attended the African Free School where he developed his position on the anti-slavery movement, became an educator, militant and Abolitionist.

He became a minister and used his leadership as the platform to drive the Abolitionist movement through religion. Not long after our meeting, on February 12, 1865, he delivered a sermon in the U.S. House of Representatives and was the first colored man who has on any occasion spoken in our National Capital on the occasion of Congress's passage on January 31, 1865 of the 13th Amendment, ending slavery.

The same manager of the Metropolitan Hotel (whose labor staff is mostly comprised of Negro workers) who facilitated the delivery of Mrs. Lincoln's very important letter was of great influence in helping me raise a large sum of money from its dining room waiters.

Later, I received a telegram from the White House that Mr. Frederick Douglass, upon hearing from President Lincoln, contributed the sum of $200 and was gracious in offering to lecture and deliver public speaking engagements on behalf of the CRA at no charge. Considering he was the most sought-after orator and speaker of the time and the most influential figure in the Abolitionist movement, I considered this one of the greatest honors and accomplishments of my life.

Mrs. Lucy Colman, a lovely white Massachusetts-born schoolteacher whose lectures focused on the anti-slavery movement requested my assistance in helping arrange a meeting between President Lincoln and a highly distinguished Negro woman, Sojourner Truth, who at 67 years of age, made the long roundabout journey from Battle Creek, Michigan.

I was happy to oblige and make the necessary arrangements. Showing no signs of slowing down to see the emancipation of slaves come to its end, Madam Sojourner Truth herself said that the President listened to her intently, offered her his generosity, kindness and support. This, among many other important incidents in my life greatly influenced other distinguished Negro men and women to contribute to the CRA generously as well.

Add to this the support from people across the world, including The Shetfield Anti-Slavery Society of England, through the help of Mr. Frederick Douglass, The Freedmen's Relief Association, The Aberdeen Ladies Society, The Anti-Slavery Society of Edinburgh Scotland, Friends from Bristol, England; the Birmingham Negro Friends

Society, and Mr. Charles Douglass of The Birmingham Society to name a few. I further received generous donations from Mrs. Lincoln as well as the President on a frequent basis.

I continued the good work for the CRA alongside my dressmaking business and committed myself in helping all freed slaves get the relief, assistance and support they deserved. I was embarking into a world imbued with a deeper sense of purpose and meaning; each stitch drew me closer and closer in seeing to it that my people where free to live rather than live to be free.

I was tenacious, determined and unshakeable in my resolve to see it through.

CHAPTER 11

The Dress of Emancipation

On July 3, 1863, the Union forces under the recently appointed leadership of General George Gordon Meade defeated Confederate General Robert E. Lee and his army at Gettysburg, Pennsylvania. Over 50,000 soldiers from both the Union and Confederate troops were killed, wounded, maimed or unaccounted for or missing. I remembered the President making several visits every day to the War Department spending long gruesome hours communicating by telegraph. The atmosphere during those days was anxious and tense.

In an unfortunate turn of events, President Lincoln learned that General Lee and his troops left Gettysburg without being pursued by General Meade and the Union soldiers; (much to the President's distress for he believed that capturing Lee and his army would further end the war.) In response, the President drafted a telegraph reproaching Meade but at the last minute refrained from sending it. Mrs. Lincoln told me that the President was so distraught by the bloody outcome at Gettysburg that he was consumed with worry and anxiety.

A lawyer by the name of David Willis was assigned to handle all the arrangements for the cemetery at Gettysburg. The task at to clear the carnage was a tall order to accomplish in such a short period of time. Not only did they need to move quickly as the bodies began to rot and decay, but they also had to navigate this process with the utmost reverence and care.

They were hard pressed to find a contractor to perform the job and so they relied on ten Negro laborers to dig graves, identify bodies, collect any personal belongings and effects to help identify the bodies to their loved ones and next of kin. This was all taking place at the height of one of the hottest summers in history, so one can only imagine the carnage, stench, disease and malodor from the casualties of war.

Makeshift tents were erected to help aide the surviving soldiers from their injuries and disease. Nurses came from far and wide to volunteer and offer their assistance for the conditions from the aftermath of the war was unlike anything anyone has ever seen before.

An invitation was sent to the President requesting him to deliver *'a few appropriate remarks'* to honor the fallen at Gettysburg. By now, it is November, and the President grew increasingly anxious spending most of his days and nights in the War Department. Mrs. Lincoln begged him not to go to Gettysburg after their son Tad, fell ill from the cholera. Torn between two worlds, the President assured his wife that he should be returning soon and settled on paying his respects at Gettysburg.

Traveling by train, he was accompanied by his valet, William Henry Johnson who attended to all the President's needs. Feeling weak, exhausted and weary, the President forged through and arrived at Gettysburg around dusk where he was accommodated in the home of Mr. David Willis. Outside the house, a growing crowd gathered for an opportunity to meet the President.

As if the President was not going through enough, he received a telegraph from the White House that his son Tad was still very ill and his wife, Mrs. Lincoln was thrown out of the carriage hitting her head on the stone pavement after a suspected assassination attempt was made against her. At this time, I ran to the aid of a very worried First

Lady who was recovering at the hospital.

The following day, the dedication to the soldiers in the cemetery in Gettysburg, Pennsylvania delivered by the Honorable Edward Everett lasted two hours long with a captive audience. The speech according to the French reporters described it as such: *"Mr. Everett was listened to with breathless silence by all that immense crowd, and he had his audience in tears many times during his masterly effort."* In contrast, the President delivered a speech that was 2 minutes long.

The Gettysburg Address

"Four score and seven years ago our fathers brought forth on this continent, a new nation, conceived in Liberty, and dedicated to the proposition that all men are created equal.

Now we are engaged in a great civil war, testing whether that nation, or any nation so conceived and so dedicated, can long endure. We are met on a great battlefield of that war. We have come to dedicate a portion of that field, as a final resting place for those who here gave their lives that that nation might live. It is altogether fitting and proper that we should do this.

But, in a larger sense, we cannot dedicate – we cannot consecrate – we cannot hallow – this ground. The brave men, living and dead, who struggled here, have consecrated it, far above our poor power to add or detract. The world will little note, nor long remember what we say here, but it can never forget what they did here.

It is for us the living, rather, to be dedicated here to the unfinished work which they who fought here have thus far so nobly advanced. It is rather for us to be here dedicated to the great task remaining before us – that from these honored dead we take increased devotion to that cause for which they gave the last full measure of devotion – that we here highly resolve that these dead shall not have died in vain – that this nation, under God, shall have a new birth of freedom – and that government of the people, by the people, for the people, shall not perish from the earth."

The audience fell silent for they did not expect his speech to be that brief. A scatter of applause could be heard here and there as the audience was taken by surprise by its short-lived theme. Despite its powerful message, it was received with mixed reviews. I was of the mindset however, that the President was worried about his little boy which could have resulted in his decision to deliver a much shorter speech than what we were all accustomed to in the past.

Soon after, the President received a telegraph that his son was on the mend. This offered him a great sense of relief and comfort. Meanwhile, as he prepared to return home, he fell ill. It was reported that during the President's speech at Gettysburg, he appeared tired, discouraged, weak and listless.

Inside the Presidential car of the train, Mr. Lincoln began to sweat profusely, suffered a terrible headache and developed a high fever. His valet, Mr. Johnson attended to the President by providing him an around the clock application of cold-water therapy throughout his forehead and limbs. He never left the President's side and nursed him back to moderate health during the train ride home.

Upon arrival to Washington, the President was admitted into the hospital until he fully recovered and then released on December 15th.

Sadly, a couple of weeks after Gettysburg, Mr. Johnson contracted the same fever and later died. He was laid to rest upon the order of the President at Arlington National Cemetery with an engraving bearing his name and the word *"Citizen"* carved beneath it. It was a great loss to me, and a great loss to the Lincoln family; especially to the President who never employed another personal valet since then.

On December 31, 1862, during the eve of the New Year, Washington planned for the declaration of our emancipation to be officially enacted.

It was nearly midnight as I gathered inside the Union Bethel Church with my fellow congregation members. I sat in quietly in prayer offering my most fervent petitions to God.

Only a few blocks from our church stood the White House where the President was slated to sign the official document that would uphold the proclamation that *"all persons held within the rebellion states as slaves are, and henceforward, shall be free."* Three years of this bloodshed was finally coming to an end.

I sat on the last bench close to the main entrance's double doors in a daze. I watched everyone milling around in a flurry of excitement mixed with a strain of anxiety. Everyone young and old arrived in their best attire and stood just a few inches taller than yesterday.

I sat quietly and observed the dress I now had on. It was a dress of my own creation and something I excitedly undertook last November upon learning of the President's initial draft of the Emancipation Proclamation. I was thrilled and beaming with joy at the prospect of seeing my people freed.

Naturally I thought I must make myself a dress of the utmost distinction to commemorate this auspicious day. Drawing inspiration from images I've seen from Mrs. Lincoln's fashion catalogues, I was intrigued by the silhouettes from the Far East and decided to create a dress of silken brocade in a deep blue shade with delicately woven silver and white blossoms upon it. To add to the mysterious tone of the dress, I created a set of Pagoda shaped sleeves and this time, mustered enough nerve to lower my neckline into a soft scoop. This act alone gave me a sense of liberation after decades of covering my bosom to avoid the jeers, advances, threats, stares and undressing eyes of my white male oppressors. This was an act of rebellion to disrupt my status quo, but felt a surge of courage to lower that neckline without a moment of doubt.

I was pleased at my decision to trim the neckline with hand folded grosgrain ribbon pleats in a contrasting color of burgundy. As it was a dress to be worn in the evening, I fashioned a matching cape in burgundy velvet lined in the same blue and silver brocade to keep me warm during my walk to and from the church. Ending the bodice at my natural waistline with a satin sash about 3 inches high, I took my time draping the flounces that created the lovely silhouette for the back of the dress.

As I sat on the bench inside the church, I smiled at the semi-sweep train peeking its way from in between my feet. I was pressed for time that I barely a few minutes to spare to finish the dress until I had to walk to the church to meet my friends for this important gathering.

Thinking of Mrs. Lincoln, a flyer blew into the church that landed on my lap as a large group of young Negro men and women entered cheering in a cadence that made me smile.

The flyer read:

"MEN OF COLOR! TO ARMS TO ARMS! NOW OR NEVER! FAIL NOW & OUR RACE IS DOOMED!"

A long list of Negro men's names were indicated on this flyer; the third one down was that of none other than Mr. Frederick Douglass whose words were printed on the circulation as follows:

"If we value liberty, if we wish to be free in this land … If we would be regarded men, if we would forever silence the tongue of Calumny, of Prejudice and Hate, let us Rise Now and Fly to Arms."

And then like the rip-roaring rumble of a train as it got closer, emerged Minister Clayton from the quiet of his prayerful office. Kneeling on one bended knee, and clasping the Holy Bible in his hands, he slowly but ferociously articulated the following words:

"The President… the President… has officially signed the decree. Let us rejoice in the arrival of Freedom's Bells! Let us ring them loudly! Rejoice Rejoice! We are free! Join me as we give thanks to the Almighty God for this day of reckoning has finally come."

Opening the Bible, the good Minister read the passage as tears from his and everyone's faces poured like the crystal life-giving water of the River Nile. The congregation erupted in a thunderous roar of jubilant praise, laughter and emotion.

"Finally..." he paused to clear his throat. Gathering himself from the passion that had taken the breath away from his lungs, he resumed to read the following Bible verse:

"Taken from the book of 1 Peter 3:8, Finally all of you, have unity of mind, sympathy, brotherly love, a tender heart and a humble mind."

In one fell swoop he raised his arms to the congregation and the room swelled with overflowing exultation. Standing amid the sanctuary, I though of how far I've come from that Black Dress and White Apron at age four. I thought of my Uncle's lifeless body hanging from the oak tree and Little Joe, Scipio, Cousin Albert, and my beloved Mother, Father, and dear Son.

I walked towards the Northeast side of the church to light a candle and from the distance of my gaze, I saw my reflection jumping back at me from the glass window and couldn't believe the stark difference of the dress I wore and the beauty within me in comparison to the days gone by of my tattered garments toiling as a slave.

In a flash, I saw my life throughout all its misery, suffering and persecution, and said a prayer in honor of my beloved son, whose life he gave for my freedom, our freedom.

I walked back home as slowly as possible, never running away again and as I neared the threshold of my workshop bearing my name, *'Madame Elizabeth Keckley, Expert Modiste,'* I smiled to enter my room and took in the first few breaths of our collective freedom.

CHAPTER 12

The Quilt of Liberty

I t had been almost two long years since Willie's death and the White House still maintained its sullen state of mourning. Everyone in the White House recognized and respected this atmosphere while continuing to conduct the business of the nation. Mrs. Lincoln was so stricken by grief that she never crossed the threshold of the guest bedroom where her son died.

The Green Room is one of the three state parlors located on the first floor of the White House and was typically used by Mrs. Lincoln for hosting smaller receptions, informal luncheons and teas. However, it was also the room wherein little Willie was embalmed in and since his passing, was no longer a room Mrs. Lincoln was willing to step into.

On any given day, Mrs. Lincoln could be heard letting out an agonizing cry and calling out her son's name. She requested that his photographs be removed from her view for the mere sight of her son's image caused her to fall to her knees and weep for hours. She was not the same woman as she was before (and rightfully so) and to some degree became coarse and short-tempered. She often spoke of Willie's spirit residing inside the White House, to which many members of the staff tried best not to pay much attention to.

To Mrs. Lincoln, it was a comforting thought. To some White

House employees, it was frightening and downright spooky.

Her other son, Tad had a personality opposite from Willie. It was known that Tad was President Lincoln's favorite son. Tad was a good-natured boy with eyes as black as a crow's feather that contrasted greatly with his fair alabaster skin. He was a mischievous little boy with an uncanny gift of humor. He offered his mother relief with his funny anecdotes especially during times when she missed Willie the most.

By now, thousands of soldiers had been killed. Bloodshed was everywhere and the smell of death loomed like a smothering thick cloud over our heads. Thousands of mothers wept the loss of their sons, wives agonizing over their husbands' passing and children instantly orphaned. It was an ominous time in the nation's history, and I was determined to live through it for my work had not yet been fully realized.

In the South, the atmosphere was the same with graves being dug not fast enough to accommodate the rising death toll. It was a terrible feeling to know that all of this was happening as a result of the aftermath of slavery's wrongdoing and to be a Negro during this time was a frightening reality.

The Confederacy began to claim a victorious trend gaining traction in the war and all rebel states were prematurely claiming victory. Their flags bearing three bars became more prominently displayed throughout the nation. Glimpses of the Union Army's flags of Stars and Stripes were sporadically scattered here and there.

I began to construct a quilt dedicated to the Union and was inspired from the word, "Liberty." Made from scraps of silken fabric, I cut all the pieces to create a beautiful design that eventually met in the center of the quilt. It was a fairly involved undertaking I hoped to finish before the war was finally over so that I may display it proudly in my workshop for all my clients to see.

Sewing the quilt in between working on a few dresses for

upcoming receptions for Mrs. Lincoln was a time to myself I looked forward to. It was a cathartic, healing and meditative process. The colors represented the richness of our nation entering the beginning of a shift that our great liberator, Abraham Lincoln set into motion.

The patterns and shapes with its sharp edges and angles represented the struggles my people faced and long endured. Stitching the pieces together symbolized the fusing of the nation towards Liberty and Freedom for all.

I couldn't wait at the opportunity each day brought me to sneak a few hours if I was lucky enough to steal some time to finish it for it was an extension of who I was as a woman born a slave who emerged from the darkest chasms of that malignant evil institution. I was set on finishing it and endeavored for it to stand the test of time.

The President's eyes sunk deeper than ever before, and his overall composure was tired and weary. Mrs. Lincoln was often in another state of mind, mostly consumed by the loss of her beloved little boy. Her headaches worsened and depression started to sink in. The President's suffering was unique in that he had neither the time nor the agency of mind to even grieve the loss of his son.

The greatest responsibility of the nation appeared to be more pressing, and I felt so much pity for him. The weight of the war was so great, and the President was doing everything in his power not to show any sign of weakness or defeat. To this day, I have not met a man so calm under such pressure, though I credit the fact that oftentimes, I would find him in the library, reading passages from the Holy Bible with utmost concentration and deep thought. This to me gave way for his ability to remain steadfast and assured of his purpose. I admired his tenacity despite so many of life's objections and threats. This man possessed a deep relationship with God which was the saving grace that helped him maintain clarity of mind.

I was attending to a dress fitting for Mrs. Lincoln when the President unexpectedly entered the room. Mrs. Lincoln and I thought that the President was in a speaking forum during this time though his presence came as a nice surprise, except the President appeared downtrodden and exhausted.

Entering the room slowly, he threw himself on the sofa while I was in the middle of adjusting Mrs. Lincoln's sleeves.

"Father? Are you ill? Where have you been my dear? Oh my God, Lizabeth please get the President a cool glass of water he looks utterly sick!"

I hurried to the adjoining dressing room where Mrs. Lincoln's water carafe was located and almost broke it in my haste trying to pour a glass of water for the President as quickly as possible.

"Darling what is the matter? You are frightening me. Where on earth did you come from that you look this bereft and worried?"

"I was just at the War Department, Mother," the President said as he began to rub his face and forehead to try and alleviate himself from a terrible headache.

"Oh, My Darling, tell me—what is the word?" the First Lady asked as she offered him the glass of water while kneeling on the floor next to her husband.

The lightly basted sleeve of the dress hung away from armhole as my tailor's pins slowly dropped on the floor one by one.

"Bad. Very Bad, Mother. Not good news. Bad. Dark, everywhere." The President spoke in broken up words and broken sentences as if he was running out of the right words to say.

Mrs. Lincoln rose from her knees and pulled a chair close to her husband while gently rubbing his back. The President then opened the drawer of the side table next to him and pulled out a small Bible and proceeded to read it quietly to himself. The room remained silent for the President was now engaged in a conversation with God.

About a couple of hours passed and I had nearly finished attaching the sleeve that got disengaged from its armhole earlier in the day when the President emerged out of the room with a look of relief. A smile on his face shifted his decorum. It was a drastically pronounced change that I could not help but wonder what the contents of such a book could possibly say to elicit this kind of improvement in one's personality.

Pretending to look for my sewing scissors, I walked over to the sofa where the President left the Bible and opened the page where he had left off, the Book of Job.

Known to many as 'The Great Comforter,' Job's words resonated back to me in a way that signaled courage, faith and hope. The passage Job 38:3 read:

"The Lord answered Job out of the whirlwind and said, Who is that darkeneth counsel by words without knowledge? Gird up now thy loins like a man; for I will demand of thee, and declare thou unto me."

I felt an utter sense of humility for the words delivered a statement of one's faith. It offered a perspective about God's greatness during a time when one is faced with the greatest of trials. It affirmed to me that the President was in fact in a deeper connection with God for it was through his word that he found assurance. The President's smile confirmed that the challenges he was undergoing would in the end serve his benefit and the nation's greatest good.

I was calmed with the knowledge that here was a powerful man carrying the weight of the nation on his shoulders and yet humbly found peace in the word of God.

The following morning, I sought out to purchase the same Bible version the President had in the sitting room and kept it close by me throughout the remainder of my life.

The White House received letters and warnings of the President's assassination and while this was of great concern to all, was not something the President chose to discuss openly. Poor Mrs. Lincoln was constantly in a state of worry for her husband's safety.

"*Father, please do not leave right now. Perhaps you can work here for now until things subside a little?*" she begged.

"*Mother, I have to go to the War Department to get some updates,*" the President explained.

"*Why can't you send one of your messengers instead? You know it is not safe for you to leave without a guard or companion. Please I beg you Abraham, please?*" she implored him.

"*Mary my dear, why must you treat me like a child? Exactly who would be remotely interested to accost or molest me? Don't be silly with your imaginings. I love you and I shall be just fine Mother,*" then giving Mrs. Lincoln and kiss on her forehead, the President put on his coat, fixed his tie, grabbed his hat and walking stick. With dexterity and ease, and no sooner, did the President close the door behind him to make his usual walk to the War Department building a few blocks from the White House.

Looking out the window, Mrs. Lincoln followed her husband's walk until he was no longer within her plain view. She was not pleased by his response and told me that she would advocate for her husband's safety. She immediately enlisted the help of his friends to sleep at the White House as growing tensions developed and more threats for his life ensued.

Their son Robert would come home for a few weeks at a time to bring his parents a sense of relief and joy. At the time, Robert was attending Harvard University and just like his father, believed in the cause of the Union and eagerly expressed his desire to enlist in the war effort.

"*Mother, I wish to quit school and enlist as soon as possible,*" he declared.

"*Absolutely positively with a resounding N-O, No, I forbid you! For one, you need to obtain higher education. Most of all, I cannot bear to lose another son Robert. Father, would you please reason with your son? Have we not suffered enough from losing Willie? Oh God Robert, I beg you please!"* Mrs. Lincoln cried.

She pled in despair and was diminished to her knees. It made me unhappy to see my friend suffer this way. In her moments of melancholy or hysteria, I would often take her in my arms during these bouts to gently rub her face with a warm soothing towel to calm her nerves a little.

"Mother, I love you so much for the loving wife and mother that you are. Your cries have not been left unheard, but I ask you to understand that our son Willie's life is not more valuable than the sons of thousands of other mothers whose lives were lost," the President gently explained.

"I understand this Father, but do you understand me? Do you understand that Robert cannot be exposed to any danger? Do you understand that he is NOT required to fight this bloody war of yours? Do you understand that you are willingly sacrificing the life of our son? Do you understand Father, do you? Do you? Do you Abraham? Do you?" she screamed.

"My dear wife, you should take a liberal view instead of a selfish view of what we are presented with. Every capable man, despite your opinion, is in fact required to serve in this war, Mother," he said as he looked out the window, far beyond what we all could see outside.

"I will never forget this day and pray that our son's life be spared for if otherwise, you shall regret the day you said these words and I shall never in a million plus forever and day ever, ever forgive you. Never!," and with that statement, Mrs. Lincoln capitulated to an agreement she was not willing to take part in by granting Robert the permission to enlist in the war. Mrs. Lincoln's anxiety grew bigger and increasingly more unmanageable with time.

Sometime later, an incident occurred that led me to further understand Robert's character during the marriage of a dwarf sized lady named Miss Lavinia Warren to little Hopo'-my-thumb Charles Stratton, who went by the stage name of Tom Thumb. Their wedding took place at Grace Episcopal Church and its reception was held at the same hotel in New York City, The Metropolitan where I met with Mrs. Lincoln during the early stages of my involvement with the CRA. Calling himself General Tom Thumb, he was a somewhat well-known circus performer affiliated with the famous combination of P.T Barnum.

It was a highly publicized wedding that made the front pages of the newspapers all throughout Washington and beyond. It was said that the couple stood atop a grand piano at the ballroom of the Metropolitan Hotel to welcome some 10,000 guests in a lavishly orchestrated wedding reception. Somehow, some of Mrs. Lincoln's friends convinced her that it would be of great interest to her to entertain the little couple and so it was settled that Mrs. Lincoln were to host a reception at the White House for them.

"You are free this afternoon and evening are you not Robert?"

"Indeed, Mother I am."

"Very well then, kindly dress up and come downstairs to meet our guests please."

"I beg to respectfully decline Mother. I will not spend my time entertaining Tom Thumb and his wife. I have a different view of what my duties entail as far as serving this nation Mother; and with all due respect-- it is not for me to spend my days in the mundane and absurd," Robert explained.

"Suit yourself Robert, but your father and I shall be downstairs to offer refreshments and merriment to the newlywed couple should you have a change of mind."

As Robert proceeded to leave, Mrs. Lincoln had some words:

"And Robert, while you might think this is an utter waste of time, it behooves you to know that sometimes we make acquaintances with people whom we may not necessarily share much in common with, but their influence and contribution towards the war effort and the overall good of all is vital to the objective of your father's administration. Might

I also remind you that your Father deserves a moment, even for a brief fleeting time to be entertained by the mundane, and I don't give a damn if the relief he gets comes in the form of a circus clown or a midget, for after all, he has been managing this war and the drudgery of the nation's woes.

Oh and by the way Robert, this extends to his cabinet, his military troops and staff, who for your edification also have wives who tend to, not only the needs of their children and their growing households at the height of a recession and a bloody war lest we forget, but also tend to their anxious, tired and weary husbands like your father, who unbeknownst to you and the rest of the God damn mundane world out there have no idea whatsoever what it is like to tender them strength, assurance, encouragement and yes, love.

Your mother is an educated woman who the greatest leader of this nation chose to be his wife, and my views about politics and the world should not be lessened and reduced by the assumption that I busy myself with matters of the mundane because for the record, Son... my political and social views were formed long before you were conceived in my womb.

My family founded the great city of Lexington, and I shall have you know, my father was a staunch Abolitionist, and I was helping fugitive slaves when I was only 6 years old.

You posture to me like the high and mighty soldier that you are? Alas my son, mind your words when you speak to me. Enjoy your afternoon of leisure and afford yourself some rest my son. I love you," and with this statement, Mrs. Lincoln picked up her fan to cool herself and motioned for me to assist her in freshening up.

The young Mr. Robert Lincoln stood dumbfounded and offered the following simple words to his mother; *"I am sorry Mother. Please forgive me, how narrow minded was I,"* to which the First Lady softly smiled and offered her son a warm hug as she proceeded to meet the President already waiting at the end of the hall to make their descent downstairs to a crowd that was eagerly waiting.

During the festivities, I diligently worked on the quilt. I embroidered on all four corners motifs of flowers and baskets of fruit. I embroidered various symbols that reminded me of what freedom meant to me, birds in flight and the stars and stripes of the Union flag. At the very center of the quilt, I planned to embroider an Eagle in silver thread with its wings wide open and the word 'Liberty' directly below it.

Heavy-eyed and nodding off, I set the quilt aside for another day. I longed for the war to be over soon and just as my eyes shut, I saw the image in the form of a silhouette of my mother looking softly over me. Her face half-smiling and the spark from her eyes glistened just as the flame from the last life of the candle's wick faded away.

CHAPTER 13

A Cabinet of Suits

The President nominated Mr. Salmon Chase to serve as the 25th Secretary of the Treasury in 1861. Before these appointments, he held office as Governor of Ohio in 1856 and later as Senator of Ohio ending his tenure in 1861.

Mrs. Lincoln was not very fond of Mr. Chase and made no qualms of her protest against his views in politics and matters concerning the best interest of the people. Suffice it to say that Mrs. Lincoln thought of herself as a good judge of character and was meticulous about her dealings with members of the President's cabinet.

Oftentimes, the President and his wife would be engaged in a full-blown debate about the character of Mr. Chase, of whom Mrs. Lincoln felt was suspect in nature. I can safely say that throughout the years of being her closest friend, she was rarely wrong about her intuition.

She abhorred Mr. Chase with great derision and was outwardly hostile when in his company.

"Mr. President, my dear husband, I will have you know that Mr. Chase is nothing but a selfish man whose intentions scream of graft and corruption. I warn you to tread carefully and be acutely aware of your dealings with him for he is not someone you should trust."

"Oh Mother Mary, I think you are far too engaged in the matter

of politics. Perhaps you should reserve your focus for the upcoming reception I will need you to organize soon. It is important to me," he jokingly said followed up with a wink.

"Stop it Abraham! I tell you now and listen to me very clearly when I tell you for the last time that Mr. Chase and his greedy intentions to advance his wealth and success will be detrimental to this nation. Furthermore, I have no interest in aligning with his daughter, Mrs. Senator Sprague nor shall I help build her social status in Washington. I cannot be associated with her ways – flaunting herself like an overdressed peacock! No Sir, I shall not!" Mrs. Lincoln protested.

It was clear to me (and to all) that Mrs. Lincoln felt a great jealousy towards Mrs. Sprague, who was a remarkable kind of beauty. Also known as Mrs. Kate Chase Sprague, she was a native of Washington who married Rhode Island Senator William Sprague during the height of the Civil War. She was an arrestingly beautiful woman even at age 19. Highly educated, she spoke several languages and was an impressive elocutionist. She was regarded by Washington's inner circle as an intelligent woman by the accounts of great leaders and politicians like Massachusetts Senator Charles Sumner, who often conversed with Mrs. Sprague about their support for the abolition of slavery.

Included in this circle was the future President Mr. James Garfield, a German American politician who considered her not only to be immensely attractive but thought her to be a highly influential political advisor to her father. In fact, Mr. Chase was later appointed by the President as 6th The Chief of Justice of the United States where he held this role from the years 1864-1873. Had her widowed father's presidential goals become successful, Mrs. Sprague would have served as the acting First Lady.

These things did not sit well with Mrs. Lincoln and her jealous tendencies towards Mrs. Sprague grew increasingly clear.

"Mother, why must you behave this way? Is it necessary for you to be in this constant need to remind me how you feel? Do you not realize

that Mr. Chase is one of my very best friends? And what may I ask does his daughter have anything to do with this? She is no different from any child in support and admiration for their parent. What is the matter with you?" said the President with a baffled look on his face.

"He is your best friend alright because he has the motivation to be so. He is only interested in himself, Father. And had you not been the President, he would not behold himself unto you for he is the kind of man who would betray you without a second thought. Lizabeth, what do you think of taking this neckline a little lower?" she continued while I pretended not to hear and kept my mouth shut.

"Ahhh Mother, you are unnecessarily far too discriminating in your views of Mr. Chase. Could you please soften yourself a little?"

"No! Never. As your wife, it is my duty to tell you the truth. Many have warned you against him and your continuous refusal to see and heed the writing on the wall is blurred by his false promises to you. Mark my words."

The President took a moment to pause before responding to his wife for he knew that many letters of warnings have been brought to his attention about Mr. Chase.

"Shame on the spineless cowards that they have stooped to this level of trying to create panic and fear. I have no doubt these letters were created by the opposing party to plot a scheme of horror and trepidation," the President said.

"My hope is that you do not learn these truths until it is too late Father," Mrs. Lincoln warned.

All throughout this period until the time of the President's death, everyone in the White House knew of his close relationship to Mr. Chase where they would often be seen in closed door meetings discussing confidential matters.

No one was exempt from Mrs. Lincoln's discerning observations of the men in the President's cabinet. Another subject of her scrutiny was a man named Mr. William Henry Seward who was appointed as the Secretary of State in the year of 1861. Earlier in his political career, he served as the Governor of New York for two terms where he signed several laws that sought to uphold the rights of and opportunities for Negros; including granting trials for fugitive slaves in New York. He was known to intervene on behalf of the freed black people who were once enslaved in the South. Later, he was elected by the state legislature to the Senate and joined the Republican Party. Mr. Seward's strong opposition against slavery caused the South to hate him.

"Please tell me you are not really going over to see Mr. Seward today, Father? He cannot be trusted, and you must steer clear of that man! He is worse than Chase."

"Do you realize that if I listened to you and all your imaginings about these men, that I would have no cabinet? Your conclusions about them have no basis Mother. These are upstanding and principled men whose intentions for this country are rooted in the same beliefs I share. Your distrust for them is unreasonable and you must stop this non-sense once and for all," the President said with his elbows on the table and his face buried in his hands.

"Unlike me, you are a saint Father. Your kindness overflows that you cannot see past these unscrupulous characters latching on to you. It is infuriating to see the scheming unfold. Better to have no cabinet if that is the kind of cabinet one has. You are best to stand alone."

"The argument is moot at this point Mother, and so I beg you to let the subject rest. My opinion will not change, Mary," he softly said.

Mrs. Lincoln prided herself in being shrewd and acute with her ability to determine a person's disposition and offered Mr. Lincoln no patience when it came to these matters. In fact, Mrs. Lincoln did not hold back her words when she said: *"Appointing Andrew Johnson to assume the position of Military Governor of Tennessee is a foolish and reckless idea! He is a miserable self-regarding inebriate."*

An old-fashioned Democrat born in Raleigh, North Carolina, his early years were spent as an apprentice to a tailor cut short when he ran away. He then moved to Tennessee and opened a tailor shop of his own and married a woman named Ms. Eliza McCardle, better known to me as Mrs. Johnson. He entered politics advocating for the common man and opposed plantation aristocracy. In Congress, he championed a homestead bill that would provide free farms for poor citizens. Mr. Johnson remained in the Senate even after Tennessee seceded, which won him the favor of the North but left him as a traitor in the South. Upon this appointment in 1862 as Military Governor of Tennessee, Mr. Johnson used the state as a laboratory for Reconstruction.

Mrs. Lincoln called him a demagogue who will *"ruin the President in the long run, Elizabeth. Oh, and that General McClellan of his, is the bane of my existence. A slug...slower moving than molasses if you ask me."*

"But why do you say that about the General, Mrs. Lincoln?" as I passed the thread through the eye of my needle like second nature and doing my best to best to stay as calm as possible. I moved quietly and softly to avoid the confrontation between the President and his wife.

"Because he is full of words with zero action! If it were up to me, I would remove him from his position and appoint someone else sprightlier and more vigorous. He is a sloth!"

The good nature of the President considered this exchange from Mrs. Lincoln amusing for he was accustomed to his wife's opinions of his cabinet members and simply let the words go in one ear and out the other.

"Ha! Mother you are much too harsh of the good General. He is a soldier trained and educated in West Point. He is a patriot who served with distinction in the Mexican American War. Why he has been subjected to such criticism is utterly dumb founding. Being newly appointed takes time, Mother. The troops are not yet accustomed to this new leadership, and it is but natural for them to be disobedient at first.

The General is young with new ideas, and many are jealous of him and would kill him off if they can."

"Oh, for God's sake Mr. Lincoln enough of all your words to advocate for him. He is full of ideas without action. If he attempted to at least do something, anything, maybe blink, then perhaps I would have a change of heart and mind, but I promise you he must be replaced if you plan to win this war. He cannot be trusted."

I must add that later, Mrs. Lincoln's warnings proved to hold merit for the President and General McClellan developed a mutual distrust. The General was privately derisive of the President and his failure to succeed in overthrowing General Lee's army following the Union's victory at the Battle of Antietam in Maryland, eventually led to the President's decision to remove him from his post in the aftermath of the midterm elections in 1862.

Two years later, McClellan unsuccessfully ran as the Democratic Party nominee in 1864 against the President. His campaign was made weak because he renounced his party's promise to end the war and close on negotiations with the Confederacy.

Mrs. Lincoln walked over to the sitting area by the fireplace to take a seat, let out a big sigh, and stared up at the ceiling as if she were looking for an answer to be revealed.

"General Ulysses Grant. Oh, there's another one. A flesher. Grant is a butcher unfit to be the head of an army. Here is Grant's tactic: If it is alive, kill it," Mrs. Lincoln scoffed.

"Excuse me Mother, what did you just say?" the President replied.

"Oh, YOU heard me, Father! Ha!" as she proceeded to straighten herself up.

"His leadership has been successful, Mother. General Grant is the most extra ordinary man in command that I know of."

"Really father? Lizabeth, shall I tell the President what I told you the other day?" I was caught off guard by Mrs. Lincoln's remark as I was

focused on finishing the hem of her dress.

"Well, Mrs. Lincoln I would consider giving this dialogue some rest for now. I think we have had enough talk about the President's cabinet for one day."

"Actually Elizabeth, I would like to hear what Mrs. Lincoln has to say," the President requested to hear.

"Very well. It is really a simple case of arithmetic. Your General Grant, while claiming victory fails to make known how he got to that point."

"I am afraid I do not follow you, Mother."

This was my cue to leave so I decided to gather my sewing tools and pack them away as quickly as possible to avoid the next discourse that was about to ensue. I knew what would come next simply based upon the many intimate moments I have spent with the First Lady.

Born in poverty in Ohio, General Ulysses Grant was an exceptional horseman who graduated from West Point. According to Mrs. Lincoln, General Grant possessed no talent or skill as a student at West Point. However, he fought in the Mexican American War and came home with great distinction. He resigned from the army in 1854 to return to his family. He was a man of modest means and spent his days as a laborer.

After the Civil War broke out in 1861, he joined the Union Army and gained a reputation after winning several Union victories. In 1863, in the Vicksburg campaign, he advanced his troops and successfully gained control of the Mississippi River. This was a huge victory for the Union as it weakened and split the Confederacy in two. His troops were victorious in Chattanooga as well, which gave rise to his promotion as Lieutenant General appointed to him by the President. For thirteen long and arduous months, General Grant and his Union army fought against General Robert E. Lee's troops in Petersburg. Fleeing Petersburg, Lee was eventually defeated at

Appomattox where General Lee surrendered in the month of April in 1865.

"Arithmetic, Father. What kind of victory is it when you lose two of your own men to one of your enemy's? How is this even remotely sensible to you? How do you not see that General Grant has no regard for the lives of his troops or that he lacks in leadership and management. Clearly he does not know how to do simple practical math. At the rate he is going, he will wipe out the entire population of the North because all the man is doing is sticking more of our men in the front lines until they all get shot down to their deaths, and he does this with no conscience for the slaughter of lives and he repeats this tactic until he tires out the Southern troops. He is willingly offering our men like sacrificial lambs and that is why I call him a butcher of the tallest order, Father. He is no such soldier and to think that our son stands on his right side is enough to make my blood curdle."

"I see. Suppose we appointed you Commander of the army troops. Do you think you would do a much better job than the current General or any of those from the past?" This time the President's was less playful and was rather sarcastic in his tone.

"Go ahead and amuse yourself, Father - because I guarantee you that if Grant were ever to be elected President, he would just as soon as leave this country never to be seen again. Ha! I pray I never live to see that day. And for your edification, in fact I would do a better job, in a silk dress to boot!"

Mrs. Lincoln had worked herself up in such a fit that she rose from her seat and left the room hurriedly, nearly tripping over her dress for I had yet to finish hemming it.

In the room stood the President gazing out the window in a state so still that when my small bowl of pins fell to the ground, it made a much louder noise than usual. I quickened my pace for I wished to follow-up on Mrs. Lincoln who was now hastily descending from the stairs.

"Why is Mrs. Lincoln so vexed? It's as if nothing pleases her anymore Madame Keckley. Tell me, am I doing the right thing?"

"Oh Mr. President, these are hard times and I wish for the South to finally surrender. Your wife is your biggest supporter and is consumed with worry for you, your son and all the sons of this nation. She is perturbed to say the least for she feels there is a plot being schemed up by someone from the inside. She trusts no one she told me, and I must admit, I too am very concerned. Mr. President, take heed to her warnings and perhaps consider getting some added protection. And thank you Mr. President, thank you."

"Thank you Elizabeth. I shall take heed. You have become her closest confidante, and at times I feel she seeks your counsel more than me."

As I began to speak, the President interrupted, *"No need to explain or apologize to me Madame Keckley. I want to take this moment to thank you for being that friend to Mrs. Lincoln. She is still stricken with grief over our boy, Willie. Thank you."*

I offered the President a smile and left the room to catch up to Mrs. Lincoln. As I turned the corner nearing the hallway, I noticed the President holding the frame by Mrs. Lincoln's writing desk. It was Mrs. Lincoln's fondest photograph of their son Willie riding his pony. I am afraid to say that in this case, Mrs. Lincoln was wrong for General Grant continued to advocate and carry on the work of the President even after his death.

He was a hero of the war, (who later became the President elected by the Republican party following Andrew Johnson) he re-enforced the post-war national economy, supported Congressional Reconstruction and the ratification of the 15th Amendment, and endeavored to destroy the Ku Klux Klan.

He restored the Union and appointed Negro and Jewish leaders to hold positions in federal offices. In a letter to General Grant dated July 13, 1863, the President wrote:

"My dear General,

I do not remember that you and I ever met personally. I write this now as a grateful acknowledgment for the almost inestimable service you have done the country. I wish to say a word further. When you first reached the vicinity of Vicksburg, I thought you should do, what you finally did – march the troops across the neck, run the batteries with the transports, and thus go below; and I never had any faith, except a general hope that you knew better than I, that the Yazoo Pass expedition, and the like, could succeed. When you got below, and took Port-Gibson, Grand Gulf, and vicinity, I thought you should go down the river and join Gen. Banks; and when you turned Northward East of the Big Black, I feared it was a mistake. I now wish to make the personal acknowledgment that you were right, and I was wrong.

Yours very truly, A. Lincoln"

Everyone in the White House knew of Mrs. Lincoln's two brothers who were soldiers of the Confederate Army. Rumors of Mrs. Lincoln being a 'sympathizer' of the South milled around in the social circles of Washington and beyond.

I never thought for one minute this to be true and proved myself right upon the news of one of her brothers' deaths while in battle. I refrained from talking to Mrs. Lincoln about her brother's passing for fear that it might cause her unnecessary hysteria, considering she was still in mourning over the loss of her son.

One morning however, I was asked to Mrs. Lincoln's room on what was supposed to be my time of rest. Thinking it was of an urgent nature, I hurried to the White House to meet her there.

"My brother, Captain Alexander Todd has been killed in the war, Lizabeth."

"Yes, Mrs. Lincoln; that is also what I was told. I am sorry for not letting you know. I was fearful that it might cause you so much heartache."

Mrs. Lincoln poured herself a cup of tea and proceeded to pour me a cup too.

"It goes without saying that I cared very much for my brother. I have nothing but fond memories of him growing up. But you see Lizabeth, my brother made a choice. And that choice was to oppose my husband, which I consider a betrayal of me, his sister. He has actively pursued to fight and kill us in a deadly war. He waged war against his own kin. My son, his nephew Robert in the front lines included."

Mrs. Lincoln continued, *"Hence, he is the enemy of the worst kind. Therefore, I have absolutely no reason to mourn his death."*

Our conversation that afternoon comprised of Mrs. Lincoln's strong position against the South.

"I have no room to sympathize with anyone who would waste no time hanging my husband. I have no sympathy for anyone willing to kill me and mine. I may have been born in the South but that does not make me a sympathizer of the Confederacy."

Unlike Mrs. Lincoln who had no capacity to absolve anyone in opposition to the President, Mr. Lincoln was a kind, generous and forgiving man who could not help but admire the courage and valor of the soldiers including those of the Confederacy. The President regarded General Robert E. Lee, General Joseph E. Johnson and General Stonewall Jackson as men of honor who were deserving of his respect.

"Stonewall is an excellent leader. Brave, honest and effective, he is a man of the Presbyterian order, a man of God. If he were to lead the Union army, we would not be stricken with so many deaths."

I repeated the President's words in my head whenever I was alone in my room right before I laid down to rest. I could not help but feel a chill down my back recollecting the scenes of my painful past. I would toss and turn in my bed at night and the scars on my back would meet the hard wood base of my bed, causing the wounds to resurface again. The whippings I endured were still so vivid in my mind and I often wondered whether the President knew of my past.

What would cause a man of his humanity and civility to be so cold? I couldn't find the proper reason to justify it and then one night as if in flash the understanding was made clear.

I opened my Bible and the book of Matthew 6:14 read: *"And when you stand praying, if you hold anything against anyone, forgive them, so that your Father in Heaven may forgive your sins."*

That evening, I labored until the sun rose and sewed a book cover for my Bible made from silk and velvet. I embroidered decorations that symbolized my life as a former slave and now a free woman. I immortalized my father and mother's names, each one with a bird in flight above their names.

At the center, I embroidered my very own name *"Elizabeth Hobbs Keckley"* surrounded by sheaves of wheat and directly below it sewed the following: *"Dressmaker and Friend to The 1ˢᵗ Lady."*

CHAPTER 14

The Second Inaugural Gown

Mrs. Lincoln was busy thumbing through the pages of a new fashion catalogue when she asked about my thoughts on a second election.

"He will serve another four years Mrs. Lincoln. Of this I am certain," I said as I proceeded to adjust the waistline of her dress.

"What makes you think so? Somehow I have learned to fear that he will be defeated," Mrs. Lincoln replied.

"Because he has been tried, and has proven himself faithful to the best interests of the country. The people of the North recognize in him an honest man, and they are willing to confide in him, at least until the war has been brought to a close. The Southern people made his election a pretext for rebellion, and now to replace him by someone else, after years of sanguinary war, would look too much like a surrender of the North. So, Mr. Lincoln is certain to be re-elected. He represents a principle, and to maintain this principle, the loyal people of the loyal States will vote for him, even if he had no merits to commend him," I said.

"Your view is a plausible one, Lizabeth, and your confidence gives me new hope. If he should be defeated, I do not know what would become of us all. To me, to him, there is more at stake in this election than he dreams of," Mrs. Lincoln explained.

"What can you mean, Mrs. Lincoln? I do not comprehend," I asked.

"Simply this. I have contracted large debts, of which he knows nothing, and which he will be unable to pay if he is defeated." Looking down on the floor, Mrs. Lincoln's could not withhold the disappointment and shame she felt in having to confide this to me.

Placing my hand on her shoulder, I asked: *"What are your debts, Mrs. Lincoln?"*

With her chin slightly up she said, *"They consist chiefly of store bills. I owe altogether about twenty-seven thousand dollars- the principal portion at Stewart's, in New York. You understand, Lizabeth. Mr. Lincoln has but little idea of the expense of a woman's wardrobe. He glances at my rich dresses and is happy in the belief that the few hundred dollars that I obtain from him supply all my wants. I must dress in costly materials. The people scrutinize every article that I wear with critical curiosity. The very fact of having grown up in these social circles, subjects me in more searching observation. To keep up appearances, I must have money; more than Mr. Lincoln can spare for me. He is too honest to make a penny outside of his salary. Consequently, I had, and still have, no alternative but to run in debt."*

"And Mr. Lincoln does not even suspect how much you owe?" I asked.

"God, no!" she retorted in her usual Kentuckian way.

"I see Mrs. Lincoln," I said.

"And I would not have him suspect. If he knew that his wife was involved to the extent that she is, the knowledge would drive him mad. He is so sincere and straightforward himself, that he is shocked by the duplicity of others. He does not know a thing about any debts, and I value his happiness, not to speak of my own, too much to allow him to know anything. This is what troubles me so much. If he is re-elected, I can keep him in ignorance of my affairs; but if he is defeated, then the bills will be sent in, and he will know all," as she sobbed hysterically.

Mrs. Lincoln was worried that Washington's circle of politicians and the press would somehow get a hold of this information and use it against her and more importantly, her husband. She knew she could not risk his reputation given he was running to serve another term in office.

The First Lady made a point of naming the many politicians who have benefited profusely from the patronage of her husband. She further declared that the Republicans should pay off her arrears and that if they refused, she would demand and force them to do so to help her get out of debt.

She spent lavishly on jewelry and clothes to rid her mind from the pressure of being the President's wife and the emotional distress of her grief. Something else about Mrs. Lincoln's need for beautiful dresses and jewelry could have been in part due to a traumatic experience during her childhood.

Mrs. Lincoln was the daughter of Ms. Eliza Parker and Mr. Robert Smith Todd who were pioneer settlers of Kentucky.

"My parents established Lexington, and when Mother died, my life was never the same," Mrs. Lincoln once proudly told me.

At age six, Mrs. Lincoln tragically lost her mother from complications during the birth of Mrs. Lincoln's youngest brother, George. Two years after her mother's death, Mr. Todd married a woman named Elizabeth 'Betsey' Humphries whom Mrs. Lincoln described as a cruel, abusive, manipulative, cold-hearted, envious and terrifying woman. Although Mrs. Lincoln belonged to the aristocracy of Lexington, with high-spirited social life and a sound private education, her childhood was sad, desolate and lonesome.

At one point in her childhood, Mrs. Lincoln's stepmother called her *"The Limb of Satan"* after Mrs. Lincoln attempted to protect her siblings from her stepmother's punishments. Considering they never got along, it was decided that Mrs. Lincoln be enrolled at a boarding school just a mile away from their home limiting her time with her father and siblings during the weekends when she was allowed to visit. Eventually, the family decided to sell their family home and move to a new home located on Main Street.

During the move, Mrs. Lincoln had requested her father to set aside her mother's writing desk and all her beautiful dresses, wraps, hats, jewelry, fans, shoes, capes, coats and shawls. Excited to return home for the weekend, Mrs. Lincoln hurried up to the attic to collect the items her father promised to give her.

To her horror, her stepmother had given every piece of her mother's belongings to a band of minstrels and strolling players who came by that same day. The one thing she was able to hold on to was her mother's writing desk her father sent by carriage to her boarding school in advance a few days prior to her return for the weekend. That same writing desk sits inside their bedroom at the White House, a most valued personal belonging she described as one of her 'greatest treasures.'

"I developed a deep loss after Mama's death, and as if that was not bad enough for a child, the loss I sustained after that evil woman gave Mama's beautiful things away to people who did not even know her was enough to bring me to a state of depression and sorrow. I dreamed of one day finding her things still in that attic, hoping to miraculously discover it had been there all along. Her dresses were beautiful, her gloves so delicate, and her shawls would have offered me comfort. Her woven blankets would have kept me warm at night. I could still smell her in those things and could have kept a small part of her with me forever. Oh Lizabeth, how it hurts. How the pain of that loss still has not ceased after all these years," she cried like a small child.

"Oh Mrs. Lincoln, I am so sorry to hear this. I cannot understand for the life of me how anyone could be so cruel. Perhaps, she was suffering her own kind of darkness for it is the only logical explanation I can surmise to explain her actions. Please don't cry Mrs. Lincoln, you will cause the President to worry about you," I said as I gently combed her beautiful long hair.

"Do you know how my father consoled me upon hearing of this news? I was hysterical and out of sorts and do you know that that evil woman had the gall to tell my father that he had better purchase yards upon yards of the finest silks, a new set of gloves, some shawls and wraps, bonnets and jewelry? And do you know that he did? The very next day a large trunk arrived, and my father was so proud of his offering. And do you know something inside me felt strangely better? Yet when everything was quiet again, and when everyone went back to their same old routines, I sat in my room at Mentelle's boarding house crying myself to sleep dressed in the silks and all the beautiful things my father bought for me. And ever since then, I have found temporary comfort in these clothes. Ever since then...Oh Lizabeth, Oh how I miss Mama."

All I could do was hold Mrs. Lincoln, who curled up in my tight embrace like a small child. She cried until the tears left a watermark stain on her dress. She cried until she could no longer and fell asleep in my arms. It hurt me to know of her suffering. It hurt me so deeply.

In the summer of 1864, Mrs. Lincoln arrived at my workshop unannounced to discuss the order of fashioning a dress for her at the anticipated inauguration. All of this of course, would be contingent on the President getting re-elected for a second term.

I must say that I preferred it much more if Mrs. Lincoln called upon me to meet her at the White House instead of her coming to my workshop for her presence during the whole time of her visit would cause an unyielding crowd of curious on-lookers. Various members of the gossip columns sniffing around for fresh material to write about would cause such disruption that it made it difficult to concentrate on my work. Knowing the kind of public attention Mrs. Lincoln would get, I cleverly devised a solution to quash the probing eyes and the eavesdropping ears of these busy bodies.

I installed heavy black curtains that blocked the view into my workshop. My clients always enjoyed the privacy and mystery it offered for often they would hint about to the excitement it caused from their inner and outer circles. *What might her dress look like at the upcoming fundraiser? What is Mrs. Keckley working on now? Where might that Mrs. So and So be wearing such an important dress? What does the wedding gown look like? How expensive is it?* These kinds of questions would all emerge at the onset of every black curtain visit without fail and clients either thoroughly loved the attention they received or abhorred it. Once they left my dress shop to walk a few steps to board their carriages (which was usually a fleeting few seconds) either someone from the gossip columns, the tabloids, the looky-loos, busy bodies and sometimes their admirers would sneak a peek at a chance to lock eyes with the lady client having a black curtain meeting. If you were inside my workshop and the black curtains were drawn, that meant only one thing: You had to be absolutely fetching and important.

I soon deduced that while initially intended as a matter of practicality to preserve my own sanity, the black curtains gave my dress shop a level of notoriety and exclusivity. Mrs. Lincoln on the other hand, preferred to be seen and hence, her time with me if spent inside my workshop would be for public consumption and display.

"Lizabeth... let them gawk. Let them talk, what else is new?" Mrs. Lincoln said as she stepped on the turn-style to get ready for her fitting. Every now and then, waving to the crowd from inside my workshop.

"Oh but Mrs. Lincoln, perhaps consider some privacy and quiet? Listen to that mad crowd!" I said shaking my head in annoyance.

"Thank you Lizabeth, but that is non-sense. Do you realize that your fashions have caused such a stir not only in Washington but also to the women in those rebel states? Ha! These dresses you've made helped reinvent my image to the public at large and dare I say, garnered me and the President the admiration of the people," Mrs. Lincoln proudly stood in front of the full-length mirror with the look of utmost approval at the beginning stages of her Inaugural Ball gown.

"Turn around please Mrs. Lincoln while I adjust the bodice here. I

cannot concentrate with those pesky peepers out there. Oh, dear God already!" I said trying to focus on my work. The crowd was quickly growing and finally I had to go outside to kindly ask them to quiet down out of respect for the other tenants in my building. It was in fact not a lie for a few of them have already raised issue with the recent attractions. I much preferred if they all simply went away for their presence in my atmosphere was creating such annoyance and disruption to my creative process. At one point, a journalist approached me with such briskness that I nearly swatted him with my measuring stick.

"Dear God, those people out there Mrs. Lincoln!" I said as I closed the door behind me, locking it for good measure. Of course, Mrs. Lincoln's guards and footmen surrounded the dress shop, but I figured locking the door was an added ounce of safety measure.

Unfazed by the delirium outside, Mrs. Lincoln said: *"Where do you think I will be next summer Lizabeth?"*

"Why, the White House of course Mrs. Lincoln. Where else would you be?" I responded as I adjusted the side seams of her dress.

"I truly don't believe so. I have no hope of the re-election of Mr. Lincoln. The race is a heated one. The people are talking about the war excessively and every horrible untruth and accusation is brought against my husband."

I replied, *"Mr. Lincoln will be re-elected. I am certain about this. In fact, I have a favor to ask of you."*

"Well, if next summer we are in the White House I shall be able to grant you any favor! Tell me Lizabeth, what may I ask is your request? And why ever is that woman wearing a winter coat outside in this inferno?" she said as she stepped down from the turn style.

"Ignore them, they belong to the mundane. Simply this, Mrs. Lincoln —I would like to keep as a memento the favor of you giving me the right-hand glove that the President wears at the first public reception after

his second inaugural." I was almost too embarrassed to ask especially after admonishing her admirers eagerly waiting outside my shop.

"It will be my absolute pleasure although are you sure of this because has it ever occurred to you how filthy it will be when he pulls it off? I shall be tempted to take the tongs and put it in the fire. I cannot imagine, Lizabeth, why ever you would want such a glove," she asked confused at my request.

"I shall cherish it as a keepsake of the second inauguration of the man who has done so much for my race. He has been a Jehovah to my people. His leadership lifted us out of bondage and directed their footsteps from darkness into light. I shall keep the glove, and hand it down to posterity," I said.

"Very well, if Mr. Lincoln continues as the American President after the 4th of March, then you are welcome to keep his filthy smelly sticky glove. Oh, really Lizabeth, sometimes I wonder about you. Such strange ideas you have," she chuckled with amusement and kissed me goodbye.

The final days of the election were tense. Everyone in the White House, including the President's cabinet down to the footmen had no recourse but to be on tenterhooks. It was as if Mrs. Lincoln herself was walking on the pins and needles in my workshop whenever she came in for a fitting. Even I grew increasingly fretful, each second spent like a bundle of nerves. I prayed in earnest on two bended knees every night after a day's work and implored God Almighty to let the President continue to be at the helm. Our lives were on the balance. My people relied on President Lincoln to continue his good work, for he had yet to scratch the surface of his plans. I knew of his plans because I spent many intimate moments behind closed doors with the First Family. They were good plans indeed. Collectively, my hired dressmakers (all twenty of them) and I were relegated to days spent in prayerful hours in between dressmaking. In my desperation, I went so far as asking my clients who came for their fittings to pray with me.

"There is power in numbers Ladies, let us pray for a victorious outcome," I urged.

Finally, our prayers were answered, and the President was triumphant in securing a second term. By the winter, the war was still unrelenting, and the Rebel states were beginning to lose their strength. Nevertheless, they pushed forward with combative unyielding resistance. The President grew more and more weary in the coming days leading up to his Inauguration.

Spring had finally arrived though you wouldn't know it for the city had a large dark cloud in the air. It was dim, gloomy and ominous enough to make you suspect a disaster was about to unfold. How I wished otherwise for this was a moment in our nation's history that would carry out the very purpose our Founding Fathers laid down for the people.

The National Capital where the ceremony was to take place was swarmed with citizens patiently waiting for Mr. Lincoln. As time passed, the gloomier the atmosphere became and the heavier the dark clouds appeared. I know this was not a sign, for the God I know would have the President in his safekeeping.

Suddenly, it was as though something greater than us orchestrated this unforgettable moment for when the President emerged from the darkness and on to the platform, he appeared to have penetrated the shadows with a bright ray of light that glistened like luminous beams. The crowd roared and cheered, many of us taken to inexplicable levels of utter joy and all that was left in our reserve, was to let out a cry. The President stepped onto the stage like a heaven-sent angel and his face, touched by the brilliance of the sun, appeared to be gilded in gold. Many of us observed that he shone like the North Star emerging like an emblematic gift from God; and there the President stood to take his oath of office and the nation was witness to the second wave of change that was about to come.

By Monday, March 6, 1865, I readied myself to the White House to assist Mrs. Lincoln in getting dressed for the grand levee. The second inaugural ball was to take place at the Patent Office Building. It was the first time that a government building was used for such an auspicious occasion. This moment of euphoria towards the end of the Civil War was an event the nation was looking forward to. All the preparations were meticulously planned with Mrs. Lincoln's leadership, keen eye for regalia and her unquestionable flair. She made sure that all arrangements were properly appointed, and no expense was spared for this re-election marked another era towards change. Mrs. Lincoln saw to it that the nation knew of their position to forge ahead.

I was combing Mrs. Lincoln's hair to pin it into its style and carefully set her jewelry and gloves aside when the President walked into the room. I had not seen him since he took his oath of office and was pleased and eager to offer my well wishes.

"Oh Mr. President, how happy I am to see you again. You are to lead this nation for another term, and I am delighted to know it is you at the helm," I said as I offered my hand to shake his.

The President took a few steps towards me and in his usual way of calling me Madam, he said: *"Thank you. Well, Madam Keckley. I don't know whether I should feel thankful or not. The position brings with it many trials. We do not know what we are destined to pass through. But God will be with us all. I put my trust in God."*

With that, he solemnly walked across the other side of the room, took a seat on the sofa, let out a big sigh and closed his eyes. He was praying. I knew this about him.

Noticing her husband's demeanor, Mrs. Lincoln motioned for me to stand closer to her to which she whispered in my ear, *"Thank you, Lizabeth; but now that we have won the position, I almost wish it were otherwise. Poor Mr. Lincoln is looking so broken-hearted, so completely worn out, I fear he will not get through the next four years."*

Everything about the war led us all to believe that the Confederate states were becoming more and more in a losing pattern. The Union Army was advancing towards a conquering outcome. Guns were constantly fired at the nation's capital in salute to mark yet another vanquishing in favor of the Union.

All evidence of the blue lines forging ahead towards prevailing against the Confederacy was apparent everywhere, yet behind closed doors, in the privacy of their quiet bowers, a husband and his wife carried the weight of the world. Perhaps, somewhere in the deepest parts of Mrs. Lincoln's spirit, she knew something portentous was ahead and I dared not to ask.

"Ah yes, thank Lizabeth. Once again, you have made me look beautiful. Are we ready for round number two, Father?" Mrs. Lincoln quipped.

"Round number two it shall be Mother, shall we?" the President obliged.

"We shall, Mr. President, we shall indeed," Mrs. Lincoln said as she grabbed her husband by the arm and proceeded to descend the long stairwell to meet their guests below.

It was one of the largest receptions held in Washington. There were thousands of people crowding the halls, and eager to shake the right hand of the President. Many Negroes tried to attend even for just a bit of a glimpse of the President or just a chance to cheer and congratulate him, however strict orders were given not to admit them. Just as things were getting hectic, a member of Congress recognized Abolitionist leader.

Mr. Frederick Douglass known as the greatest orator of our time was standing in the outskirts with the crowd.

"How do you do, Mr. Douglass? A fearful jam tonight. You are going in, of course?" said the Congressman.

"No, that is, no to your last question," Douglass replied.

"Not going in to shake the President by the hand! Why, pray?"

"The best reason in the world. Strict orders have been issued not to admit people of color," Mr. Douglass replied sarcastically.

"It is a shame, Mr. Douglass, that you should thus be placed under ban. Never mind; wait here, and I will see what can be done."

The gentleman entered the White House, and working his way to the President, asked permission to introduce Mr. Douglass to him.

"Certainly," said Mr. Lincoln. *"Bring Mr. Douglass in, by all means. I shall be glad to meet him."*

The gentleman returned, and soon Mr. Douglass stood face to face with the President. Mr. Lincoln pressed his hand assuredly onto Mr. Douglass' hand and said, *"Mr. Douglass, I am honored to meet you. I have long admired your course, and I value your opinions highly."* The President and Mr. Douglass shook hands and exchanged some kind words to each other.

Later that evening, I was in attendance to a gathering with some friends where Mr. Douglass' presence was received with great adulation and surprise. He spoke of his satisfaction by the way the President welcomed him. He spoke of the work ahead and the necessity of our participation in ensuring the end of slavery. We listened and we concurred. Mr. Douglass, had it not been for the color of his skin would have made the best President and I reckon that decades from now, the people would have agreed with me.

The Monday following the White House reception, the staff was immersed in the final preparations for the Inaugural Ball to be held at the Patent Office Building. Mrs. Lincoln upon learning of Mr. Frederick Douglass' attendance at the White House became perturbed.

"I did not know Mr. Douglass was in attendance Lizabeth, why was I

not introduced?" she implored.

"I am not quite certain Mrs. Lincoln. Perhaps it was due to the order that no Negroes were allowed entry to the White House," I explained.

"Ridiculous! Father? Abe? Would you please come in here?" she called out loud.

Upon entering the room, the President found his wife standing erect with a look of disgust in her face.

"Father, I do not understand. Lizabeth here said you had the distinct honor and pleasure of meeting Mr. Frederick Douglass. Father, is this true? How could you not have looked for me when you know I have been dying Father, dying to meet him? I am so upset I could cry!" and she did cry.

"I do not know. I thought he was presented to you," the President explained.

"But he was not! He was absolutely not Father!" she cried some more.

"It must have been an oversight then, Mother. I am sorry you did not meet him. I know you are his biggest fan," the President apologized in full sincerity.

"Utterly unbelievable! I am terribly disappointed Father, how could you?" was all Mrs. Lincoln could say from the sheer disappointment she felt. I realized then the magnitude of Mr. Douglass' effect on people while Mrs. Lincoln lamented her misfortune.

He was by all accounts a living ball of radiant magical light. He was a luminary, a sta. Thw loost opportunity to be in his presence was enough to make the First Lady of the United States cry like a possessed banshee. How I felt so bad for Mrs. Lincoln and her massive disappointment.

After calming her down, I finally finished arranging Mrs. Lincoln's hair in a soft low bun and proceeded to dress her in the inaugural ball gown. I would be remiss not to mention the beauty and disposition Mrs. Lincoln possessed. Standing at a mere five feet and two inches, Mrs. Lincoln had a pair of glass-like, clear blue eyes framed together with lush dark long eyelashes that curled at its tips. She had soft silky light-brown hair with glints of blonde, red and bronze colors. Her skin complexion was a milky porcelain-like alabaster hue and her cheeks slightly pink (especially when she was happy or angry.) She possessed small delicate hands with fingers that were evenly balanced throughout. Her high-pitched voice was almost child-like although a rumbling roar would present itself during heated debates.

She moved gracefully and enjoyed dancing the waltz and had the coordination of an athlete. She was a highly-skilled equestrienne and was often seen galloping her pony in her township as a young child. She was a woman of finery and was undoubtedly self-assured. She was intelligent and scholarly. She loved to read books of every subject and was open to learn new things all the time.

She was curious, inquisitive and dared to challenge ideas with a willingness to learn. Fluent in French, she sounded so convincing that there were simply no hints of that deep Southern twang in her diction whatsoever. She was the epitome of a Southern Belle, a true Coquette, a specimen of Gentility contrary to popular belief.

She was proud of her heritage and often reminded those in her presence of who she was, where she came from and all the reasons why.

She was the kind of woman who would not hesitate to burn bridges either, and one would not be surprised if they found her dancing on and licking the ashes of the bridges she chose to burn.

Made from a most beautiful fine silk in pure white, and an overdress of French lace with pointe lace bertha, I created a gown with a deep V-neckline festooned with ruffles with a natural waistline silhouette. An additional five layers of ruffles at the hemline of the crinoline skirt was a perfect balance to the design.

In a bold move, I purposely created the front center hemline of the gown approximately three inches shorter than the sides of and back of the dress that transitioned into a soft sweep train to ensure Mrs. Lincoln's ease of use and balanced footing.

I considered the fact that it was her first time entertaining guests in an unfamiliar location inside the Patent Office Building and while Mrs. President was quite adept and nimble in her self-awareness, I decided to err on the side of caution just in case.

Her sleeves were smocked underneath the layers of ruffles that showcased her beautiful bosom and shoulders. Red embroidered florets throughout the gown commemorated the coming of the spring season. I designed a demi-tiara of fresh flowers in violets and jasmines to adorn her head that lay perfectly atop her soft low bun.

A decision to sway away from a crown of jewels was a wise choice considering her critics might find every reason and excuse to besmirch her character, and since I was not willing to take the risk, opted to take a more wholesome approach with her adornments. Instead of gemstones, we selected a demi-parure customized by Tiffany jewelers, a treasure from Mrs. Lincoln's personal collection. It was a lovely set made from delicate pearls for her necklace, earrings and wrist cuff. What better way to showcase Mrs. Lincoln's collection of flowers from her garden than to fashion a garland of fresh jasmines, violets and greenery worn like a sash across her bodice. A pair of white evening wrist length gloves was the final touch to her ensemble.

I lightly sprayed Mrs. Lincoln wrists with a soft French perfume that mimicked the fragrance of the flowers of her headdress and sash. I neatly folded and perfumed the silk handkerchief that once belonged to her late grandmother bearing her initials *"E.P."* (Elizabeth Parker) and placed it inside a dainty little beaded Reticule gifted by Mrs. Lincoln's friend from France.

Looking at the full-length mirror, Mrs. Lincoln softly spoke: *"When I was a little girl, all I had were Grandma Elizabeth and Mammy*

Sally to stand up for me. After mother's passing, life became so very sad and I vowed one day, I would live in the White House. I never once doubted that dream. Isn't it curious to you that the two most important women in my life shared so much in common with you? One shared your name Elizabeth, who too was an excellent seamstress who lavished with me beautiful dresses with bows and frills; and the other was also Negro woman born a slave like you and loved me like her own. Mammy comforted me in the wee hours of the night when I longed for my mother. Do you realize that this is no coincidence? And here we are, the closest of friends; you are like a sister to me really. You are my dearest. Thank you Lizabeth. I do not know what I would have done without you."

It was one of the most poignant moments between us. Throughout my relationship with Mrs. Lincoln, she shared some of her most intimate experiences to me and I kept them in my safekeeping. Many of these stories were of her childhood in Kentucky. Endearing stories of her great Grandmother Jane's wedding dress made from woven leaves, tree bark and willow sticks.

She told me of the cream-colored pony named 'Peaches' her 'Pa' gave to her when she was thirteen, how her stepmother forbade her to ride it any other way other than sidesaddle. She was a harsh and bitter woman who did everything in her power to make life difficult for young Mary. One day, young Mrs. Lincoln rode her pony with both legs astride and bareback straight to the home of a family friend and prominent citizen named Senator Henry Clay to let him know, *"There isn't a soul in all of Lexington who wants you to become President more than me, and one day I too, shall live in the White House,"* young Mrs. Lincoln once declared.

"My forebears founded this town and named it Lexington after the town in New England where the war started," she told her stepmother one day when she became embroiled in a dispute about her character as a 'Lady.' Her Grandma Elizabeth lived just minutes up the hill and since the passing of her daughter, (Mrs. Lincoln's biological mother) never set foot inside their house again.

Grandma Elizabeth was a tenacious and proud woman who did not hold back her tongue when it came to Mrs. Lincoln's stepmother. And then there was Mammy Sally, the Negro slave who raised Mrs. Lincoln. Mammy once belonged to Grandma Elizabeth but after the death of her daughter, decided to send Mammy Sally to watch over her grandchildren, specifically Mrs. Lincoln.

One day, Mammy Sally was painting the fence with beautiful flowers and the young Mrs. Lincoln picked up a paintbrush to help.

"What lovely flowers Mammy. What brings you to make time for such a task? Don't you have enough work to do?" Mrs. Lincoln asked in genuine curiosity.

"Now hush yo' mouth when I tell you sumthin' important. Promise you aint gunna be runnin' yo' mouth to nobdody 'bout dis here fence?" Mammy Sally asked.

"Cross my heart and hope to die. I will not say a word to anyone about our secret Mammy," Mrs. Lincoln said.

"Alright, Miss Mary. Dis here picket fence is full of flowers 'cus dis here tell all da runaway slaves we is a safe house where dey can git dem sumthin' to eat, some clean clothes and shoes, en a few minutes to rest before the head on out der. Now you promise you ain't gunna tell nobody, not yo' Daddy, yo' brothers or sister, nobody 'bout did here little secret we got goin' on. Mammy gon' git a serious whippin', maybe even killed on account of dis here thing we doin', " she whispered.

One evening shortly after, Mrs. Lincoln heard a shuffling downstairs. Here, she saw Mammy giving a runaway slave a basket of food, some clothing and a jug of water. When Mrs. Lincoln asked Mammy what the fuss was all about, Mammy explained that the fence was a sign to invite runaway slaves to stop for some food, clothing and drink, sometimes to rest for a few minutes even. Mammy made Mrs. Lincoln promise to never tell anyone of this operation that continued for some time.

Her childhood was filled with fascinating stories growing up as part of the well-to-do society in Kentucky. She spent summers at Crab Orchard Springs where they would swim, play, and socialize with the many distinguished families in high society. She attended the prestigious private all-girls academy called Ward's and later attended Madame Mentelle's Boarding School where she learned to write in French and speak it fluently. She was exposed to all the fine things in life, played instruments and traveled to far away and foreign places.

At age twenty-one, she moved to Springfield, Illinois to live with her older sister, Elizabeth Todd who married Mr. Ninian Edwards, son of one of the founding fathers of the state of Illinois. The junior Edwards himself served as Attorney General to Illinois and served in the Illinois House of Representatives. Mrs. Lincoln met the President during a social gathering the Edwards' hosted in their home. Mr. Lincoln at the time described himself as *"a poor nobody then,"* who studied law by borrowing books and rigorously studying legal cases and disputes.

By age twenty-five, the young Mr. Lincoln obtained his license to practice law. Most of his work involved settling contracts and debts, business disputes, some criminal cases and divorce. Three years later, after a stormy and bumpy courtship, a broken engagement, Mary and Abraham married on November 4, 1842.

"Lizabeth, do you know that when a friend asked Mr. Lincoln while he was preparing for the nuptials as to where he was going, he said 'To Hell, I guess?' I suppose he was right!" she laughed loudly waking up the President who was now running behind schedule. It took all my composure not to laugh myself and Mrs. Lincoln was nearly in fits.

"Oh, Mother Mary, what would I have done without you? You are simply too much," as he kissed her on her forehead, held her in his arms for a long moment and motioned for her to resume getting dressed. As she turned to walk away from him, his eyes looked upon her with the greatest admiration. A half-smile with his head held high, the President at that moment was simply a loving husband.

Feeling his gaze, Mrs. Lincoln turned around, put her hands on her waist, and said:

"Mr. President, you are running behind. Where is your valet? Should you not be grooming and readying yourself soon? Now, perhaps?" Mrs. Lincoln said while she nudged him to exit the room to his dressing room where his newly appointed valet awaited.

By now, Mrs. Lincoln was fully dressed, and she looked resplendent. About half an hour later, the President entered the bedroom in a custom black suit coat made specifically for his measurements by haberdashery and master tailor Brooks Brothers. Mr. Lincoln, who stood at six feet and four inches, was not a standard sized man. This meant that all his suits required an expert tailor. Sometimes, I would take charge of the basic sewing, mending and adjustments however most of the President's suits were assigned to his tailor.

Due to his exceptional height, he required a special mirror and enlisted the help of Brooks Brothers to appoint this undertaking. The President's inaugural suit was beautifully decorated with silk twill embroidery on the inner lining of the jacket. It depicted the image of an eagle holding a banner at its beak that read: *"One Country, One Destiny."* I paid close attention to the President's formal white gloves, for soon, the right one would be a cherished possession in my personal collection.

The Presidential Barouche was polished and impressive. As they entered the barouche, four black horses gleaming like balls of midnight magic stood in attention for the President and his First Lady to be taken on a short ride to the Patent Office Building.

I followed along behind them with several other members of their personal staff assigned in a separate less deluxe carriage, (yet still quite impressive) to attend to their needs if necessary. I felt quite special myself for this role of distinction. With me, was my sewing basket, a small pouch of crackers for Mrs. Lincoln typically failed to eat during receptions, spirit of hartshorn to aide Mrs. Lincoln (in the event of another headache to break out), and the bible to keep me busy while waiting to be called upon. Washington looked like a brilliant gem in the night.

The Patent Office halls were brilliantly lit and decorated with flags. A band played as guests entered the reception hall where the dinner and ball were to take place. Everyone was dressed in their best formal attire, with their heads held high, standing erect and proud of this celebratory moment. The evening delivered an air of prophecy that Mr. Lincoln would finish what he started and lead the nation towards a new order.

A special dais was built for the Lincolns' grand entrance and promptly at 10:30 in the evening, the band played 'Hail to the Chief' as they walked into hall to the swell of beaming guests.

The President entered the ballroom side by side with Speaker Shuyler Colfax while Mrs. Lincoln entered upon the arms of Senator Charles Sumner, whom she liked very much. Colfax and Sumner were especially invited as a declaration to the nation that there was no breach between the Executive and Legislative branches.

The First Lady and the President were delighted to see the attendance of their eldest son, Robert, who was granted a special leave of absence to attend his father's inaugural reception. In his arms was Mary Harlan, the daughter of Iowa Senator James Harlan, who was an acquaintance of the Lincolns.

Shortly after midnight, supper was served. Beautifully decorated tables dressed in the finest of linen, serve-ware and silver accommodated three hundred persons at a time. Ornate and elaborate centerpieces were positioned lavishly throughout the hall. A sculpture done in sugar and gum paste mimicked Admiral Farragut's flagship. They served delicacies like pate, oysters, smoked meats, breads, beef, poultry and game provided by T.M. Harvey, the Culinary Chef.

A tower of jams, jellies, carved ices, sweets, cakes, tarts, chocolates, candied fruit and a variety of nuts accompanied coffee and tea from the expert craftsmanship of Mr. Balzer, the Confectioner. Guests were ravenous by this time and thousands of people practically ran to the beautiful tables of food that ended up in shambles. Entire platters of food were removed from the main tables by male guests who ventured to take them outside and laid them upon the grassy areas to picnic under the trees and in the alcoves.

The women whose gowns were of the utmost quality and craftsmanship were torn, stained and damaged from boats of gravy and fine sauces. Most of the glasses were broken. Flatware, silver, fine China and serve wares were pilfered and strewn all over the place. Nothing was spared, including the linen napkins. Anything not nailed down was taken as souvenirs.

Guests were in a state of drunken stupor smattered all over the place. Some were fully asleep on the cold marble floors. Even the coat racks were left in such disarray, guests were leaving with capes and coats that did not belong to them.

I could not help but wonder about how they stayed an order preventing Negroes to attend in the celebrations for reasons unbeknownst to my people, other than perhaps the assumption that we were not decent enough to partake in the regalia, yet the most elite, highly educated, poised citizens of the nation were unable to maintain a level of basic manner and decorum. How curious it was indeed. Nonetheless, a good time was had and perhaps, they all deserved it.

I was simply glad to know that before all this melee occurred, the barouche led by the four black horses of midnight magic whisked the President and the First Lady away from the maddening crowd, landing them safely home; and while Washington reveled in the moment's marking, the two fell asleep in each other's arms in a rare but well-deserved occasion of rest.

The following morning, a delivery from the First Lady's footman arrived at my door. I opened a beautifully wrapped box and within it a handwritten card that read; *"Some promises are never meant to be broken, Signed Mrs. Mary Todd Lincoln."*

My friend kept her promise. The glove becoming one of my most cherished mementos, imprinted with the marks of the thousands of hands that held the honest hand of Mr. Lincoln on that historical night.

CHAPTER 15

"Crowdy," a Union Soldier Dressed in Blue

On Monday, April 3, 1865, one of my prominent clients, Mrs. Secretary Harlan arrived at my dress shop with some fabric for a dress she wanted made. As we went over her notes and specifications, Union soldiers armed with artillery marched past my shop window.

Mrs. Harlan indicated, *"Oh dear Lizzy...what is happening you think?"*

"Your guess is as good as mine Mrs. Harlan," and I proceeded to draw the black curtains just in case we might be witness to something we did not want to see.

"Oh no, Lizzy. Don't do that. Perhaps something of importance is about to unfold. Let us just sit here quietly and wait," she said.

Mrs. Harlan's suspicions proved to be correct for the soldiers were preparing to fire a gun salute, which meant good news was received from the War Department. I recalled the day Mr. Lincoln arrived at home from the War Department at the onset of the Civil War and telling Mrs. Lincoln how dire and bad the days ahead would soon be. Finally, I thought, one less weight upon the President's shoulders.

My receiving and consultation room was on one side of my dress shop, while the other side was dedicated to my workshop where all the sewing, pattern making, and construction took place. Stepping out of my receiving side door, I inquired with a passerby what the gun salute was intended for.

She replied, *"Richmond has fallen!"* as she jumped up in the air unable to contain her excitement.

"Lizzy come here and let us hold hands to pray," Mrs. Harlan grabbed my hands tightly as we stood together in silent prayer. I peeked to observe her face which was half in devotion whilst the other in smiling in sheer delight. Mine was reflective of a smile from ear to ear and I could not wait to share my excitement with Mrs. Lincoln.

I hurriedly ran across to the other side of my workshop and found my workers doing their best to contain their excitement until finally, unable to hold her composure any longer erupted in delight, *"The rebel capital has surrendered to the colored troops Mrs. Keckley! My cousin just snuck inside the workshop to let us all know!"* she cried as every single one of my employees jumped for joy.

I had previously promised my girls that *"when Richmond falls, everyone shall be given a holiday with pay."* This news was doubly pleasing to them, and I was utterly happy to keep my promise.

Back in my receiving room, Mrs. Harlan could barely contain herself and said that her dress could wait for she was *"just too excited to focus on anything else at this time,"* and for me to *"join my girls on the promised holiday treat."* Mrs. Harlan entered her carriage and headed home to celebrate with her family, while I gathered up my staff to commence our celebration for the day.

We took our time all throughout the capital, enjoying the streets, eating sweets, laughing, singing and joining the jubilation of the city. Many other departments took the day off to celebrate and become stupefied with joy. Some men walked past us with blank looks on their faces as if living in a state of limbo, unsure of themselves and what was next. I pitied them and prayed for their humanity to prevail.

Later, Mrs. Lincoln sent for me to join her at City Point near Petersburg, my old home. I was happy to join her and packed a suitcase for the trip and gave Mrs. Lincoln notes on what to pack for her wardrobe.

Two days later, we set aboard the steamboat The Queen River designated for City Point. It delighted me to know that Mrs. Secretary Harlan with her lovely daughter, Senator Charles Sumner and several other prominent gentlemen were also traveling with Mrs. Lincoln. A few days prior to our departure from Washington, President Lincoln headed for City Point in advance and then made a stop in Richmond then to Petersburg and a few other places.

Disappointed to learn that her husband arrived earlier to visit the Confederate capital, Mrs. Lincoln expressed how deeply she desired to make an entrance on conquered soil. After some careful planning, we steamed ahead to the once impassable James River.

There was a benign tranquil feeling in the air; the river was quiet and serene with the first installations of the sweet perfumes of spring blossoms. It was a long journey and for many hours I stood aboard in quiet repose absorbing the scenery before me. It was wide, vast, calm and soothing.

With outstretched arms, I opened my chest to let out a significant exhale as if to welcome the river into my soul. The lush green trees whose branches swung and swayed in exalted movement symbolizing our welcome into sovereign grounds gave me a sense of vigor and a reclaiming of a youth I always longed to have.

The birthplace where my story was set into bondage even before I let out my first breath of air has now transformed into a homecoming I've always prayed for. Somewhere in the deepest chasms of my soul I envisioned that I would return to the place where my beloved mother Aggy pushed me out of her weary, beaten yet glorious and sacred body on the coldest, rainiest season of the times inside a dark dreary cabin, with nothing but a quickly fading candle to offer some light. And now here I was, the only Negro woman aboard this steamboat whose human cargo comprised the wife of the greatest leader of our time and perhaps this nation's history, along with the men and women who were ever ready to come to blows with anything or anyone who stood against Freedom's way.

I have journeyed far and wide to return full circle to my birthplace and wonder whether the changing of tides would finally bond all Americans into one common understanding towards the soothing balm of Peace.

I reflected quietly in abject amazement at the suffering I endured, and yet despite all its agony and suffering, found it within myself to recast the foundations of bondage and alter its purpose of disablement into the fulfillment and attainment of experiencing what it is to be human.

In every ripple of the river's water, in every leaf fallen from the trees, in every slight nuance of a breeze and the lulling sounds of the white-crowned sparrows, I for the first time saw my birthplace from a set of newfound eyes. I felt the souls of my father, mother and the forebears who arrived in bondage long before me some hundreds of years ago.

This river held within its vastness the stories of all their lives once sunken to the bottom and now bubbling and rising to the very top, its headwater transformed into hallowed and sacred streams consecrated by their spirits nevermore to be forgotten. Like a rebirth, like a baptism, their spirits sang through the river in a triumphant chorus like noble ghosts no longer running, no longer fighting, no longer hiding; ghosts whose souls have been restored and made forever free.

One by one, each of us disembarked as the helmsman dropped the anchor marking our journey's end. Arriving to the main city a few days before, the President and his party entered Richmond with great curiosity.

Meanwhile, a caravan of barouches led by footmen met us at the loading station to carry us to important points of interest within the city. Signs of defeat were all over the Confederate Congress building; from broken signs, desks turned upside down, papers strewn and scattered about, and the evidence of hurried flight palpable in every nook and cranny of Richmond.

By happenstance, I picked up a newsletter indicating the resolution to prohibit all free colored people from entering the State of Virginia. I saw the chair Mr. Jefferson Davis sat on in the Senate Chambers, along with the chair of the Vice President Alexander H. Stephens.

A chill ran down my spine just at the imaginings going on in my mind of what the scene might have looked like a few days ago.

We visited the Davis family mansion where they once lived whilst the white Southern ladies of the Confederacy given charge to clean and organize the remains of its once spectacular and eminent grandeur offered us nothing but scowls and venomous stares.

The Confederate White House, surrounding buildings and its contents would soon be seized by the Union army's troops as contrabands of war. Mrs. Lincoln entered each room to inspect them with meticulous observation as we walked in silence throughout the assessment. *"Hail to the Chief!"* I kept reciting privately in my head and wondered if the party I traveled with held the same thoughts in their private minds.

Returning to City Point, inside the dining cabin of the Queen River, we gathered for dinner around the warmth of a beautifully set table as guests began to arrive. I was assigned a seat directly next to Mrs. Lincoln's right with a handwritten place card indicating my name *'Mrs. Lizzy Keckley.'* A wink from Mrs. Lincoln confirmed that she was the commander behind this arrangement, and I was thrilled for the experience.

An officer from the Sanitary Commission was also seated next to Mrs. Lincoln's left side and midway through dinner he said, *"Mrs.*

Lincoln, you should have seen the President the other day on his triumphant entry into Richmond. He was the cynosure of all eyes. The ladies kissed their hands to him and greeted him with the waving of handkerchiefs. He is quite the hero surrounded by so many pretty young ladies."

How I wished I could have forewarned the young gentleman but am afraid I was too late. Mrs. Lincoln met the officer's eyes with the most glaring scrutiny and offered words that cut through him like double-edged forged blades of steel.

She was offended and vexed by the gall of his audacity and invited him to be excused.

"You look tired Officer. I suggest you be excused from the table, and I shall have the valet deliver your dinner to your cabin in case you wish to eat later. Thank you for making an appearance tonight but please be excused. Good night," she dismissed.

The room fell silent, and the young gentleman acquiesced with no argument for he knew that the memorable evening inside the cabin of the Queen River was marred by his lack of propriety. Quietly, he rose from the table and excused himself giving the reason that he had important matters to attend to that required his attention.

"No more words from you. Goodnight, Sir." Mrs. Lincoln uttered the audible words ending this gentleman's welcome at the table and any future dinners with the Lincolns. As he left, Mrs. Lincoln stood up to offer a toast making sure the young gentleman was within earshot of what she said. *"Good riddance to all who no longer serve the best interest of this nation! Cheers!"* she announced as each guest (including myself) held glasses high for a celebratory toast.

The following morning the President and his party agreed to visit Petersburg with me alongside as Mrs. Lincoln's personal companion. I was so thrilled to visit Petersburg and could barely sleep a wink after the dinner. Upon arrival to Petersburg, a little Negro boy skittishly approached the President and in replying to several questions used the curious word "tote."

Just then, the President bent down and asked, *"What do you mean by 'tote' little boy?"*

"Why Sir, you tote 'em on 'ya back like this," he eagerly said.

"Very definite my son. I presume when you tote a thing, you carry it. By the way, Sumner, 'What is the origin of tote?" the President asked.

"Its origin is said to be African. The Latin word totum, from totus, means all, an entire body, the whole," Mr. Sumner explained.

"But my young friend here did not mean an entire body, or anything of the kind, when he said he would tote my things for me," said the President.

"Very true. He used the word tote in the African sense, to carry, to bear. Tote in this sense is defined in our standard dictionaries as a colloquial word of the Southern States, used especially by the Negroes."

"Then you regard the word as a good one?" Mr. Lincoln said as he turned his gaze back to the little boy.

"Not elegant. I should like to use a better word, but since it has established its usage, I shall not refuse to recognize it," Sumner replied.

The President reached out to shake the little boy's hand and said, *"You are quite an enterprising young man. I would like to ask the favor of your assistance to kindly 'tote' my things and carry them to the car that is waiting for me please. I think it sounds rather elegant Sumner... Tote! Hahaha!"*

Pointing to the carriage, the President handed the little boy some money and let out a hearty laugh as he watched him eagerly carry his things to his car.

The President and his party visited various forts and other areas of interest while I ventured out separately in search of the familiar faces I knew of in my early days. The aftermath of the war took its toll on the once scenic landscape of my birthplace.

Just several yards in front of our carriage, Mrs. Lincoln and I watched as the President talk to a troop of Union soldiers who appeared to be surveying a captured wagon that had been used to smuggle flour into Petersburg, Virginia during the siege of Richmond.

Curious to know what the delay was about, Mrs. Lincoln shouted from the carriage's window, *"Abe, shall we move ahead while you meet us at the end of the road?"*

The President turned and nodded, *"Yes Mother, I am just finishing up with this young soldier Private William Crowdy here, who tells me the details of how they captured this Confederate flour wagon! Oh what a bunch of brave lads!"*

I took a moment to observe the way these Negro Union soldiers were dressed in their uniforms. Private Crowdy was smiling from ear to ear as he told the President of their victory in Richmond. He was wearing a black woolen forage hat, tipped slightly at an angle, with one brim being secured by way of an embroidered eagle. Their knee-length jackets in Prussian blue were trimmed with the arm of service with piping along the collar edges. The bright gold-hued buttons lined up in a row at the center of the coat glistened as the sun hit them in certain angles while they moved about, lifting trunks filled with seized items from the Confederate Army.

"Meticulous," I said under my breath.

Their trousers were made from a well-bodied broadcloth woolen fabric in sky blue with a stripe down each side in a darker hue. A leather belt around their waist held them up in a posture that kept them erect and standing straight. Their shoes called 'brogans' went up to their ankles, a critical design feature to protect their feet and keep them warm and dry while at war.

Private Crowdy spoke on behalf of his fellow-soldiers and said succinctly, *"On behalf of our regiment, it has been an honor to serve our country Mr. President.*

"Thank you for your service Private Crowdy, and to all of you

soldiers. Gentlemen I bid you goodbye for now, carry on," the President removed his stovepipe hat to salute the soldiers as he bid the soldiers goodbye, beaming with pride.

Despite the victorious feeling in the air, the changes to my hometown were drastic in my view and drew upon me a certain feeling of sadness. I discovered some old friends of my youth however most of them were unfamiliar faces to me now.

The atmosphere was grim, sullen and brought back painful memories of my time spent here with the Burwell clan. I hurried myself back to the city where Mr. Lincoln urged his party to pay a visit to a lone old oak tree he observed during his first visit a few days prior. I knew of the tree he spoke of, for many years it was the guardian that wrapped me in its embrace. If anything good were to come of this visit, it would have to be my reunion to this majestic old oak tree.

"A magnificent specimen of grandeur!" said the President as we finally arrived to see it. We all stood there in deep admiration of its stately and noble beauty.

There my old oak tree stood, braced to the earth- unharmed by the wrath of war. My old oak tree welcomed me with an otherworldly force as its branches swayed as if purposely in my direction that even Mrs. Lincoln took a calculated step back to somehow suggest that the tree might be speaking, that it perhaps could have some deeper understanding than the average tree in the woods. Isolated in its magnificence in the forest, the old oak offered to the enjoyment of all, a sense of quietude from the event of the day. I, on the other hand had a much deeper experience I preferred to keep to myself.

On the train to City Point, the President asked the conductor to stop for a moment as he observed a turtle basking in the sun by the wayside.

"Bring the little guy to me would you please?" he asked one of the third men to take the terrapin from the ground and into his cabin. Throughout the ride back, the President and his son Tad, delighted

in laughter while playing with the lumbering little creature until we reached City Point. Mrs. Lincoln was so pleased to finally see her husband display a moment of relief and normalcy.

For about a week, we traveled aboard the Queen River. Guests included General and Mrs. Ulysses Grant along with many distinguished officers of the Union Army. The President lounged around the boat when not stopping for duty and enjoyed talking about subjects that interested him. His cabinet members too, enjoyed the time spent aboard.

A day before our arrival to Washington, Mr. Lincoln entered Mrs. Lincoln's cabin while I was preparing to help ready Mrs. Lincoln's dress and shoes for her arrival to the White House. The President entered the room with a weary and tired look on his face.

"Mother, I have shaken so many hands today that all I wish to do is go to sleep," the President said as he lay on the bed faced down with his feet dangling past the edges of the bed for he was too large of a man.

"Oh Father, indeed you are exhausted. Your work is unrelenting, and you must know that the people of this nation owe you a debt of gratitude. Take a brief nap and you shall be good as now for this evening," she said while she gently ran her fingers through her husband's hair. Within seconds, the Chief was asleep.

The sun's setting was replaced by the evening sky filling the expanse of infinite space above all of us aboard. Like a gem sparkling in the night, the Queen River was brilliantly illuminated with brightly colored lights like fireflies in flight.

The steamship stayed afloat like a magical enchanted kingdom while the sweet soft music of the military band filled the air.

I stood at its bow to make my final goodbyes offering my sun-drenched face to the midnight sky where a lone star shined above me. The North Star that once led my people to freedom hung above me like an aide-memoire of the work still ahead and the uphill roads still waiting to be traveled.

After excusing himself from the evening's revelry, the President proceeded to retire in the privacy of his cabin where his wife awaited, and within the following hour, all the lights were taken down, the band with its final song playing in the background as the Queen River geared itself into the water to make her way back to Washington.

By 6:00 a.m., the Queen River arrived in Washington and each guest taken back to their respective homes. It was one of the most indelible experiences of my lifetime that filled my soul with the fondest of memories.

CHAPTER 16

The Dress of the Final Act

Shortly after our arrival back to Washington from City Point, Mrs. Lincoln visited me in my apartment to invite me to witness the President deliver a speech. It would be the very first time I were to witness the President deliver a public address of this magnitude and knowing him as closely as I did, was very eager to attend this event.

"Lizabeth, if you take any interest in political speeches, you must come and listen in welcome," Mrs. Lincoln urged.

"I do not wish to sound presumptuous but may I bring a friend along with me?" I asked.

"Why of course Lizabeth, please do bring a friend and be sure to arrive in time to assist in getting me dressed," she winked.

I confirmed as she whisked herself away from my apartment and into her carriage to be driven away by the same barouche led by the four black horses that gleamed like balls of midnight magic.

I worried a little for she appeared distracted and deep in thought. Perhaps, (still recovering from her recent accident while aboard her carriage where she hit her head on the pavement causing her to suffer from a severe concussion) she was just tasked with various things leading up to the President's public speech. Nonetheless, it left an uneasy feeling throughout the day.

I entered the White House during the early part of the evening and proceeded to walk upstairs towards Mrs. Lincoln's dressing room when from the corner of my eye, glanced at Mr. Lincoln's room through the door that was half-ajar.

Seated on the desk, I saw the President reading his notes and talking under his breath. Reflective in thought, he was focused in a way unlike anything I had ever witnessed before in all my years in the White House.

It was as if he was in a world of the supernatural; a transcendental state of being and I could not remove myself from the intrusion of his privacy no matter if I tried for what I saw before me was short of something mythological or mystical in nature.

I witnessed before anyone else in the nation had ever witnessed, the unfolding of the spectacular dramatization that was soon to commence before the people's eyes, to be heard by thousands of listening ears.

Slowly, the President shifted his weight from the seat of his leather chair and turned to look at me, his eyes smoldering with curiosity underneath the mayhem of his disheveled brows.

"Hello Madame Keckley, Good Evening," he said as he cleared his throat as if to signal me to go away. I found myself fumbling through my sewing basket embarrassed at getting caught for eavesdropping.

"My apologies Mr. President, I was just making my way to Mrs. Lincoln's dressing room when I heard you in your office. Please forgive me for intruding on your time as I know you have much to prepare."

"That is quite alright Madame Keckley. I pray that I shall not have to look too hard for you in the audience yes? You will try your best to make your way towards the front of the stage I hope," his eyes still smoldering at me.

"Yes Sir, yes indeed Mr. President, indeed." Mortified, I swiftly headed to Mrs. Lincoln's room.

"Ah Lizabeth, thank you for arriving early," Mrs. Lincoln greeted.

"Shall we begin the ritual of Mrs. Lincoln's toilette?" I teased as the relief from the embarrassing incident that had just occurred started to settle in.

"Yes we shall Mrs. Keckley. Lock the door would you and pour me some spirits. Let the games commence!" said she with glee.

Through the years, I have taken care of all Mrs. Lincoln's needs from head to foot with exacting detail. The 'Toilette' as it is commonly referred, was the act of getting prepared for the day. It first became a ritual during the reign of great Absolute Monarch Louis XIV of France.

This ritual was performed like a ceremony making dressing a form of Art. The process of dressing called 'Lever' and undressing which Mrs. Lincoln called 'Coucher,' gave nobles in the royal favor the privilege of watching the great monarch prepare for the day or night.

This ritual then spread to other courts in Europe, and to the nobility, with different levels of formality accompanying the event. Eventually, the art of dress made its way to members of the elite society in America. Most of the time, the toilette was practiced in private for its most intimate portions involved undergarments not meant for all to view. I considered this ceremony to be meditative in nature allowing me to dress Mrs. Lincoln slowly in her most relaxed state. Bathing was also part of this process and a favorite of Mrs. Lincoln's. She enjoyed getting her hair washed, dried, fragranced and then combed into a suitable style for day or night.

Gently, I applied lavender and rose oil on her face, neck and ears. A light layer throughout her body gave her skin a lovely glow. Like a rite of passage, the Toilette was a process that not only paid reverence to the role fashion played in society, but it was believed that the art of dress in its ritualistic form gives it an almost religious connotation that brings deeper appreciation for what seemed to be a mundane daily occurrence.

By ritualizing the process, each layer of "dressing" is given its importance not only through what is seen but also through what is unseen. This act alone signified Mrs. Lincoln's desire to identify herself as a woman of her own choice, her own doing and her own purpose. Every layer was symbolic of her nature as a woman, an abolitionist, a mother, a wife, a friend and daughter of God. This gave her time to think through her woes and challenges, sometimes seeking my counsel and advice on matters that she felt needed by my guidance. I was happy to perform the tasks because it was an extension of my expression as a Modiste.

Finally, after a the calming ceremony, Mrs. Lincoln was ready to get dressed and face her husband's audience. She looked beautiful.

The crowds gathered quickly in front of the White House and I, along with my friend positioned towards the front of the stage just as I promised the President. Like a vast ocean, the swell of people that formed behind me grew increasingly larger by the minute. I was agog at the attendance of people that evening and fathomed at the presence the President commanded.

The magnitude of this moment was something out of a fairytale book told when a great leader of some faraway land arrives for but a fleeting moment to make a once in a lifetime appearance to his admirers. From his mouth, words were uttered to transform heavy hearts into hopeful ones and the promise of renewed life to its people would come to action. This was the very thing the people came here to witness, the very thing they longed to hear said, the very thing that brought them to the battlefields in pursuit of upholding the nation's promise of liberty for all. And then from the right side of the stage, Mr. Lincoln emerged and advanced himself forward to the center of the platform to speak.

Before thousands of people, the man who sat at his desk just merely a few hours ago, transformed into a God, no different from the Olympian Zeus, the strongest deity possessing both power and intelligence. The roar emanating from the audience was so deafening and arresting that it could stop hearts from beating. It was a phenomenon etched in the hearts and minds of all those in attendance.

"A Light! Give the President a light!" the crowd screamed, stomped and applauded; tearing through every possible reasonable thought I had at the moment.

To the stage entered the President's son little Tad, who rushed to his father's side. A lamp was brought to echo the audience's cries.

"Papa! Let me hold the light Papa, let me hold it!" Tad yelled.

Mrs. Lincoln granted her son's request and the lamp was handed to little Tad Lincoln. The older Lincoln stood on the stage in front of thousands of people about to deliver a statement of expressive and powerful ideas, while the younger Lincoln looked up proudly at his father. It was a sight to behold as the light from the lamp traced the silhouette of the Commander in Chief as he stood before his audience. Then, raising his left arm, the President motioned for the audience settle down. The once maddening roar of the crowd fell eerily silent that if a pin dropped, it would be a dissonant and unwelcome distraction.

As the crowd settled, the President spoke with a cadence that increased in both volume and emotion leading to the culmination of his speech. And then he knelt to his son to take the lamp from his tired hands. Holding his son on the other arm, he then stood up to face the audience; his eyes surveying each of the onlookers before him with intense concentration.

In delayed response, the audience remained silent only for a few seconds upon which a thunderous, ear-splitting applause raised the ground to a reverberant fortissimo of monumental proportions. My body was uncontrollably shaking, and my mind raced into an irrational frenzy. I was worried. I was paranoid. I was suspicious of the crowd behind me.

"I tremble at the thought of anyone attempting to assassinate the President. This crowd is too big for anyone to even determine who the

assassin may be," I whispered to my friend that evening as we headed our way home, though I do not know why such a horrible thought even entered my mind.

There have been many warnings and threats during this time and the following morning, I confided my unrest to Mrs. Lincoln.

That same night while getting Mrs. Lincoln ready, she said the same thing: *"The President's safety is always at risk. Oh, the drudgery of a life in constant fear of such threats. Lizabeth, I have told you many times and over that I pray for my nightmare of Mr. Lincoln's life meeting a sudden and violent end to never ever come true. Oh, Lizabeth...please pray that my presentiments and paranoia are mere imaginings of a worried wife."*

"Yes I shall pray with you that none of these things ever come true." We held each other's hands tightly as we prayed in silence. Mrs. Lincoln was breathing heavily and began to cry and all I could do was hold her; her face buried deeply in my chest, I held her until her breath slowed down; until she was no longer lamenting, until she fell asleep like a child in my arms.

The following Saturday afternoon upon Mrs. Lincoln's request to assist her with her toilette, I was surprised to be greeted by the President himself in the White House garden. There he was, playing with some goats for what seemed like an hour or so. Little Tad was playing along with his father and laughed in delight.

"Madame Keckley, you are fond of goats aren't you?" asked the President.

"Oh, indeed I am Sir."

"Won't you come here and look at my two goats Madame Keckley? These are the kindest and very best goats you will ever meet. Notice how they breathe the crisp air, how they seem so happy skipping and hopping around? My Oh my! Have you ever seen a jump as lofty as that one yet?" the President chuckled in delight.

He was known to have a deep fondness for animals and kept a

menagerie of them in the White House. Fido was the President's favorite pet. He was a sweet mixed-breed dog who was around as early as the time the President was a lawyer in Springfield, Illinois. Willie and Tad enjoyed running around and playing fetch with him at the White House during the early part of the Presidency.

Unfortunately, **Fido** cowered from the crowds who greeted the President. Add to this the business of fireworks, not being used to strangers and the increased attention surrounding his master caused him much distress. With the activity of people going in and out of the White House, the social scenes surrounding it, and all the bustle relating to the Presidency, Mrs. Lincoln and the President decided to leave Fido in Springfield under the care of a family friend who was given specific instructions from the President:

"Fido must be allowed to have the run of the house. He is never ever to be scolded for tracking mud. He is to be allowed to wander around the family dinner table and fed all the scraps he begs for."

"Fido is spoiled rotten indeed, and those cats are the bane of my existence," according to Mrs. Lincoln who was not fond of animals at all.

The President would often seek refuge in the quiet moments spent with his cats. Secretary of State, Mr. William Sewell gave the President two cats after learning of his love for these feline creatures. 'Tabby' and 'Dixie' were his closest companions. He would sit quietly and talk to them for half an hour at a time.

During a military meeting at General Ulysses Grant's main station, Admiral David Porter witnessed the President with bent knees petting three stray cats and telling them *"Kitties, thank God you are cats and cannot understand this terrible strife that is going on."*

He went on to give his military staff the following instructions before departing Grant's headquarters: *"Gentlemen, please ensure the kittens are well-taken care of."*

One time during a formal dinner at the White House, Mrs. Lincoln chastised the President in the presence of their guests at the sight of the President feeding one of his cats at the dining table.

"Abraham, this is shameful behavior!" scoffed Mrs. Lincoln.

"If the gold fork was good enough for former President James Buchanan, then it is good enough for Tabby," he said with a smile as he fed the cat from his spoon.

For a moment, I had forgotten where I was for I was too busy reminiscing until the President's voice awakened me back to reality.

"Madame Keckley, I realize Mrs. Lincoln is waiting for you but do indulge me for a few minutes won't you?" motioning for me to take a seat next to him while he plays with his goats.

"He feeds on my bounty and jumps with joy. Do you think we can call him a bounty jumper? But I flatter the bounty jumper for my goat is far above him," he said.

"What do you mean Sir?" I asked.

"I would rather wear his horns and his hairy coat through my life than demean myself to the level of the man who plunders the national treasury in the name of patriotism. The man who enlists into a service for a consideration and then deserts the moment he receives the money, but to repeat the play, is bad enough; but the men who manipulate the grand machine and who simply make the bounty-jumper their agent in an outrageous fraud are far worse. They are beneath the worms that crawl in the dark hidden places of the earth."

A withered look was in his eyes; his lips curled in a scathing way that made the words difficult to escape from his mouth.

He paused at the same time one of his goats began to baa and bleat to his master. *"You see Madame Keckley, my pets recognize me. Look at them, what sweet beasts they are. There they go again, what jolly fun they are,"* he uttered then let out a laugh that caught me by surprise for I had never seen the President this light-hearted about anything.

The goats running and hopping about to the next yard caused the President to rise from his seat to run after them. What a curious scene this was to witness the President running vigorously to catch up to a few little mischievous overfed goats.

Just then, *"Lizabeth, come! I must finish dressing and you must stop playing with those silly goats,"* Mrs. Lincoln beckoned.

Inside the dressing room, I began to lay Mrs. Lincoln's fineries on her bed beginning with the undergarments and stockings.

"Have I ever told you how much I despise those goats? For the life of me, I can never understand the President's fascination with them. In fact, after Willie's death, I cannot bear to see the President love anything so much, not even a singular flower. Forgive me Lizabeth, but it is my truth as peculiar as it may seem," Mrs. Lincoln confided.

She continued, *"Anyway, on more exciting things. In a few days from now, I shall be attending a show at the Ford's Theater with the President to watch a performance of play 'Our American Cousin.' I heard it is quite hilarious and I am very much looking forward to it. Lizabeth, I should like to give you a day off from having to attend to my toilette. How does that sound to you?"* she asked.

"Thank you Mrs. Lincoln but surely you know it is of no inconvenience to me whatsoever to assist you in getting dressed," I said as I combed her hair.

"Oh, but I insist Lizabeth. The evening shall be a night of rest for all of us. The President and I are looking forward to this time with friends, enjoying the show and all the merriment afterwards. You should too make merry Lizabeth! Do make plans with your friends and let us meet the following day for an afternoon of tea," she excitedly said with her eyes wide open.

"I suppose you are right. I shall make plans with Mr. and Mrs. Walker then and perhaps take a nice stroll in the Capital after supper, and turn in early for once," I laughed sheepishly.

"Yes my darling, what joy this brings to my ears Lizzy, my dearest friend Lizzy..." uttered Mrs. Lincoln.

Setting aside the petticoat and all the accoutrements in the correct order for her ease-of-use since she will be dressing by herself for the theater, I gave Mrs. Lincoln an embrace goodbye.

On the evening of April 14, 1865, I maintained my promise to to enjoy an evening of respite though I secretly wished to have been able to attend to her toilette instead for such a special occasion. I had already spent an afternoon with Mr. and Mrs. Walker (who were a respectable free citizens of my own race) the day previous and decided instead to spend a quiet evening at home alone instead.

In the White House, unbeknownst to me, Mrs. Lincoln had experienced a terrible headache and considered to cancel attending the show but after some convincing from her husband, proceeded to get herself dressed. In a strange turn of events, General Ulysses Grant and his wife declined the Lincolns' invitation to visit their son instead. With two extra tickets, the Lincolns extended the invitation to Major Henry Rathbone and his fiancée Ms. Clara Harris to attend in Mr. and Mrs. Grant's place.

Minutes before departing the White House, the President's footman Mr. William H. Crook advised the President not to go after Mr. Lincoln had told him that he had been having dreams of being assassinated for three consecutive nights. Mr. Crook tried many times and more tried to persuade the President not to attend the performance that night, or at least allow him to go along as an extra bodyguard, but Lincoln said that he promised his wife they would attend the show and for Mr. Crook not to be too concerned.

"I suppose it's time to go though I would rather stay," the President told Speaker of the House, Mr. Schuyler Colfax before assisting Mary into the barouche with the black horses on the ready.

As the President disembarked from the carriage, he turned to his footman, Mr. Crook and said, *"Goodbye, Crook."*

"Good Night Mr. President," and with the tip of his cap, Mr. Cook drove off until it was time to return to collect the President and his wife once the show ended. As he drove away, a thought entered Mr. Crook's mind.

In all the years he served the President, he always said *"Good Night, Crook."* It was the first time that he neglected to say, *'Good Night'* to him and it was the singular time that the President ever said **"Goodbye."**

The Ford's Theater was a full house that evening, and as Mrs. Lincoln adjusted her gown, she looked up to her husband with a the most dazzling smile.

The President, in his usual manner, took his wife's arms and said, *"You look beautiful darling. Shall we Mother?"*

With one deep breath, she said to her husband, *"We shall Father. We shall indeed."*

The President and the First Lady entered the theater in full regalia. The Military band played; the theater doors opened wid; the people jumped in sheer excitement. Their raucous cheers bounced off the four walls of the theater and they screamed *"Hail to the Chief!"* as the President and his wife made their way to theater's balcony to enjoy the show. The crowd fell silent as the curtains opened on the stage.

Little did Mrs. Lincoln know that it would be the last time she would ever hold her husband's arms again for somewhere near ten o'clock, during the second scene of the third act of the show, a man named John Wilkes Booth entered the Presidential Box and fired a single bullet into the President's head.

Inside my apartment, at around a quarter before midnight, a loud bang shook me, yet I couldn't wake myself up from a terrible nightmare. I heard screams but I was paralyzed, transfixed upon the bed and laid there in a cold sweat. It was as if I was possessed again with the incubus that tormented me for 47 years. I attempted to scream. Nothing but the force of the demon kept at me. Suddenly,

I awoke disoriented but relieved by the pounding coming from my door.

"Who is it?" I trembled as I called out. It was my neighbor, Mrs. Brown whose face jumped at me when I opened the door.

"Lizzy...The President has been shot," her dilated eyes frightful and spooked. She was panicked and stricken by the shock of the news.

CHAPTER 17

Sorrow in Silk

I disembarked Mrs. Lincoln's carriage upon arriving to the White House and frantically ran up the stairs to the President and First Lady's bedroom. From a distance as I hurriedly made my ascent, I heard the echoes of Mrs. Lincoln's anguished cries. As I drew closer, her deafening panic-stricken screams terrified me.

"Lizzy! Lizzy! Where is she? Someone please get me Elizabeth! Somebody get her for me! Get me Elizabeth now!!!" Mrs. Lincoln howled liked an animal trapped in a cage. I was transfixed. I was petrified and unsure whether to move forward or stay still. Something gruesome is happening or has happened. I did not know what to think, do or say.

Standing outside the bedroom was a line of staff members. Both of Mrs. Lincoln's sons Robert and Tad had their faces buried in their hands.

"Robert, dear God...Robert? Why are you not inside the room with your Mother?" I asked Mr. Lincoln's oldest son who was doing his best to stay composed.

He did not offer me an answer. His face still buried in his hands. I then turned to one of President Lincoln's aides to ask the same question and was given no response either.

Finally, I asked Mrs. Lincoln's nurse who leaned close and whispered to me, *"The First Lady has ordered everyone, including her children to remain outside for she only asked for you, Mrs. Keckley. Mrs. Keckley, the President is dead. We are told to remain here with Mrs. Lincoln but... "* The nurse fell to the floor as if all the life had been drawn out of her.

"How long has Mrs. Lincoln been alone in her room?" I demanded to know yet no one could offer a response. Everyone stood there paralyzed and consumed by an insurmountable sense of shock and grief.

I was frightened at the uncertainty of what I would discover. I entered Mrs. Lincoln's bedroom. Everything looked collapsed, askew and ramshackled. The bedside lamp had fallen to the floor to meets its end, the drapes were pulled leaving its rods dangling for life, chards of broken glass were everywhere and the President's handwritten papers and notes strewn all over the floor. The room was dark and the chill that lingered was ominous and gut-wrenching. I was terrified and stunned.

Like a small child, my dear friend lay sprawled in the middle of the bedroom's cold floor, listless and limp with grief.

In her blood-soaked hands, she held her husband's Bible as she gently called his name, *"Abraham, Abraham, Father, my darling."*

"Mrs. Lincoln? I am here now Mrs. Lincoln, I am here, Lizabeth is here," walking slowly towards her, I knelt and held her lifeless body in my arms.

The silk dress soaked in the President's blood was still warm from the violence and terror that just came to pass. By now, my own dress fused together with hers, leaving it bloodied and stained.

I could not find the strength to mobilize myself from this unspeakably spine-chilling moment. I stood there terrified and shocked.

Mrs. Lincoln finally looked up to face me. Her face covered in blood was only discernable from the streaks of her tears that exposed her beautiful alabaster skin.

Like the wrath of a thousand evil spirits in Revelations 17, the scarlet-colored beast, having seven heads and ten horns lingered inside the President's chambers as if to gloat at its doings. The demon's name was Slavery.

There inside the chambers, Mrs. Lincoln let out the deepest and most deafening cry I had ever heard in my life. She struggled, convulsed and quivered to speak in between moments of losing her breath and consciousness.

"Help me. Please don't leave me. I need you Lizzy, I need you my friend. Stay with me Lizzy, I beg you...Please stay!."

On bended knees, I sat still, frozen and shocked. I held my dearest friend's airless body close to my chest and cried with her like the sister and friend she was to me. I wept for the loss of our President. I wept for the nation. I wept for my own people and all I could do was stay like she asked me to do. I promised to stay even if it meant I had to stay there forever. I stayed and held her as tight as I could and vowed never to leave her side. There was a time when I believed that clothing was the armor of life but today none of it mattered because there was only thing for me to do for Mrs. Lincoln, my dearest friend of all.

I was to stay and remain with her for so long as she needed me.

CHAPTER 18

The Reverend's Sunday Suit

225 CLINTON STREET, BUFFALO, NEW YORK CIRCA 1938
(at the height of the Harlem Renaissance where we are taken into the "Future")

Seated by the fireplace in the living room of his home, is the Reverend James Stansil, whose congregation from The Church of God and Saints, patiently await him in the basement below for their usual Sunday service.

He is the son of Elijah Stansil and Emma Mitchell; both of whom had been enslaved in Virginia. James was born in Spottsville County, Fredericksburg, Virginia in 1868 shortly after the Civil War.

Not much of his life was known however on June 19, 1901, he married his wife Lora Francis in Boston, Suffolk, Massachusetts.

James Stansil is a tall man, with large round eyes, high cheek bones and a well-groomed mustache to add to his dignified posture and poise. His hair is parted in the middle and combed neatly, the curls resembling the waves of the ocean. He is in his 60's though his appearance does not show any trace of his current age. His vim and vigor would rival the energy and endurance of most young men.

Seated across in the living room is his colleague, friend, and roomer, Reverend Erastus Lee; a former slave. He, on the other hand appeas to be older than his age. Perhaps having been enslaved had an affect on his appearance. Both men are in deep thought and seem to be engaged in a very important decision-making process.

Reverend Lee pulls a small book from the inside pocket of his coat and hands it to Reverend Stansil who takes the book with the utmost of care. He held it as if it were alive like an infant baby and he says to Lee: *"Well Reverend Lee? Now do you understand why?"*

Lee says nothing and instead closes his eyes, takes one big deep breath and offers Stansil a clear nod of resounding agreement.

"Very good," Stansil says and proceeds to open the book to a particular chapter he knows all too well.

He is reading the following excerpt from a chapter called *"Crowdy, A Negro Soldier Dressed in Blue,"* out loud to Reverend Lee, who listens intently to the following words:

'Just several yards in front of our carriage, Mrs. Lincoln and I watched as the President talking to a troop of Union soldiers who appeared to be surveying a captured wagon that had been used to smuggle goods into Petersburg, Virginia during the siege of Richmond.

Curious to know what the delay was about, Mrs. Lincoln shouted from the carriage's window, **"Abe, shall we move ahead while you meet us at the end of the road?"**

The President turned and nodded, **"Yes Mother, I am just finishing up with this young soldier Private William Crowdy here, who tells me the details of how they captured this Confederate flour wagon! Oh what a bunch of brave lads!"**

I took a moment to observe the way these Negro Union soldiers were dressed in their uniforms. Private Crowdy was smiling from ear to ear as he told the President of their victory in Richmond. He was wearing a black woolen forage hat, tipped slightly at an angle, with one brim being secured by way of an embroidered eagle. Their knee-length jackets in Prussian blue were trimmed with the arm of service with piping along the collar edges. The bright gold-hued buttons lined up in a row at the center of the coat glistened as the sun hit them in certain angles while they moved about, lifting trunks filled with seized items from the Confederate Army.

"Meticulous," *I said under my breath.*

Their trousers were made from a well-bodied broadcloth woolen fabric in sky blue with a stripe down each side in a darker hue. A leather belt around their waist held them up in a posture that kept them erect and standing straight. Their shoes called 'brogans' went up to their ankles, a critical design feature to protect their feet and keep them warm and dry while at war.

Private Crowdy spoke on behalf of his fellow-soldiers and said succinctly, **"On behalf of our regiment, it has been honor to serve our country Mr. President."**

"Thank you for your service Private Crowdy, and to all of you soldiers. Gentlemen I bid you goodbye for now, carry on," *the President removed his stovepipe hat to salute the soldiers as he bid the soldiers goodbye, beaming with pride.'*

Stansil gently closes the weathered and frayed book, with its spine nearly falling apart and its pages barely holding on to its binding. He stares at its cover, smiles and proceeds to make his descent down the stairs to the basement with Reverend Lee following behind him to meet the congregation patiently waiting below.

As he opens the basement's door, he puts the book back inside his coat pocket to meet his audience and begin his sermon.

"Good morning my friends. Today I shall have no sermon to share, no words of wisdom to give you. Today, I would simply like to take this moment to read to you the words of our founding father, William Crowdy. He said and I quote: 'Now this country is then so sadly burnt up, that nobody cares to come at it;... It was of old a most happy land, both for the fruits it bore and the riches of its cities, although it be now all burnt up," Reverend Stansil declaimed.

"Amen, Amen!" said the crowd.

The Reverend continued, *"Reverend Crowdy also once said that it is related how for the impiety of its inhabitants, it was burnt by lightning; in consequence of which there are still the remainders of that divine fire; and the traces or shadows of the five cities are still to be seen."*

The congregation listened and acknowledged as Stansil continued to read Crowdy's words out loud. By now the crowd is cheering from the frequency Stansil raised in the room.

"These were the words of our founder Pastor William Saunders Crowdy, who in 1856 was a soldier of the Union Army whose regimen seized and captured the Confederate Army's flour wagon being smuggled into Petersburg, Virginia during the siege of Richmond! Can I get an Amen?" preached Reverend James Stansil to a crowd of church goers.

"Amen! Hallelujah! Thank you to the Good Reverend Crowdy!" yelled the crowd. By now, the choir began to sing a song of praise as the church goers joined along.

"Bless his spirit as he lives on!" another member of the church said as Reverend Stansil stepped off the podium to greet the crowd one by one; the music echoing from the four walls of the basement reverberating in the movement and style of the Harlem Renaissance era.

"Lee? You ready?" Reverend Stansil asks his colleague.

"As ready as the sun will rise in the morning, I am ready Reverend Stansil," Reverend Lee acknowledged. His smile from ear ear quivered at each corner of his mouth in excitement at what was about to unfold. His perfectly straight teeth chattered as he tried to restrain himself from making too much noise, all the while nodding his head.

"Very good, let's go-" Stansil says as both men walked up the stairs of the basement leaving a very jubilant congregation behind. As they come out from the basement, past the kitchen and into Stansil's living room, the voices singing from the congregation below projected a resonance unlike anything both men have ever heard before. It's as

if heaven was rejoicing for this auspicious afternoon. Stansil takes a moment to stop in his tracks to pause and offer a prayer as he steps out of his home and on to Clinton Street to meet a man just two short blocks away.

They are met by a white-haired, bearded short man whose smock was stained in ink from the many years of doing his work, printing books.

"Ah Reverend Stansil, Reverend Lee, how do you do? Glad you made it just in time. I was just about to hang up my smock. How was Sunday service?" the short man said.

"I apologize for being late. Service was most enlightening, thank you Sir," Stansil replied.

"Well, did you bring it? May I see it?" the white-haired man asked as he proceeded to put his smock back on again.

Reverend Stansil carefully pulls the book from the inner pocket of his coat and gently hands it to the white-haired man.

"Behind the Scenes: Thirty Years a Slave and Four Years in the White House by Elizabeth Hobbs Keckley," the white-haired man slowly said as he read the book's title out loud.

He stares at the book in his hands, looks up to Reverend Stansil and says, *"She must've been something...this here woman Elizabeth Keckley for you to want me to do this some seventy years later. How did you ever come across such a lost treasure? You do want me to do this...right Reverend?"*

Reverend James Stansil turns his gaze from the white-haired man and looks dead straight into Reverend Erastus Lee's eyes, never leaving his gaze to say, *"As sure as the sun will rise tomorrow morning Sir."*

The white-haired man nods when Reverend Stansil utters, *"Yes, do it! Run three hundred copies to start. It's about time her story is told. Finally."*

With a slight tip of their hats, the two men say goodbye and exit the print shop to walk back to Reverend Stansil's home where the second half of Sunday's Service continues, gathered aound the big table to say grace and break bread.

THE END

EPILOGUE

A few months after the death of President Abraham Lincoln, Mrs. Mary Todd Lincoln left the White House and moved to Illinois with her two children, Robert and Tad. Mrs. Lincoln had amassed so much debt that in late September 1867, she sought the assistance of her best friend, Mrs. Elizabeth Keckley to help sell some of her jewelry and clothing to raise money to pay her bills.

Mrs. Keckley made the difficult decision to leave Washington and put her business on hold in order to assist Mrs. Lincoln in accompanying her back and forth from Illinois to New York. She secured a broker to manage and handle the business of selling Mrs. Lincoln's personal effects under the agreement that the transactions were to be conducted under an alias to protect Mrs. Lincoln's privacy. The effort proved unsuccessful when word of Mrs. Lincoln's financial hardships became publicly known and she was heavily criticized by Washington society.

To assist her friend reclaim her reputation, Elizabeth sought to write her memoirs and use the proceeds from the sales of her book to give to Mrs. Lincoln. Entitled, _"Behind The Scenes: Thirty Years a Slave and Four Years in the White House,"_ the endeavor resulted in a terrible recoil and misfire that caused Elizabeth's reputation to be compromised as the media and press portrayed her to be an avaricious social climbing former slave capitalizing on her notoriety as Mrs. Lincoln's confidante and best friend.

The book was labeled a 'literary thunderbolt' and the publisher, Carleton & Company, joined in by declaring it as a 'great sensational disclosure.'

News of this reached Mrs. Lincoln who felt that Elizabeth had betrayed her trust by divulging the most personal and intimate accounts of her life. In truth, Elizabeth was questioned by the publishing company as to the trueness and validity of her memoirs and was ordered to submit proof of the authenticity of her story by providing some form of documentation that would prove her story to be accurate. Trusting the publishers had her best interest at heart, she loaned them all the personal letters of correspondences between her and Mrs. Lincoln in their safekeeping. Unbeknownst to Elizabeth, the letters were published in the Appendix section of the book without her consent or approval.

By the time Elizabeth found out, it was too late; the book was already on the shelves for all to read. Vilified by society and with her reputation under scrutiny, her business began to suffer and all her clients in the elite social circles refused to have their dresses made for fear that Elizabeth would divulge their private lives to the public.

By this time, Mrs. Lincoln stopped all communications with Elizabeth while Mrs. Lincoln's son, Robert Todd Lincoln convinced the publisher to cease further production of the book as he felt it to be a huge embarrassment to the Lincoln family legacy.

Robert Lincoln then published his own parody and entitled it _"Behind the Seams: by a Nigger Woman who took work in from Mrs. Lincoln and Mrs. Davis,"_ and signed it with an _"X", the "mark of Betsey Kickley (Nigger)"_ to imply that the author was illiterate.

Forced to dissolve her business, Elizabeth struggled to make a living as a dressmaker until around 1890, where she eventually moved to Ohio and was offered a position at Wilberforce University (a college she helped rebuild after suffering severe damages from a fire where she donated money and help fundraise for) as the Department Head of Sewing and Domestic Science Arts. In 1893, she held an exhibit at the Chicago World's Fair for Wilberforce University but after a mild stroke, retired from teaching. Living off her son's military pension of $8.00/month, Elizabeth moved back to Washington to live in the *National Home for Destitute Colored Women and Children*, an institution she helped found. Residents and staff members of the institution described her as a *"Reserved, poised, educated, cultured, polished and elegant woman."*

On May 1907, Elizabeth Keckley died as a resident of the National Home on Euclid St. NW, in Washington, D.C. She was interred at Columbian Harmony Cemetery. In 1950, the cemetery stopped accepting new burials, and the Columbian Harmony Society struggled to afford the annual upkeep. A real-estate investor named Lewis N. Bell offered to buy the land and relocate the graves to what is now known as the National Memorial Park. When the graves were moved to a new cemetery, Elizabeth's unclaimed remains were placed in an unmarked grave like those of her mother, stepfather, and son.

As it turned out, an unknown number of headstones and bodies that were supposed to be moved were not. Instead, the headstones were unceremoniously dumped on the Potomac River, used as riprap to prevent erosion, while workers found human remains when digging on the site in the 1970s.

An intended memorial was never built. On May 26, 2010, 103 years after her death, a marker was placed at her grave in National Harmony Memorial Park.

In a most poignant part of her life story tells the message of the love of a friend for another, and that despite all the years of unresolved differences between her and Mrs. Lincoln, Elizabeth Keckley left a powerful message of the loyalty and devotion she had for her friend when her body was discovered inside the single room unit at the National Home for Destitute Colored Women and Children where she lived. There, she was found peacefully on her bed covered in the quilt she made from the scraps and remnants of Mrs. Lincoln's dresses. The room was sparsely appointed without any decorations except for one sole framed photograph that hung directly above her headrest, a photograph of Mrs. Mary Todd Lincoln dressed in one of her creations.

Nearly seven decades later, after her book was first published and forcibly removed from the shelves shortly thereafter with the intention of it to never be seen again, a fire and brimstone preacher by the name of Reverend James Stansil, (along with a colleague and friend named Reverend Erastus Lee) whose congregation "The Church of God and Saints of Christ" located in Buffalo, NY decided to re-publish Elizabeth Keckley's memoirs again.   According to an article published by Uncrowned Community Builders, *"Because of Stansil's actions, the book has subsequently been republished at least three times, with new introductions and numerous journal articles have been written examining the manuscript as well as Keckley. On December 7, 1948, Stansil died at the old A.J. Meyer Hospital in Buffalo. He was funeralized at the Sherman L. Walker Funeral home and was buried in Rochester at Mt. Hope Cemetery on December 13, 1948. He is survived by grandchildren including Joseph Johnson and Naomi Johnson of New York City. Rev. J.H. Stansil is celebrated as an Uncrowned King for rescuing the work of Elizabeth Keckley from continued literary obscurity. Because of Stansil's actions, the book has subsequently been republished at least three times, with new introductions and numerous journal articles have been written examining the manuscript as well as Keckley."*

In interesting case of fate, Reverend James Stansil's church was founded by Reverend William Saunders Crowdy, who in between the years 1864-1865 during the Civil War, served in the Union Army as a laborer and supply storeman, and participated in the successful capture of a confederate flour wagon being smuggled into Petersburg, Virginia during the siege of Richmond. Crowdy remained in the Army after the war to become a Buffalo Soldier. He was promoted to quartermaster sergeant in the 5th Cavalry in 1867, receiving his discharge in 1872 and in 1896, formed The Church of God and Saints of Christ whose branch in Buffalo, NY was headed by Reverend James Stansil sometime in the time frame of 1910 through the 1930's during the Harlem Renaissance era.

It is unclear as to how Reverend Stansil acquired an original copy of Elizabeth Keckley's memoirs but some speculate that *"he could have heard about the book from a vast network of friends and associates including Frederick Douglas who was a colleague of Elizabeth Keckley. He could also have learned of the book during the Pan American Exposition of 1901 of Buffalo where the Phyllis Wheatley Club petitioned to have the Negro Exhibit on display in Buffalo. Keckley's book was in that display. It is likely that Stansil acquired the book shortly after the Pan American Exposition which he may have attended. Or, he might have acquired it in 1893 at the Columbia World's Fair where Keckley gave presentations discussing her book,"* according to an article by Uncrowned Community Builders.

The decision to have it published was an act that not only kept her written work protected and preserved, but also kept Elizabeth Keckley's legacy alive for generations to follow.

✻ ✻ ✻

LEGACY

• The dress that Keckley designed for Mary Todd Lincoln to wear at her husband's second inauguration ceremony and reception can be seen at the Smithsonian's American History Museum.

• Keckley designed a quilt made from scraps of materials left over from dresses she made for Mrs. Lincoln. The quilt is held under the stewardship and care of the Kent State University Museum.

• A life-size bronze statue in her likeness is located at The Virginia Women's Monument in Richmond; a state memorial commemorating the contributions of Virginian women to the history of the Commonwealth of Virginia and the United States.

•   The former school in Hillsborough, North Carolina, where Keckley worked for Rev. Robert Burwell, is now owned and operated as a house museum, the Burwell School Historic Site, by the Historic Hillsborough Commission.

•   On December 12, 2018, New York Times published an obituary for Keckley, as a part of their Overlooked series of stories of remarkable individuals whose deaths went unreported by the newspaper.

•   She has been written about in many books and articles. "Lincoln" was a biographical drama feature film directed and produced by Steven Spielberg starring Daniel Day Lewis, Sally Field, Tommy Lee Jones. Featured in the film was the character of Elizabeth Keckley played by Gloria Reuben.

•   In 2022, Hollywood actress Sarah Jessica Parker wore a dress designed by Fashion Designer Christopher Rogers to the MET Gala based on one of Keckley's designs from 1862 for Mrs. Mary Todd Lincoln.

C. Georgina C.

The author who goes by her writer's name C. Georgina C. was born and raised in the Philippines to an American father and Filipina mother.

Her family immigrated to the United States while she was a young girl where she first learned about Frederick Douglass after borrowing a book from the local library entitled, "Narrative of the Life of Frederick Douglass, an American Slave." This newly found knowledge opened her world to learning more about American History.

Fast forward some 30 years later when she opened her first bridal shop where she designed and created made-to-measure wedding gowns and evening dresses. A self-taught dressmaker with no formal training, she became a student of the trade, learned from the experts and leaned on any information she could access to broaden her knowledge and fine-tune her technique and skills.

One night while doing some research, an image of a gown from the 1860's caught her attention. She learned about Elizabeth Keckley, a formerly enslaved woman who became the official dressmaker to the First Lady, Mary Todd Lincoln.

After over a decade of research, she was inspired to write a book to celebrate and honor the life of a woman who left behind a remarkable and brilliant legacy. The author considers Elizabeth Keckley as her biggest influence outside of her own mother.

Now retired from dressmaking, the author is working on her second book centered around the love story of Frederick Douglass and his wife Anna Murray.

She is an advocate of The Healing Arts Foundation, a 501C3 dedicated to helping improve the lives of the marginalized and underserved members of the AAPI and LGBTQ+ communities through the Arts.

She is also a Multiple Sclerosis survivor, an avid horse enthusiast/equestrian, a Reiki practitioner and full-time Mom who enjoys spending her days raising her children, cooking at home. She loves listening to Jazz, enjoys a good book and anything art-related and occasiionally sews for special projects and special people.

PRAISE FOR AUTHOR

"A remarkable true story about a former slave and single mother who defied all odds during one of the most harrowing times in U.S. history where she became a highly skilled and sought-after dressmaker of the Haute Couture catering to high society and ultimately, for the First Lady, Mary Todd Lincoln; while being a Single Mother, Abolitionist, Human Rights Advocate, Philanthropist, Entrepreneur, Author, Professor and more.

Lizzy is a page turning heart-pounding book that will leave you inspired. The author takes her readers to the hidden and untold stories in U.S. History that we have yet to know about; propelling one to realize how incredible the human spirit is and what an astounding WOMAN Elizabeth Keckley was!" Ryan Jordan, Artist, Designer, Entrepreneur

Made in the USA
Middletown, DE
11 April 2024

52817679R00139